Pride Publishing books by C F White

Responsible Adult
Misdemeanor
Hard Time
Reformed

St. Cross
Won't Feel a Thing
Won't Be Fooled Again

Pink Rock
Love & Tea Bags

St. Cross

WON'T FEEL A THING

C F WHITE

Won't Feel a Thing
ISBN # 978-1-83943-815-8

Interior text design by Claire Siemaszkiewicz
Pride Publishing

Published in 2019 by Pride Publishing, United Kingdom.

Pride Publishing is an imprint of Totally Entwined Group Limited.

WON'T FEEL A THING

Dedication

To all the doctors and nurses who tirelessly work the night shift and care for all the children who'd rather be somewhere else. You lift their smiles, and brighten their days. Thank you, from a mother who has sat beside her child's hospital bed twenty-four-seven with only the staff for company.

Chapter One

New Year's Resolutions

"You want my opinion?"

"Yes."

"My honest opinion?"

"Yes," Ollie repeated. "Please."

"Brutal honest opinion?"

"Yes."

"Even if you don't like it?"

"Even if I never want to talk to you again." Ollie took a sharp slurp through the straw of his smoothie and winced, his glasses tipping to the end of his nose. "Until tonight, anyway."

"Then leave well alone."

Ollie sighed. He sucked up another mouthful of his daily fruit and veg intake, flicked back his blond hair that had lost its vigor after a twelve-hour night shift and glanced away from Taya's wide brown eyes. The eyes that signified she meant every damn word. *Bitch.*

"Told you."

Taya freed her dark, waist-length hair from its curled bun and stroked it over one shoulder. She wrapped the band around her slender dark-skinned wrist then sipped her dainty cup of pink hot chocolate. The blue edges of her lips, caused by the freezing weather, were subsiding back to their usual reddish tinge with each guzzle of the pink cream and rainbow of chocolate candies scattered over her ridiculous sickly concoction. She hadn't even offered a spoonful to him. Twelve hours straight on night shift clearly meant she needed the sugar all to herself.

"He's not worth your time, your worry or your respect." She clanged the cup down onto the glass surface of the table, pulled her winter trench coat over the scrubs she hadn't bothered to change out of and reached for her packet of menthol slims.

"Neither are they." Ollie pointed to the cigarettes.

Taya glared across the table. She unhooked the top of the packet, took one of the white sticks between her teeth and lit it with her pink lighter. Blowing the smoke into the freezing cold air, she waved her hand.

"We all have our vices, Oliver."

Ollie stuck his middle finger up. He slapped it back down and shoved it into his jacket pocket. It was freezing, and Taya had to bloody sit outside the corner coffee shop in order to smoke her way out of the trying night shift. She was right. Everyone needed their vices, especially with what he and Taya did for a living. He sighed.

"I think he needs patience."

"He's got plenty of those." Taya pointed her two fingers clutching the death stick at Ollie.

"Har fricking har. Patience with a *c*."

"He's a *c* all right." Taya took another drag. At Ollie's glare, she sighed and rested her elbow on the tabletop. "What? He is."

"I think you may be the only female in the entire hospital who doesn't like him." Ollie slurped the dregs of his raspberry-ripple smoothie and shivered. He should have gone for a hot drink, but it was hard enough to sleep during the day as it was. Caffeine would only make it infinitely more difficult.

"That's because I know him," Taya replied.

"Urgh. Not you, too?"

"Ew." Taya grimaced around her cigarette. "No, thank you."

Ollie leaned back in the chair. He waved a hand to waft away the smoke drifting into his face. To give her some credit, Taya was trying to blow it out of the side of her mouth to avoid him, but the icy-cold January breeze from the earlier sleet downpour blew it straight back. Ollie zipped up his puffer jacket, folded his arms and jiggled on the cold metal chair.

"You nearly done?" He nodded to the half-full cup of violently pink chocolate.

Taya blew another puff of smoke into the air, stubbed out the remains of her cigarette and downed the rest of her drink, leaving a foam mustache on her top lip. She licked it away. "Yeah. Home to bed, miss the snowfall, back at eight. You?"

They scraped back their chairs and Ollie tucked a five-pound note under the ashtray for the servers. Anyone willing to come outside and serve drinks in this weather should most definitely get tips, even if his wages would no doubt be far less than those of the coffee baristas working this part of London.

"I should go see my dad," he replied.

Taya linked her arm in with his, curling her slender fingers around his quilted sleeve. Checking both ways along the crossroads lined by independent boutiques, high-class restaurants, unconventional cafés and health-food shops, she steered him across, narrowly missing a black cab speeding over the mini-roundabout. The glass-enclosed bus stop's bench overflowed with waiting passengers, so he stood, his freezing toes within his inappropriate-for-the-weather slip-on loafers numbing with each passing second, and checked the time on the electric board for when the next bus was due.

"How's he doing?" Taya asked.

"Good days and bad days." Ollie sighed. "Keeps calling me Tilly."

Taya tried to hold in the chuckle but failed miserably. Ollie didn't mind so much. A good sense of humor was always best in these situations, not to mention their line of work. He pulled Taya in closer. It was fricking freezing and snowflakes fell from the overcast sky. How would he get back to work later that night? London came to a standstill if even one flake hit any mode of public transport. Him living in the other end of the city—the cheap end—would make it all the more difficult to travel across town. On occasions when there wasn't a downfall, he would have cycled in. But that was out of the question with the ice on the roads. And the fact that he hadn't woken up in his own bed last night. Ollie shuddered at the memory.

"Right." Ollie bounced to keep warm while awaiting the number 252. "It's January. So that means New Year's resolutions. What's yours?"

"Quit smoking."

"Good luck." Ollie meant it.

Taya stuck out her tongue.

"Well, we both know mine—"

"Which you broke last night." Taya was a bitch like that.

"I don't believe New Year's resolutions should start until the second week of January." Ollie rubbed his hands together, digging Taya's arm into his side, and wondered why he hadn't thought to bring gloves. Ah, yes, he hadn't had any where he'd been before his shift started. He wasn't allowed to leave any trace of his existence there.

"Riiight," Taya said. "So that means from today, you'll be steering clear of arsehole men?"

"Sadly, no. Unfortunately, I will no doubt encounter many of them in my time without realizing until it's too late."

"Amen." Taya saluted.

Ollie wasn't sure what the salute was about. But he wasn't particularly religious, so maybe that was how it was done in church these days? Or temples, considering Taya's family were Hindu.

"So, what *is* your resolution, then?"

"No baggage," Ollie replied.

"Baggage?"

"Yep," Ollie confirmed.

The gleaming new red Routemaster bus edged along the narrow High Street, bumping over the speed mounds meant to slow the traffic down, which Ollie thought ridiculous as the morning rush-hour pileup tended to last all day in central London. The streets were filled with scuttling people carrying takeout coffee cups, cyclists braving the ice, and the occasional honking of a taxi horn. This time of the morning, most people were trying to get to work and not home from it like Ollie and Taya. He was never quite sure who was keener to reach their destinations.

"I don't mind a complete arsehole—"

"Obviously." Taya cut Ollie off with a raise of her smoothed-out eyebrows. That new rainbow hot chocolate had clearly contained one too many e-numbers and sent her loopy. That and the long night shift. Not that she hadn't been a little bit loopy to begin with.

"Ha ha." Ollie pushed her forehead. "Like, I can handle a dickhead—"

"We all know."

"Jesus Christ," Ollie muttered. "No more white hot chocolate with pink dye for you, okay?"

"Sorry." Taya pressed her lips together. She rose up on her tiptoes to check on the bus's progress but needn't have worried, as it had traveled all of a millimeter since the start of their conversation. At this rate, Ollie might get home in time to have a shower and come straight back.

"What I mean is—"

"You don't want a man who can't commit because of circumstance," Taya finished for him.

Ollie was capable of finishing his own sentences, but Taya was getting warm from flapping her lips, so he allowed it. "Exactly. I'm married to my job. I love my job. Therefore, I should have the occasional fling and become the arsehole myself." He pointed a finger at Taya. "Don't fricking say it."

Taya shrugged and mimed zipping her lips up.

"What do we nurses say daily?"

"'No, you can't have McDonald's'?"

"Not that one."

"'You're going to feel a little prick'?"

Ollie sniggered. "Not that one either."

"Oh, I know. It's 'Of course I'll change your TV channel for you—it's not like I have anything better to do with my time.'"

"No! I mean the big one—'You won't feel a thing.'"

Taya nodded. "So?"

"So, my resolution is to no longer feel a thing."

"Good luck." Taya smiled. *Bitch.*

The bus pulled up and Ollie jogged on the spot, waiting for the doors to open. They hissed to the side, and even though he and Taya were standing correctly at the hop-on part of the Routemaster with the exit farther along the double decker, a tall man with floppy dark hair jumped straight off and bashed Ollie's arm as he rushed up the high street, heading toward the gleaming glass frontage of St. Cross Children's Hospital.

"Ouch." Ollie pouted and rubbed his arm.

"Ha!" Taya jumped the step onto the bus.

"What?"

Amusement shimmered across Taya's face as she bleeped her Oyster card onto the yellow reader. "You just felt something."

"Oh, bog off."

* * * *

Ollie jangled the keys in the lock of his third-floor flat and burst in out of the freezing cold. He slammed the door, wriggled free of his coat and slipped out of his comfortable loafers. Rubbing his numbed hands together, he hurried up the corridor and decided to forgo the shower in favor of sinking under his fluffy down duvet instead.

He stripped out of his jumper and jeans, threw his glasses onto the bedside table and collapsed onto the bed. Grabbing the side of the duvet, he wrapped it around his shivering body, rolled onto his front and made a human sausage roll out of himself. He shut his eyes. Of course, that would be when his house phone decided to ring. He wasn't going to answer it. That time of the morning, it'd only be personal-injury-claim chasers or some double-glazing salesman. The answer phone clicked on and Ollie's recorded voice wafted down the hallway into his bedroom.

"Hey, you've reached Ollie," it sang out. "I'm way too busy and important to come to the phone right now, and if you're not with me then you're missing out! So leave a message, and I'll decide whether to call you back. Oh, and if it's PPI, I've claimed four times and turns out I'm still not owed anything. Oh, and I haven't had an accident in the last three years. Oh, and I'd simply luuurrvve to take your survey on local facilities I use in my leisure time, if I had any. Much love—bleeeeep."

Ollie chuckled. Until the caller's voice boomed down the phone.

"Oliver?"

It seemed like a question, especially with the pause. Ollie held his breath.

"Oliver?"

Ollie hoped he'd either hang up or get to the point before Ollie passed out from asphyxiation. And considering he was naked, wrapped in a duvet, he could just see the local paper headlines misconstruing his accidental death as some sort of sex game gone wrong.

"Right. You're not there. Or ignoring me."

Bright man, this one.

"You left your watch here."

Ollie scrambled to get his arm out from under the duvet and checked his wrist. *Bollocks.* He shut his eyes.

"I've had to throw it out."

Ollie shoved a hand over his mouth, adding to his suffocating possibilities, and ignored the sinking feeling in his gut.

"I'll get you a new one."

Ollie shook his head and sank farther into the duvet to cover his face.

"Don't call me back. I'll see you later."

The answer phone bleeped, indicating the end of the message and signifying the beginning of Ollie's New Year's resolution.

The one where he wouldn't feel a thing.

Chapter Two

All in a Smile

"There he is!"

Ollie glanced over his shoulder to Patty and Lily at the front nursing station of the cardiology ward, where he was starting his next night shift. Patty had been the one to whisper the words loudly as she shoved Lily next to her. Ollie rolled his eyes. The two veteran nurses started with their usual fluttering of eyelashes and sticking out of bosoms for the arrival of Dr. Rawlings. Ollie, not having breasts in his arsenal and not bothering with the rapid blinking, turned back to the whiteboard. He scrubbed out the name of the child who had vacated Bed One during the day shift and squeaked his blue pen across the shiny board to write the new one.

"Evening, ladies."

Dr. Rawlings, tall, dark and ridiculously handsome even for a bloke in his middle years, passed by the desk. He gave a tight nod, and the two girls giggled. Considering Patty was forty-one, married with three children, and Lily, in her thirties, had been with her boyfriend for a fair few years, it was nauseating how they melted into teenagers each time the pediatric cardiology consultant entered the unit.

"Evening, Doctor," Patty replied. "I trust you had a good sleep?"

"Thank you, Nurse." Dr. Rawlings' deep-gravel voice resonated off the whitewashed walls. He flashed his pearly whites. "Unfortunately, I was kept up most of the day preparing for the hospital's annual charity fundraiser. I'm organizing the auction this year." He stroked his combed-back dark hair. "All in the name of those in the Third World who need urgent medical attention and aren't as lucky as our patients here."

Patty and Lily swooned. Ollie rolled his eyes. Until he realized that would come across as though he didn't care about the sick children in war-torn countries. He did. Obviously. He just got a little weary at the doctor's constant need to bang on about how fucking great he was. Everyone already knew how perfect the man was.

The doctor marched off to the first private patient bay and Ollie let out the breath he hadn't realized had been gathered in his lungs.

"The things I would let that man do to me," Lily said, flicking through the files on her lap.

"I know, right!" Patty replied. "I think I might need a thorough examination."

Ollie snapped the lid on his pen and spun on his heels to face his two fellow nurses. He was about to offer his disapproval of their blatant sexual harassment when Dr. Rawlings slinked out of the bay he'd just entered.

"Oliver," he called, rather sternly. No nods and casual greetings now.

"Yes, Doctor?"

"We'll need some help in here."

Ollie stood straighter with a curt nod. He was rather proud it had been him chosen for the task and not the two veteran nurses who bowed to the doctor's every whim.

"Bucket of water, cloths. PDQ."

Ah. "Yes, Doctor," Ollie repeated. His shoulders slumped, but he straightened them out when Patty nodded with an encouraging smile. Nursing meant cleaning up shit and vomit as much as it did aiding doctors.

Rushing with buckets and cloths, Ollie hurried into the private room in time to see the second hacking-up from the patient whose name he had just written on the board. The sick landed all over Dr. Rawlings, midway through listening to the little girl's heart with his stethoscope, dirtying his pristine white lab coat. Luckily, Dr. Rawlings had it buttoned up. Ollie froze for a moment as the doctor stood, popped open the lab coat in one swift rip and shrugged free of it. The shirt beneath was one of his tighter and more expensive ones and tucked nicely into a pair of fitted dark blue chinos that rounded the man's perfectly constructed arse.

"Oliver," Dr. Rawlings demanded, waggling an impatient hand.

Ollie snapped to. He passed over a cloth, and the little girl threw up again, but at least the vomit landed in the cardboard tray Dr. Rawlings held out for her. Ollie took the sick-covered lab coat to throw it into the waste bin outside the door. Dr. Rawlings waved again and Ollie rushed forward to clear up the mess.

"Probably a bit more to come out," the doctor said.

The small, pale and fragile little girl whimpered, snorted and hiccupped, tears trailing down her blotchy cheeks. Her mother stood on the other side of the bed, chewing on a manicured nail. Worry washed over her pale features, but she dodged to avoid having any more vomit splashing on her. There was no doubt that this wasn't the first time the mother had been covered in her daughter's sick, and, more likely, she'd only just cleaned up in the en-suite bathroom from the last lot, considering the splats of wet patches blotting through her top. The girl cried, hacked up a bit more then belched.

Ollie wiped his wet cloth across the girl's lips. She peered up at him, her blue eyes bloodshot but full of gratitude. Ollie smiled. Being a pediatric nurse meant learning to perfect the delivery of a smile. There were gradients of them. Sympathetic ones, friendly ones, humoring ones, sincere ones and the ones he had to stick on all day, which fell into the 'slightly unnerving' column. The one he gave the little girl was his best friendly smile. It made his eyes sparkle beneath his dark-rimmed glasses. Placing a soothing hand on her back, he rubbed in small, gentle circles.

"It's okay, sweetie." He attempted to soothe her—tense vomiting caused the belching, and relaxing the body helped vomit to flow more freely. "I was sick in my own hair once."

The little girl twitched half a smile.

"Don't ask." Ollie shrugged with one shoulder. "Nursing school is for more than just nursing."

The girl giggled. Ollie was pretty sure that, at eight years old, she wouldn't understand what he was getting at, but it helped relieve her fear, and that was what he was there for. The giggle led to continued coughing, and Dr. Rawlings shoved the cardboard container at Ollie. He held it in front of the girl's mouth while she threw up yellow bile more freely, this time into the already filled pot of lumpy canteen food.

"Right, well." Dr. Rawlings patted Ollie's back while acknowledging the mother. "Oliver can take it from here."

Ollie offered a smile to the doctor. He wasn't sure which type it would be labeled as. 'Incredibly awkward' could be used to describe its delivery. Dr. Rawlings didn't seem to notice, or care, and marched out of the room. Sighing, Ollie watched through the gap in the window blinds. The doctor stopped at the nurses' station, offered his dashing smile with whatever few words he bestowed upon the ladies this time, tapped the desk and stalked out of the cardiology wing. Sticking on his friendly smile, Ollie turned back to the little girl.

"How are you feeling?"

"Sick," she replied.

Her mother stepped forward, uncrossing her arms with a *harrumph*. Ollie quickly merged the friendly into sympathetic.

"I thought we'd get some answers," she hissed.

"It's a long process," Ollie replied. "The doctor needs to check in every so often. He has to consult with the other doctors and make decisions based on her recovery." He continued rubbing soothing circles on the little girl's back but stood to speak at the mother's level. "I know it can seem like a waiting game—"

"That's all I fucking do," the mother snapped and ran a hand through her long blonde hair, which appeared as though it hadn't been washed in a few days. "Wait around for men to decide what to do."

"That's life, honey." Ollie removed his hand as the little girl leaned back into the bed. "But perhaps keeping the language at a child-friendly level would be best all around."

The mother glared back. Ollie was used to it. Parents thought they could say anything, considering it was their child stuck in a hospital. They had a point. But swearing should never be tolerated while in the presence of a child, sick or not. The woman re-crossed her arms and glared past Ollie as a figure approached the doorway.

"Of course, you turn up."

Ollie twisted to see who the recipient of such disdain was, figuring the woman wouldn't be speaking that way to a doctor in charge of her child's care. The man at the doorway clutched a soft pink teddy bear, possibly purchased on a whim from the ground-floor shop. He smiled. His, however, was in the 'not really wanting to but having to' category. Ollie knew all about those.

"Daddy!" The little girl's voice was hoarse and light.

"Hey, Daisy," the man greeted, then paused at the frown displayed across the features of the girl's mother. "I came this morning, but they told me she was being moved. I had to go to the office to sort a few things and came back as soon as I could."

Remnants of white snowflakes dotted the broad shoulders of the man's black trench coat, beneath which he wore a white shirt and thin blue silk tie. He ran a hand through his thick dark hair that flowed freely, quite longish, down to his cheekbones. He wiped it away from his face to reveal deep blue eyes identical to the little girl's and once again tried a smile.

"Well." Daisy's mother slapped her hands down to her sides. "If you're staying, then I'll go home. I need a shower. And sleep. Considering I've been the one to be here the whole fucking time." She bent to kiss the tip of Daisy's nose, then stalked around the bed.

Ollie did a quick check of the name above the bed and hoped he wasn't going to make the same faux pas he'd made many times in his short career. He'd soon gotten used to it and cared less and less about offending mothers whose names didn't match their children's. But he also hated the one-size catchall 'mum' that most medical professionals used. He knew how much it pissed off the mothers of regular patients when medical carers never bothered to learn their names.

"Mrs. Monroe," Ollie started. "I do urge you again to keep the language child-friendly. We are in a children's hospital."

The man's eyes closed in a wince, and Ollie knew he'd done it and braced for impact. The woman spun around and Ollie was hard-pressed not to recoil from her scowl of hatred and contempt.

"I am not Mrs. Monroe," she growled through gritted teeth.

Ollie guessed this wasn't her first time having to utter those words.

"And my child has undergone heart fucking surgery, so I'll fucking swear if I fucking well want to!"

"Becky," the man urged, and if Ollie thought the scowl he'd gotten had been bad, it was nothing in comparison to the one she now shot at the man Ollie figured was Daisy's father and who no longer shared a bed or bodily fluids with Daisy's mother.

"Fuck off, Jacob. You no longer have any say in how I act."

She stormed past Ollie and brushed a shoulder against the man, making him bump against the doorframe. Her heels tapped on the linoleum flooring all the way out to the exit. Not even the bleeping of machines and crying of children drowned out those raps—those stomps demanded to be heard. Just like her curse words.

Ollie caught the eyes of the man he would hazard a guess was called Jacob, although he probably should ask as his assumptions weren't going down too well that evening. He offered one of the smiles from his back catalog.

"Daddy?" Daisy croaked. She scraped her head along the pillow, her long dark hair spreading over the cheap white cotton case.

Jacob perched on the edge of the bed and took her hand in his. "I'm here, pumpkin."

The smooth-as-silk voice, not to mention the man's sincere compassion and concern for his daughter, made the hairs on Ollie's arms stand up. Ollie smiled, his genuine one he didn't struggle to put on. He went to clear up the sick and vomit that had landed on the floor. Such was the lot of a nurse.

"I was sick." Daisy's voice was hoarse from the obvious strain it had undergone, not only from the vomiting but also from the breathing tube she would have had plunged down her throat the last couple of days.

Jacob wiped Daisy's clammy hair from her forehead and felt her skin with his palm. He glanced down at Ollie, concern flickering across his face.

"Is she okay?" His voice cracked.

"The canteen food sometimes does that to me." Ollie stood, scrunching the dirty cloth in his hand, and smiled. Obviously.

"It wasn't the meds? The pain relief?" Jacob near stuttered.

Ollie shook his head and nodded for Jacob to follow him outside the private room. The concern on the man's face was unmistakable. A man so in love with his daughter, he feared all news, good or bad.

"What is it?" Jacob asked, outside in the main ward, trepidation in his voice. He divided his gaze between Ollie and the gap in the window blinds.

"We don't like to say that medication might be the thing making children sick, if they can hear or understand," Ollie explained. "It can bring fear of trying any new medicine. So, we make light of it. The canteen served pasta today. Lord knows what they put in that sauce, right?" He shrugged.

Jacob ran his floppy hair back from his face and scrubbed a hand under his nose. "Sorry, this is all—"

Ollie cut him off. "It's okay." His fresh-faced, genuine smile came to the forefront without any coercing. "The best we can do at this stage is to keep her smiling."

Jacob nodded, glancing through the gaps in the blinds to his daughter, exhaustion across his otherwise handsome face.

"I'll bet she's a firecracker, am I right?"

Jacob tore his eyes away from the window and slowly chuckled, giving a fond nod. "She can be, yeah."

"Then she'll be just fine."

"The surgery went all okay?"

That was a question and not a statement. If this was the girl's father, it seemed a little off that he hadn't already been informed how the open-heart surgery had gone, by either a doctor or the girl's mother. It would have been a couple of days ago, at least—one day for the patient in Intensive Care, two in the High Dependency Unit, to today moving into the main cardiology wing. Clearly the man had a tempestuous relationship with the mother, but still, this was their daughter who'd gone through a major operation. *Surely differences should be put aside?*

"Nurse?"

Ollie snapped out of his thoughts and quickly offered a smile. "Sorry." He wasn't normally one to ponder so much about his patients' family lives. "Let's go check her notes. I've just come on the night shift, so wasn't here during the day."

Ollie gestured for Jacob to reenter the private room where Daisy sprawled out on the thin mattress, eyes closed and hugging her pink teddy bear. Ollie picked up the clipboard at the end of the bed and checked through all the written observations and notes collected during the day shift. He'd been given a handover on arrival and brought up to speed on all his patients, but it never hurt to check through the written words to be sure. The doctors sometimes added in their own notes from time to time, so it would have been foolish to think he would know it all on a twenty-minute handover from the day nurse.

"All went according to procedure," Ollie said, skimming the notes. Jacob nodded, pulling up the comfy chair beside his daughter's bed and gripping her hand. "It says here surgery lasted four hours. The ASD repair has been patched and patient is responding well. She woke up approximately five hours after surgery and has been in and out of consciousness since then. All obs normal."

Ollie hooked the clipboard back onto the end of the bed. Daisy was out cold again, and Ollie understood she looked a lot paler than how her father would be used to seeing her. Ollie was more used to pale children. *Unfortunately.*

"Tough cookie, really," Ollie remarked. "To be on the ward so quick. If she's already been up, eating, talking and throwing up, then she's on my list of all-time greats. She'll be home by tomorrow, building a snowman by Wednesday, dancing by Thursday and running you ragged by the weekend. You'll be begging me to take her back."

Jacob snorted in amusement and his piercing blue eyes, with their now added sparkle of relief, caught Ollie off guard. Ollie had blue eyes himself, but in comparison to the dark features of the man before him, Ollie's seemed washed out and gray. Jacob's eyes could light up a room.

"Thank you, Nurse." Jacob stroked his thumb along his daughter's delicate hand, being careful not to catch the IV drip stuck into her vein.

"Ollie." Ollie moved around the bed and held out his hand. "The name's Ollie. I'll be Daisy's night nurse until she's discharged."

Jacob shifted in his seat, slipped his hand from his daughter's and took hold of Ollie's. His grip was firm and his cold skin scraped against Ollie's palm. "Jacob," he said. "Jacob Monroe."

Jacob's fingers curled around Ollie's and he gave one shake before sliding his hand away to cover his daughter's once more. Ollie twisted on his loafers, the rubber bottoms squeaking against the floor. He walked over to the door to leave the man alone with his daughter. She seemed in good enough care now, and Ollie had another three children to check half-hour obs on.

"I suppose you think I'm a bad father."

Ollie stopped. He wasn't sure if the man was talking to him or his daughter. Jacob's eyes were firmly on the girl in the bed, so Ollie thought perhaps he was intruding on a moment and went to walk out, until Jacob lifted his bowed head.

"I didn't know."

Ollie smiled. It was all he had as a comeback.

"Me and her mother aren't together anymore. Haven't been for quite some time."

Ollie was used to parents treating him as a confessor. Under strenuous circumstances, people often chose nurses to open up to. All that was required of Ollie during those situations was to offer a sympathetic ear. And add it to his list of patient confidentiality. He nodded and smiled the category of smile that went into 'this holds no other meaning other than the fact I have heard you'.

"I work away a lot. Came as soon as I heard," Jacob continued. "So, thank you for letting me know about the surgery. Means I don't have to beg Becky to explain it all."

Ollie fixated on the man's voice. It was deep and subdued yet had a smooth undertone, like the low buzz of bees wading through honey. He couldn't help noting the sheer regret in it, too. Whether that was about Jacob not being there for his daughter during her surgery or about his breakup with her mother, Ollie wasn't sure. But he guessed which female had most of Jacob's attention as Jacob leaned forward to kiss his daughter's forehead.

"The surgery is usually a waiting game for parents," Ollie offered. "Long hours hanging around, not able to do anything. Then ICU and HDU—they mostly drift in and out of consciousness with no real idea what or who's there. This bit here"—Ollie nodded at the bed—

"is the hard part. The part where parents are needed most. You've got perfect timing, in her book."

"Thank you, Ollie," Jacob replied, giving a somber smile in return.

Ollie hated to admit the tingle he felt at hearing his name uttered by this near stranger. He nodded and scuttled out of the door before any further feelings could be felt. He bumped into Taya trotting his way, coat slipping off her arms and dark ponytail swishing as she ran. He smelled smoke as she trundled past.

"When do you start your resolution, then?" Ollie asked with a smirk.

Taya twisted around to stick her tongue out. Ollie shook his head. He didn't blame her, really. Second week of January and all that. Which would officially start in... He lifted his wrist, then slapped it down to his side with a mumbled curse. He no longer had the watch he'd worn since he was sixteen. The one his father had given him. He pulled at the fob watch clipped to his scrubs pocket by a plastic monkey face, and the retractable wire zipped free for him to check the time. Three hours. Three clear hours until the second week of January.

Seriously, what can happen in three hours?

Chapter Three

Touch a Life

"Then guess what he said."

"I can't imagine."

"Guess, though."

"I don't have the brain capacity right now to make a blinking guess," Ollie replied, a little exasperated and whacking the file of two-year-old Dylan Anderson onto his stack.

"Guess," she repeated and grinned.

"Urgh." Hands on hips, Ollie twisted around behind the nurses' station to face Taya. "I don't know." He looked up at one of the child-made butterfly drawings pinned to the ceiling, spinning on its thread against the air conditioner. "Wait, was it 'will you marry me?'"

Taya burst out laughing. She had one of those high-pitched laughs that never failed to cause a commotion, and in a quiet nighttime children's hospital wing, ever so much more so. Ollie went to offer a quick apology, aka smile, to whichever parent might still be awake this late. There weren't many. Just the one. Jacob. He hovered by the door of his daughter's room, probably wondering if Taya's laugh was a fire drill.

"No." Taya wiped her tear-filled eyes.

"Oh, flipping tell me," Ollie urged. "I need to observe Daisy Monroe in—" He lifted his arm to reveal his bare wrist, then quickly changed plan to pull the zip wire on his lapel fob watch. "Two minutes."

"What happened to your watch?" Taya asked, calming her outburst.

"Nothing," Ollie replied a little too quickly, not to get the wrinkled brow from Taya. He sighed. "I left it at his place." And winced at the inevitable comeback.

Amazingly, there wasn't one. Taya hummed an idle response and shifted along the desk to tap at the computer. Ollie waited a few moments and, thinking he might have dodged a bullet, picked up his implement tray and walked around the desk toward Daisy's room.

"Your dad bought you that." Taya tapped sharp fingernails along the keyboard, eyes fixed on the screen.

Ollie stopped on his way to Daisy's room. Head bowed, he nodded. He could make out Taya uttering the C word under her breath and hoped that she was referring to the man who she knew would have thrown out that watch. He couldn't be certain, though. Ollie deserved the retort himself. The last remaining gift his father had bought him with a sound mind was now discarded to a waste dump simply because Ollie had needed comfort and release from a man who had given neither.

Remembering his New Year pledge, Ollie straightened his scrubs and continued to Room One.

"Ollie, hi." Jacob's piercing blue eyes penetrated Ollie as though the man was able to read every sordid detail in Ollie's memory bank.

"Need to check Daisy's obs."

Ollie kept his voice low. Daisy still slept soundly, clutching the pink teddy bear, and Ollie could feel that comfort radiate through his body. He wasn't ashamed to admit he had a soft toy just like it at home and regularly hugged it at night when he needed soothing. He didn't get hugs that often anywhere else. *Never underestimate the power of a St. Cross-emblazoned teddy bear.*

Jacob nodded and shifted in the doorway for Ollie to pass. He hovered as Ollie placed the tray down on the moveable table at the foot of the bed, and when Ollie leaned over to press the various buttons on the observation screen, he caught Jacob watching him.

"It was bleeping earlier." Jacob nodded at the screen. "I was worried. Should it do that?"

"It'll bleep occasionally," Ollie assured him. "When she's asleep, her blood pressure drops." He wrote down the latest results on Daisy's file. "I get notified out there of any alarms." He pointed his pen at the nurses' station. "Anything abnormal, and I'll come running."

Jacob nodded, but the perpetual tension in his shoulders was still visible. Ollie had a sudden urge to massage it away. But he gave what he could—a smile.

"If you're worried about anything..." Ollie clapped the file on the table. "Anything at all, there's a button over there to call me." He nodded at the headboard with its multitude of buttons, plug sockets and wires. "Ignore that it's a silhouette of a dress. Hospitals can be very gender stereotypical."

Jacob snorted a laugh and tucked his hands into his jeans pockets. Ollie pulled out two disposable gloves from the packet on the tray, slipped them on and picked up Daisy's wrist to feel the pulse. Pulling his fob watch from his pocket, he counted the beats.

"Doesn't your machine do that?" Jacob queried.

"Yes." Ollie strove to focus on the pulsating wrist rather than the voice drifting across the mattress. "But we do manual spot checks to make sure. Can't rely on technology all the time, I'm afraid. Often fails."

"I could take offense at that, you know."

Ollie placed Daisy's arm under the blankets and glanced up.

"I work in IT," Jacob explained. "Consultant. Software developer. I build technology, so I'd have to argue that it isn't the technology that fails." Jacob smiled, leaning forward so his knees knocked against the side of the bed. "It's the end-user base."

Ollie laughed. He leaned over for the syringe on his tray and picked up Daisy's other arm with the IV cannula taped to the back of her hand. "I can probably agree with you there." He inserted the syringe through the infusion. "Give me human patients any day. Can't give a computer a hug when they're not working properly."

"Do hugs work, then?" Jacob's gaze fixed on his daughter.

"Of course!" Ollie stepped to the foot of the bed and wrote the obs on the clipboard. "It's a whole year at nursing college on hugs alone."

Jacob chuckled. His deep, soft laughter made Ollie's stomach flutter. He quickly brushed it off to keep to the job in hand and sorted through the items on his tray. *Focus on what I love. Nursing. Keeping children comfortable when they are clearly uncomfortable.* Things he should be doing.

"What made you want to be a nurse?"

Jacob took a few steps toward him and sat on the edge of Daisy's bed, eyeing the items on Ollie's tray. He was no doubt wondering what they could all be for and how they aided his daughter's recovery.

"I like helping people." Ollie snapped off his gloves. "Children especially, as it seems so unfair that any of them have to go through this."

He moved over to the orange flip-top bin and shoved the gloves in. When Ollie turned, Jacob stood with his arms wrapped around his body, as if giving himself one of those therapeutic hugs.

"Plus, I always find it truly amazing how these kids take it all in their stride," Ollie added. "Adults cower and curse and feel the unfairness of it all. Children accept this is their life, rather cruelly. And the power of a hug to a child is far more effective than to an old grizzly guy in for a stubbed toe."

Jacob breathed out a laugh. Ollie could tell he was finding the whole situation unbearable. By talking to him, Jacob was able to keep his mind off things. Ollie didn't mind. The night shift was always so deathly quiet, with most of the children dreaming their way to a better life. A life without operations, needles and sickness. Most parents used the opportunity to catch up on sleep, some by their child's bed. Others went home, leaving the responsibility to the professionals for a while, to recuperate for the next trying day.

"My little sister was a poorly child," Ollie offered. "Matilda. We call her Tilly. Cancer. Lots of stays in hospital. I used to kinda love coming to visit her. I thought it was all fun. None of my friends got to come into London after school. It felt special." Ollie shrugged. "Of course, it doesn't feel like that for the parents. But I learned a lot about nursing from my visits and couldn't see myself going into anything else."

"I can see why you would choose it, then." Jacob lowered his head to get into Ollie's eyeline. "Is your sister okay now?"

Ollie waved a hand. "Oh yeah. She's fine now. Been in remission a fair few years. Sixteen and into the Vamps." Ollie shuddered. "Can't protect her from that, unfortunately."

Jacob chuckled. "Not a fan, then?"

"God, no. Boy bands are not my thing. Although…" Ollie lowered his voice and spoke out of the side of his mouth. "Take That are considered a man-band, right?"

"Afraid I wouldn't know." Jacob returned his gaze to his daughter. "Last I heard, she was into Disney Princesses and Peppa Pig."

"Keep her that way for as long as possible." Ollie clucked his tongue. "Because when boys come to town, they bring a world of trouble."

Jacob nodded solemnly, as if the statement held a multitude of truths. Ollie sure knew it did. He hovered for a bit, checking all was in order around the bed.

"What made you go into IT?" Ollie finally asked, tucking his hands into his scrubs pockets. It was rather novel to have someone to talk to who wasn't Taya or any of the other female nurses or the occasional frantic mother.

"Oh. I was always a bit of a nerd." Jacob shook his head, his hair falling around his face. He swiped it back. "Plus a bit of an oddball. Making friends wasn't easy, so I made friends with a computer." He chuckled as if at a memory. "I had a knack with them. Hacked into my parents' online banking accounts when I was a kid.

Hacked into a few other places I probably shouldn't mention."

Ollie laughed. Jacob's smile brightened up his otherwise dark features. "Well, at least I know who to come to when I lock myself out of my online banking for forgetting the answer to my pre-prepared questions." Ollie picked up his nurse tray. "Seriously, you'd think I would remember the name of my first pet, but apparently the bank knows better."

Jacob chuckled again. Before the deep vibrations could reach Ollie's groin, he clanged the tray over to the door.

"Mine was Frodo."

Ollie turned back to catch the desperation in Jacob's voice and those blue eyes.

"A fish. Goldfish. Had a circular bowl for a home. So, he had the one ring to rule them all."

Ollie laughed. The tray in one hand, he curled the other around the door handle to pull it open. "Budgie," he offered. "Mine was a budgie, but I think I must have spelled it wrong or something."

Jacob grinned with a nod. He stepped forward, then back again, his eyes remaining fixed on Ollie. The pleading in the dilating pupils was unmistakable. Ollie had seen that same appeal many a time. Especially from parents who undertook the night shift beside their children's beds. Jacob didn't want to go back to sitting in silence, listening to a bleeping machine, one that made no sense to him for once. Talking obviously made him forget where he was and what had happened to get him there.

"You should try to get some sleep," Ollie suggested. "I know it's not the ideal place for a nap, what with all the weird noises. And that sofa bed is as hard as hell.

But you should still try. I'm here for Daisy, too, remember."

Jacob nodded and just before Ollie could leave the room, he heard it. The loud growl from the pit of Jacob's stomach. Jacob shifted, his cheeks blushing crimson under the dark stubble on his face. "Sorry," Jacob said. "I haven't been able to eat all day. Not since I heard."

Ollie smiled in sympathy.

"Is there anywhere open for food?"

Ollie went to check his wristwatch, until he remembered it wasn't where it usually was and slapped his arm down. Again.

"Lost my watch." Ollie wasn't sure why he felt the need to explain his strange arm-flap. He switched the tray to his other arm and pulled his fob from his top pocket. "Sorry, the canteen closed a while back. They have those god-awful vending machines if you want something that gets microwaved and burns your tongue on the first bite but is still frozen in the middle?"

Jacob scrunched his nose, emulating a cute bunny rabbit twitching his whiskers. Ollie glanced down to the floor not to have to look at it.

"It's okay." Jacob shook his head. "I'm sure I won't starve."

Another loud growl of his stomach came with perfect comedic timing.

Ollie snorted a laugh and tugged the door open. "There's a late-night pizza place down the road. They do an amazing seafood topping. If you like seafood, that is. Why don't you go fuel up for the night ahead?"

"Oh, I don't want to leave her." Jacob glanced down at his daughter, still snoring in the bed.

"She's okay," Ollie assured him. "She has the best nurse on the ward, I promise."

He offered up a wink, and Jacob smiled, but it was short-lived.

"I don't think I could sit and eat, not being with her," Jacob admitted, voice low and melancholy. "I've not been around enough as it is."

Ollie heard his own heart beat. He was used to listening to little hearts and could easily notice an out-of-time pulse, but his own was harder to put a finger on. Yet he knew it was beating out of time at hearing such sincerity and sadness. He took a deep breath, attempting to even it out.

"Listen," Ollie finally said. "I probably shouldn't allow it, but why don't you go order it, and I'll let you bring it up here?"

Jacob's face lit up with gratitude. "Really? You wouldn't get into trouble?"

"Nah. The things parents sneak up here without us seeing are bad enough. I'll just plead ignorance."

Jacob smiled. "Thank you, Ollie."

Ollie nodded, and Jacob rooted around in the pocket of his jacket, laid out on the chair, for his money. He met Ollie at the door and held it wider for him to pass through. Jacob's breath trickled down the back of his neck and Ollie's arms erupted with goose pimples. So he strode hurriedly to the nurses' station which was vacant for once – all the other nurses were off with their own patients. Jacob jogged over to the swinging exit door and rammed it open with his shoulder.

"I really appreciate this, Ollie."

Ollie waved a hand. "You get the seafood, and I may have to steal a slice."

"Done!" Jacob bounded out of the ward, the swinging doors flapping shut.

Ollie slapped the tray down on the counter and sighed. Pinching the bridge of his nose, he checked the time on the computer screen and wondered if, at the stroke of midnight, it would happen automatically. This whole not-feeling anything? It was easy. That was how Elliot did it. Elliot, the c—

"I need a smoke." Taya slipped up behind him and rested her chin on his shoulder.

"One hour, T," Ollie said. "Then resolutions just happen, right?"

"Sure," Taya replied, rather unconvincingly.

Ollie huffed.

"He said, 'I like you, I just don't like being around you.'" Taya plucked out a mint from the bag she always kept in her scrubs pocket and offered Ollie one.

He refused with a shake of his head. "He sounds like a keeper."

"Yeah," Taya agreed. "I think I'll just stick to the sexting with this one."

* * * *

"The first time I ate an oyster, I nearly chucked it back up." Ollie bit into the luxuriously hot and creamy pizza slice. He tucked it to the side of his mouth to continue talking. "Felt like I was eating snot."

Jacob laughed, holding a hand up to his lips not to spit his own mouthful of pizza across the room. He had come back to the ward quite quickly, and Ollie had managed to sneak him through into Daisy's room, with the door now firmly shut. The offer of the one slice had made him not immediately back right out. He was hungry, and it was another two hours until his official break. All his patients were asleep, obs up to date, and while he should be catching up on the paperwork, he thought he could use a quick bite.

Sitting at the end of Daisy's room on the pull-out sofa, Ollie had closed the separating curtain in case anyone peeked in through the blinds. It wasn't exactly against the rules to bring food into children's rooms, although it was frowned upon if it wasn't food from the hospital canteen. It was probably ever so much more frowned upon for Ollie to be eating it with a patient's parent.

The pizza box lay open on the sofa between them, and Ollie perched on the armrest while Jacob sat on the cushions. Jacob devoured the pizza as if he hadn't eaten properly in days. Ollie couldn't blame him. The seafood topping was to die for. But he suspected it was the first time Jacob had allowed such a meal to pass his lips in a while, fear and worry taking over the hunger pangs in his stomach. It made him wonder what sort of person wouldn't tell their child's father about their child's operation.

"I don't mean to pry." Ollie knew that was the age-old saying for actually, *yes I do* and *I'm so gonna* but he continued regardless. "How come you didn't know about Daisy being here? Did her mother not tell you? The operation would have been booked in for months."

Jacob swallowed his last piece of pizza and wiped his hands on a paper napkin to rid them of the crumbs and leftover grease. Falling back in the seat, he rested his head against the wall and drifted his all-consuming bright blue eyes to Ollie's.

"She doesn't particularly like me anymore." Jacob winced. "We don't really speak. Most of our conversations are conducted through lawyers and the CSA—the Child Support Agency. I used to see Daisy every other weekend, but when she got sick, Becky stopped turning up. I believe she also has a new boyfriend who may be the cause of some of that."

"I'm sorry." Ollie wished he hadn't asked on witnessing the torment on Jacob's features. "That must be tough."

Jacob shook his head against the wall. "I deserve it, I suppose."

"Nothing merits being shut out of your daughter's life." Ollie was surprised at how gallant it came out.

Jacob picked at the skin on his hand. "Perhaps not. But I don't think she really trusts me." He shrugged one shoulder. "Lying to someone for so many years often has that effect."

Ollie nodded, sympathetic smile on display, and decided to leave that there. It wasn't his place to know the whole goings-on in the man's life, even if it did affect his patient.

"I found out Daisy was having surgery from my many phone calls to Becky's parents." Jacob met Ollie's gaze and held it. "They also choose not to have any dealings with me. So, they rarely answer my calls. I called from a pay phone in the end, and as that wasn't my number, they had to answer."

"Well, they all sound extremely petty. Whatever happened, the way you love your daughter is commendable, and they shouldn't hinder that, no matter how they feel about you." Ollie stood and brushed down his scrubs. "I'm going to assume you're not an axe murderer or anything and it's more to do with your love life?"

Jacob snorted. "Yes. As in no." He shook his head. "I'm not an axe murderer or any other type of murderer." He held up his hands. "These break into computers all day and not people's skulls."

"Good. 'Cause sharing a pizza with a murderer was not on my list of things to do in the new year."

Jacob laughed. "I hope it isn't, because I hear they can end pretty nastily…and the world would be a duller place without your smile."

Ollie paused, stunned, and wondered if he'd even heard the mumble from Jacob correctly. But his mouth overtook any rational response and simply offered up the aforementioned smile. Jacob scrubbed a hand over the lower half of his face, as though attempting to shove the words back in, so Ollie gave it no further thought.

"I'd best get back to work. If you need anything, I'll be out there. Or ring the bell."

At Jacob's nod, Ollie ripped open the curtain and rushed out of the room as fast as his comfortable shoes allowed.

Chapter Four

The Doctor Will See You Now

"Um, hi, um, Ollie?"

Ollie glanced up from the mound of blue card files he had been flicking through for the past couple of hours. He couldn't stop the beam radiating from his face. His mouth curled upward, replacing his previous frown. Of course, he always had a smile for patients and their families. But this smile had erupted before he could even decide which one to put on. It grew tenfold when the nervous flicker of lips opposite curved up into a returning grin.

"Jacob." Ollie flopped the files onto the desk. "How can I help?"

Jacob scratched his short and, Ollie noted, perfectly manicured nails across the surface of the nurses' station reception desk. Ollie stared at the hands that screamed *all male.* Apart from the tended-to fingernails, Jacob's hands were as masculine as they came, thick, chunky and scattered with dark hair that protruded from under his long-sleeved shirt, over the back of his thick-veined hand and up to his knuckles. It wasn't a grotesquely hairy hand. The man was no hobbit, regardless of what he'd called his fish, but Ollie could almost feel the touch of the silky-smooth hairs, and he licked his lips involuntarily.

"Oh, I, er," Jacob stammered.

Ollie's grin grew to Cheshire-Cat levels. His hand barely covered it.

"Wondered if there were any cups about? For the machine?" Jacob waved a hand at the watercooler that was, indeed, absent of any of the plastic variety of cup.

"Right, yes, of course," Ollie replied. "I'll need to go get some from supplies. Can you hang tight for a couple of minutes?"

"Sure." Jacob cleared his throat to rid the deep crackle, then laughed. "Thanks."

"If you're overly parched, I have a bottle under my desk you can use?" Ollie then offered up the sweetest smile he had probably ever given in his entire life. It seemed his face had overtaken his ability to categorize his choice of responsive lip curling. Jacob was beginning to have a category all to himself.

"Oh no, that's okay." Jacob backed away from the desk. "I can wait."

"I promise I don't have mouth cooties," Ollie replied with a suggestive tilt of his head.

What am I doing? That was not the sort of thing I should say to a patient's father. Maybe to a stranger in a bar or club. Perhaps he could blame the recent lack of social life and the involuntary need to flirt, like his resolution had allowed, was now seeping out in his place of work. He needed to get a grip on that. It wouldn't bring him good fortune. *Not here.*

Jacob stumbled, almost hitting a passing bed being pushed by an orderly. The child within displayed a multitude of tubes sunk into his body, and Jacob grabbed the traveling mattress, offering up an apologetic hand to the little boy. The orderly didn't stop for pleasantries, and Ollie knew that kid was heading somewhere he'd rather not. It didn't help to curtail his tickled smirk at Jacob's misfortune, though. Jacob blew out a puff of air from rounded lips and stroked his super-silky hair from his face, the locks flowing between his fingers. The man could be in a medicated shampoo commercial. Not that he needed it—the guy clearly didn't have dandruff. But Ollie doubted any of the football stars they used to endorse the product suffered from a flaky scalp either.

"Oliver?"

Ollie ripped his gaze from Jacob to address the incoming interruption. And probably for the first time that night, his smile faltered.

"Yes, Doctor?" Ollie replied in his all-professional tone. He even added a bit of height to the delivery. He needn't have bothered. Dr. Rawlings was a good six foot three and he a mere five-ten.

Dr. Rawlings did his usual scan, glancing around the reception area. Ollie rolled his eyes while the doctor wasn't looking. Jacob backed off toward his daughter's room and Ollie snapped out of his blatant ogling of the man when the doctor slapped a hand down on the counter and leaned forward.

"I need to see you."

Ollie supposed the doctor could have been attempting a whisper, but his deep and vibrating voice simply came out a hushed baritone.

"Here I am." Ollie smiled with his mouth, not his eyes.

"End of shift." Dr. Rawlings either didn't notice Ollie's standoffishness or chose to ignore it. "Not my place. We'll go to the Radisson."

Tapping the desk, the doctor twisted to walk off.

"Er, Doctor?" Ollie called, leaning forward on the desk. "No."

"I beg your pardon?"

"I said, no."

Him folding his arms across his chest made Ollie's pen and timer flick up from his top pocket. He stood his ground, but the deep, penetrating dark eyes firing their lasers across the desk made Ollie sink back. He loosened his arms and couldn't help the quick glance across the corridor to Room One. Jacob had his back to him, standing by the door to his daughter's room. Ollie was pretty sure that, from there, he could hear every damn word. Ollie faced Dr. Rawlings and awaited the inevitable reply.

"That isn't welcome this time, Oliver."

"I'm busy. This time. *Doctor.*"

"Doing what, may I ask?" Dr. Rawlings' brow furrowed as if he couldn't believe that Ollie would have another life outside this hospital. And the occasional fraternizing with him. *Not that he isn't far wrong.*

Ollie picked up the paper files from his desk and continued to idly flick through, avoiding looking directly into those eyes that had had him rooted to the spot and caving in numerous times before, until he realized that he could do this. It was the new him. The New Year's resolution. He wouldn't feel a goddamn thing. "I'm seeing my dad."

"Fine." Dr. Rawlings, unperturbed, tucked his hands into his chino pockets. "That's fine. We can do that first."

"We?" Ollie widened his eyes. "And first?"

"Yes. I'll drop you there. I can go to the coffee place around the corner. I have some charity work I need to catch up on, and you'll be, what, an hour?"

Ollie snorted in utter contempt. He violently shook his head, and his eyes shuttered closed, so he wouldn't be able to see the doctor's next reaction.

"No," Ollie said again with more conviction this time. "No, Elliot." He gritted his teeth, bold enough to utter the first name here. "I don't want a time limit as to when I can see my father. I don't want you to wait around the corner like some shameful pay-for-play. And I don't want to go to the bloody Radisson. It's sleazy. You're sleazy." Ollie waved a hand across the desk, moving it up and down the doctor's tall and muscular frame he knew intimately yet had no desire to ever see again. His voice rose as he spoke, but he no longer cared.

"Oliver," Dr. Rawlings warned, making a quick scan of the ward.

"Ollie!" Ollie barked through clenched teeth. "My name here is Ollie. Everyone calls me Ollie. The only person who is allowed to call me Oliver is my father!" He stomped out from behind the front desk and around the side to head off toward the supply cupboard. "Well, when he isn't calling me Tilly, that is."

"Right." Dr. Rawlings had his hands on his hips. "I see you're being this way again. We'll talk later."

Ollie wanted to scream, but instead he listened out for the slap of dress shoes on the linoleum floor and the swing of the exit doors before scratching his nails through his closely cropped blond hair. If he had hair like Jacob's, he would be yanking it right now to get some cathartic release. But he didn't, so he took a deep breath and slapped his ID badge on the reader to the supply cupboard. It buzzed, turned green and Ollie shoved open the door. He grabbed a couple of the piled tubes of plastic cups and grumbled his way back up the corridor.

Jacob stood waiting at the water machine. His smile said it all. He had heard. His opinion had changed and he now awaited the cups to grab some water and never venture from his daughter's room for the entire night shift. That was fine. Ollie had far too much work to do to waste it chatting with someone he wouldn't ever see again after his daughter's discharge in forty-eight hours.

"Thanks." Jacob held out a hand for Ollie to pass him the cups. "I'll put the rest in for you, if you have things to get on with?"

And there it is. Bugger off, Ollie, you disgusting prostituting specimen of a man. I can't believe I wasted my precious time here with my daughter talking to someone who sleeps their way to the top.

It wasn't like that, but Jacob wouldn't know. No one would understand. Ollie had a hard time understanding why he'd let it happen. All the women around the hospital would slap him on the back with a 'well done'. He didn't want that either. And he certainly didn't want that look from Jacob. Because that hurt.

"Dr. Rawlings and I," Ollie started before he even realized his mouth was speaking. He tucked the tower of cups to his chest, cradling them like a protective barrier. "We had a sort of thing. It's totally over, though. Like, totally."

"So I heard," Jacob replied and the nod indicated that he didn't believe a word Ollie had uttered and chose to believe his ears.

Ollie squeezed past Jacob to the watercooler and began tucking the tower of cups into the holder. It didn't require as much brute force as Ollie was giving it, and he was sure he'd cracked a few of them in the process. He made a mental note to fill the paper towels too, just so the nurses wouldn't have to clean up when the inevitable spill happened. He was then momentarily stunned when Jacob curled a hand around his and tugged him away. A few of the cups fell to the floor with a clap.

"People make mistakes, Ollie." Jacob began tucking the cups into the tube more cleanly. "You've met mine, remember."

Ollie breathed out a laugh. He crouched and gathered up the spillage. As he stood, he handed them to Jacob to ease into the holder.

"I mean, Daisy isn't a mistake," Jacob rushed out. "I love Daisy with all my heart." He swallowed. "She was an accident, yes. But never a mistake. Becky was the mistake. I sometimes think this is all my fault. My penance."

"That's ridiculous!" Ollie blurted, then instantly bit his lip. One thing never to do was give his own opinions on things he didn't know the full story on. But there was something about Jacob that screamed he was a decent sort and not being treated fairly. Ollie's overprotective nature spilled out, unannounced. "What I can honestly tell you from all my years being in a hospital is that illness is completely unprejudiced. It doesn't care who it attacks."

Jacob nodded, his smile solemn. He appeared stacked with guilt. Ollie didn't know how to assure him that, no matter what he did with his life, Daisy's hole in her heart would have been there regardless. Just like his sister's cancer.

Ollie filled a cup with water and handed it to Jacob. He took it with gratitude and downed the lot in one gulp. The hospital's air-conditioning often made people parched. Jacob refilled the cup and swished the contents before taking a slower sip this time. Ollie knew he needed to back away, but his overwhelming desire to hear more kept him rooted to the spot.

"If you don't mind me saying…" Jacob lifted his eyes from staring at the swirling water. "I'm sure you can do better than him."

Ollie's throat caught, and he had to hack up a bit, Daisy-style, to rid it of the congealed saliva. He glanced down to the floor and suddenly felt the need to explain. To make someone understand why.

"He's a great doctor," Ollie said. "One of the best. Daisy's in good hands with him."

Jacob nodded. "I'm sure she is. But doctors aren't known for their bedside manner, right? I mean, that's why they have nurses."

Ollie snorted. "Good point." Nodding, he filled another cup to wash down his guilt. "I've known him since I did my placement here. I really wanted this job when I'd finished my course. I guess…" Ollie shrugged. "He could help with that."

"Aren't nurses in demand?" Jacob asked, his voice light and low, with no trace of judgment in it. A mere statement.

"Yes," Ollie replied. "But pediatric nurses not so much. And especially in this place. It's the best hospital in the country. The pay is better. The conditions much better. Getting a job here straight out of nursing school is rare."

Jacob nodded and glanced away, scanning all the pictures and thank-you cards scattering the walls and desk. There were a fair few written and drawn directly for Ollie. No one gives thanks like a child who'd enjoyed playing with their nurse.

"My dad has dementia," Ollie blurted out, still trying to rectify his actions and how they came across to a complete stranger. It had been hard enough for Taya, with whom he'd been friends for years, to understand why Ollie continued to fall back into bed with Dr. Rawlings, when each morning he was made to feel as unworthy as something stuck on the bottom of the doctor's shoe. "He's in a good nursing home. The best care." Ollie took another swig of water and, swallowing, he met Jacob's concerned gaze. "It costs a fortune, and I need to help my mum pay for it. Getting this job was vital in that."

Jacob simply nodded. No further conversation. No further sweet mutterings about Ollie's smile making the world a better place. No further offer of pizza. In a mere couple of hours, Ollie had managed to make someone devalue their opinion of him. He had to remember that he wasn't going to feel anything about that. Or Dr. Rawlings. Or his lost watch. Or his father calling him by his sister's name, seemingly forgetting he had a son as well.

"I'm sure he offered you the world," Jacob finally muttered, pressing his cup to his lips as though to hide his next words. "Anyone would if they could."

Ollie stopped breathing and his brain tried to process what those words meant. He wasn't able to comment further because a loud alarm bleeped from the nurses' station, followed by a distinctive childlike wail. Ollie spun and checked his monitor. As he turned, Jacob was already in Room One, arms around his daughter as she threw up all over the bed, the obs machine's bleeps drowning out her tears.

Jacob clung to Daisy as she curled over to vomit once more. Ollie rushed around the bed, picked up another cardboard pot from the side unit, and held it out to Daisy, while pressing the buttons on the obs machine to stop its incessant shrill.

"What's happening?" Jacob demanded. "What's the alarm?

"Her heart rate and blood pressure will go up when she's sick," Ollie explained. "As they do usually. It's not abnormally high. She's just clearly upset, and the machine is letting us know."

Daisy continued to sob through her vomiting.

"I'll call the doctor to come check, anyway." Ollie handed the pot to Jacob and slipped off the bed to use the phone mounted on the wall by the door. "Just to be safe. But I'm sure all's fine." A few taps, and Ollie was through. "Room One, Daisy Monroe," he said into the receiver. "She's been sick again. Can you come check?"

Ollie paused and offered over a wink to Daisy. Vomiting over, she leaned back into her father's warm embrace. Jacob wrapped his arms around her frail body and slid his hands up and down her arms, kissing her forehead.

"Yes, all meds up to date. Yes, I gave her that about a half-hour ago. Yes."

Ollie slammed the phone down harder than he needed to. With a deep breath, he turned to his patient. "Dr. Rawlings is on his way." He did his best not to catch Jacob's eye and remain fixed on Daisy, but the urge overtook him. As his gaze landed on Jacob, relief washed over Ollie on witnessing the comforting curvature across Jacob's lips.

A few moments later and Dr. Rawlings burst into Room One, his presence both foreboding and alleviating over the scene. Ollie gave him the rundown on Daisy's obs, status and sickness whilst the doctor stood at the end of the bed, rubbing his chin, reading and rereading the notes. Ollie stood back, allowing Jacob to give Daisy the comfort she needed. Plus, he felt ridiculously uncomfortable with Jacob now knowing his history with the doctor. If Dr. Rawlings found out, Ollie would be in a world of pain that in no way compared to Daisy Monroe's.

"Right." Dr. Rawlings slapped the clipboard down on the table. He turned to Ollie. "You gave the oral morphine at the stated time?"

"Yes, Doctor," Ollie replied. "Eleven twenty-five."

Dr. Rawlings's gaze didn't flicker. Ollie felt ever more uncomfortable.

"I was here, Doctor," Jacob said. "That was the time Ollie gave Daisy the drug."

Dr. Rawlings turned his gaze on Jacob. The hum of his reply was the only other sound in the room now that all the machines had been turned to silent. Jacob didn't move. He kept his eyes on Dr. Rawlings, arms firmly around his daughter. Eventually, the doctor turned back to address Ollie.

"Dosage?"

"Naught-point-one milligrams."

Dr. Rawlings sighed. He shook his head.

"I do apologize, Mr. Monroe," Dr. Rawlings replied. "It would seem my nurse has been distracted and gave the wrong dose of morphine to Daisy." He turned back to Ollie. "I clearly stated on my notes to reduce the amount to naught-point-zero-five milligrams, due to the nausea-induced side effect. Perhaps keep your mind focused on the job, Oliver?"

Ollie sank, his stomach plummeting to the floor. He was fairly certain he looked as pale as Daisy right then. Racking his brain, he tried to remember the notes or even the verbal notification on the reduction of medication. He couldn't. All he could remember was sitting on that sofa behind him, eating seafood pizza.

"Hopefully, she has thrown that all back up now," Dr. Rawlings continued, eyes back on Jacob. "I think we will give her a night off morphine and stick to paracetamol should she require it." He turned to Ollie. "Can you make a note of that, Oliver?"

"Yes, Doctor," Ollie muttered. He straightened his shoulders to appear more confident than he was. "Paracetamol only."

"Good." Dr. Rawlings turned his attention back to the bed. "Mr. Monroe, I can only apologize once again on behalf of the hospital and my staff. There is no immediate concern. I'm afraid Daisy is having an intolerance to the morphine. Her body is acting accordingly. Which is a good sign."

"Thank you, Doctor," Jacob replied, and Ollie noted it was said with trepidation as he flicked his gaze from the doctor to Ollie.

"Oliver?"

Ollie glanced up, chewing his bottom lip to stop it quivering.

"My office, half an hour."

Ollie nodded. Dr. Rawlings marched out of the room, and it took a couple of moments before Ollie could make eye contact with Jacob.

"I'm so sorry." Ollie swallowed. "I will check all the notes, but I don't recall a change in dosage."

Jacob nodded.

"I'll get some more sheets, change the bed and get Daisy a new gown."

There was no further eye contact.

* * * *

Ollie tapped on the door to Dr. Rawlings' office lightly, in the hope it wouldn't be heard. The bark from behind indicated it had been, and Ollie opened the door with a resigned sigh.

"Close the door," Dr. Rawlings ordered, not looking up from his computer screen.

Ollie did so reluctantly. Being alone in this office didn't fill him with much confidence. Adjusting his scrubs, he stood to the side of the desk and clasped his hands together behind his back. At least his glasses lenses would mask some of his fear. Dr. Rawlings gave a few more fierce taps to his keyboard, twisted around in the swivel chair and clasped his hands over his stomach.

"Rookie mistake, Oliver."

"I checked all the notes." Ollie attempted to inject his voice with confidence. "There was nothing on there about a change of dose. I maintain I gave the correct amount to Daisy Monroe according to the doctor in charge."

"That being me."

"Yes, Doctor."

"Well." Dr. Rawlings waved a nonchalant hand. Slapping it down on his leg, he leaned forward in the seat. "What's done is done. The girl will feel a little nauseated for a while, but that's the extent of the concern."

"I trust then this won't be taken any further?"

Dr. Rawlings smiled. His pearly white teeth shone as he shook his head with a chuckle. Ollie was hard-pressed not to knock a few of the caps out of alignment.

"As always, Oliver," Dr. Rawlings said, twisting the seat from side to side, "this will remain between us."

Ollie nodded. He knew the drill.

"As long as we can think of some way for the father not to report it to the Patient Advice and Liaison Service?"

"I'm sure he won't," Ollie muttered.

"Yes." Dr. Rawlings tapped his clasped forefingers over his lips. "I can see your undeniable charm has worked miracles on him, too."

"I don't know what you mean."

"Oh, come off it, Oliver." Dr. Rawlings slapped his hand down viciously. "You could bend the straightest of straight men."

"I beg your pardon?"

The doctor stood, strode toward Ollie and leaned forward to breathe into his ear.

"Don't say no to me again. It's not nice. And we both know how I like you being nice to me." He lowered his voice to a deep rumble. "Unless I deem it necessary for you to act otherwise."

Ollie shuddered and stepped back.

"Dr. Rawlings," he snapped. "I ask you not to speak that way to me again or I will file a sexual harassment case against you." Turning on his heel, Ollie ripped open the office door. "And I ask that all further work-related discussions are conducted in an open space or accompanied by a chaperone."

The doctor chuckled. Ollie shivered, straightening out his shoulders and attempting to get his jelly legs to move out of the office. It was as if he were stuck. He knew why.

"Are you insisting we play it this way again?" Dr. Rawlings dragged his hand down the nape of Ollie's neck.

Ollie glanced over his shoulder, his chin hitting the doctor's thick fingers. "It's over, Elliot. *Over.* I don't want to play it any way, anymore. Not with you."

Dr. Rawlings pouted. "That hurts, Oliver." He pressed his lips to Ollie's ear and dug his fingers into his neck. "You'll have to make that one up to me."

Ollie squirmed out of the doctor's grip and marched up the corridor, the soles of his shoes squeaking with every hurried step away. He was going to make it all the way back to the cardiology wing without feeling a goddamn thing. He was—

"Oliver?"

Oliver stopped dead in his tracks at that tone.

"How's your father?" The doctor's cruelest words yet rebounded off the sterile walls and stabbed Ollie right through the heart.

Fucking New Year's resolutions.

* * * *

Ollie marched through the double doors and into the gusting snowfall. It was freezing, obviously, so he wrapped his quilted jacket over his scrubs and around his shoulders. When he looked up at the night sky, the flakes landed with a delicate tickle on his lenses. Now, where could he go in the middle of the city of London to scream as loudly as his lungs allowed?

"Taking up smoking, Ollie?" Taya leaned up against the wall, drawing on her usual menthol cigarette.

"The resolution going as well for you, then?" Ollie inquired with a nod.

"I have a whole year to achieve it." Taya sucked in another lungful. "Seems a bit rushed to do it on the first day. You okay?"

Ollie nodded. He soon changed his mind and shook his head. He sighed, and the steam billowing from his mouth rivaled Taya's menthol breath.

"He really can be a wanker," Ollie remarked.

"Amen, sister." Taya waved the hand clutching her cigarette. "Finally over him, then?"

"I've been over him a good long time," Ollie admitted. "Trouble is, I don't think he's quite ready to give me up."

Taya took a long drag, sucking it almost to the end of the butt, and exhaled with one elongated blow. She flicked the cigarette end to the floor, stamped on it with her black Crocs and tucked her arm through Ollie's. "Don't go dwelling on things that happen on shift."

"I did not make that mistake." Ollie's jaw clenched, and not just because of the freezing-cold air. He took pride in his work. Giving the wrong dose of controlled medicine to a child wasn't something he could come to terms with. He'd thoroughly checked every note and every file—there was nothing mentioned about a change in dosage. His only doubt was due to Jacob. Maybe Ollie had been paying too much attention to the man to have heard any verbal instructions.

"I know you didn't, hun." Taya lifted up on her tiptoes to kiss Ollie's cheek. "He'll find a new toy to play with soon."

What she said wasn't meant to be hurtful. Ollie had been the doctor's toy, for far too long. Ollie had always known that Dr. Rawlings liked to have a favorite nurse, or more often than not a student nurse, which was where it had started with him. The doctor's previous playthings had all moved on. Ollie wasn't sure when or where because Elliot didn't speak of them. But Ollie knew they'd existed. The doctor kept mementos from past relationships. Ollie had been shown them, Elliot brandishing them like trophies. Ollie hadn't been sure why. Perhaps it was that sick part of the doctor's character that liked to 'collect' people, the way he'd collected Ollie. Having then been ordered not to leave any trace of his existence at Elliot's place, Ollie had meticulously followed the rule in some insane attempt at not providing the man with any more keepsakes. Leaving his watch there had been a mistake, one he would no doubt pay for in more ways than one.

Ollie sighed. He'd expected Elliot to toss him aside as soon as Ollie became part of his medical team, and move on to someone who didn't work directly under him. But it seemed Dr. Rawlings hadn't quite finished with Ollie yet. "I pity the toy he chooses next," he said. "That common doctor's phrase that it 'won't hurt a bit' isn't strictly true in Elliot's case."

"Lucky for you, that pain ceases in a few minutes, right?"

She meant the resolution. Ollie nodded. "Abso-bloody-lutely."

Taya sniffed. She opened her mouth. Then closed it.

"Go on. Say it," Ollie urged.

"Do you really mean it?" Taya's banter and playfulness morphed into a concern Ollie couldn't accept. "This time?"

Ollie exhaled heavily into the freezing air. The loud blast of sirens cut him off as an ambulance bolted from the side road and screeched past them toward the crossroads, throwing a bumpy left over the mini-roundabout and vanishing out of view. Ollie hung his head and tapped the toe of his shoe on the pavement. *Lucky ambulance.*

Doctors are meant to perform miracles. Mend broken hearts. Why is mine so unfixable?

"Let's go back in." Ollie nodded at the door, avoiding Taya's last question. He wasn't sure he could lie anymore. "I'm freezing my nuts off out here."

Taya laughed. Before they had a chance to walk through the sliding doors into the hospital's main reception, Ollie's phone buzzed in his pocket. He stopped, fished it out and, on checking the incoming message display, his stomach wrenched.

"You go." Ollie nodded toward the hospital.

Taya did, and once she was out of view and the double doors closed, Ollie spun on his heel to put his back to the hospital entrance. With a shaky thumb, he clicked on the incoming video message. The screen opened up to blackness, but it was the doctor's deep, resonating, and gruff command of 'strip' that made Ollie immediately switch it off. He couldn't watch. That had been another side to him, one he desperately needed to forget. And he promised *himself* this time that he'd never revisit.

Chapter Five

Kiss It Better

Ollie glanced up at the clock on the wall. Nearly four o'clock in the morning. Four hours until his shift ended. He'd spent the remainder of the night avoiding Room One and dedicating himself to his other patients, checking, double-checking and triple-checking every note and observation chart thoroughly. Even though he was fairly certain Dr. Rawlings had been the one to make the mistake, using Ollie as a way not to have to admit it, Ollie was still shaken by the whole thing. And he was loath to admit how much that was to do with Jacob Monroe and whether the man could read the sordid images still playing on his mind from the doctor's earlier message.

He was due to take Daisy's next set of obs, and the trembling in his hands got the better of him. His stomach twisted into knots at the thought of entering that room and Jacob being awake. He hadn't seen or heard much from him since Daisy's bout of sickness, although Jacob's silhouette through the window blinds when he moved around in the room was unmistakable.

Ollie hadn't seen it for a while and he crossed his fingers with the hope that Jacob had finally succumbed to sleep.

Picking up his tray and trying not to let the contents on top rattle, he tiptoed over and peered in through the blinds. Daisy slept in the bed and Jacob, seated in the chair next to her with his back to the window, had his head propped up on his arm. Ollie swallowed, easing the door open with practiced caution. Jacob didn't stir, so Ollie walked in and slipped the tray down onto the revolving table.

Taking out his disposable gloves, he risked peeping at the chair. Jacob's eyes were closed, and his even breaths indicated he could well be asleep, so Ollie set to do everything he needed to with quiet speed. Of course, his trembling hands wouldn't allow it, and as he picked up the disposable thermometer, the tray fell to the floor with a *ting*. Ollie cursed under his breath and knelt to pick up the now unusable utensils and syringes. He dumped them into the bin, the lid clanging shut after. Ollie winced.

"Ollie?"

Ollie met Jacob's bleary expression. "Sorry. Was trying not to wake you. Which evidently means throwing a bunch of metal equipment onto a hard floor."

Jacob chuckled, leaning forward in the chair. Ollie's whole body seemed to relax from its previous tension. How did Jacob do that? It was purely the sight of an exhausted man—it brought out his inner caring side. *That's all.*

"Did you get much sleep?" Concern outweighed Ollie's decision to keep his distance.

"A little," Jacob replied. "Not much. I can sleep later. No doubt Becky will be back by morning and won't want me hanging around."

Ollie nodded, trying not to let the statement affect him either way. "I'll just go get some more equipment." He used the moment to take a deep breath and compose himself. He returned to the room with a new set of syringes and thermometer, hoping no more conversation was needed. Ollie ripped the plastic casing off and walked around the side of the bed to pop the thermometer into Daisy's armpit. He tugged on his fob watch to count the time.

"I know you didn't do anything wrong," Jacob said after exactly twenty-four seconds of silence.

Ollie peered over the bed, not knowing what to say.

"I believe you. I don't want you to think I blame you."

"We all make mistakes." Ollie involuntarily uttered the same statement Jacob had used earlier. Funny how they could both be referring to the doctor's mistakes. "We're human. Not computers," he added, to lighten the mood.

"You don't have to cover for him, either." Jacob stood. "I'm not here to make things difficult for anyone. Least of all Daisy and most certainly not Becky. I'm chalking the incident up as just one of those things. Daisy has been fine since." Jacob leaned forward to tangle his gaze with Ollie's. "But don't think you need to protect him."

Ollie nodded again and avoided looking into those deep-blue eyes. Zapping his fob watch back, he lifted Daisy's arm to take out the thermometer and checked it. Jacob retired into his chair as Ollie got on with all his other Daisy-care tasks. Once finished, he settled the tray on his forearms and paused to look over at Jacob.

His eyes were fluttering shut, and Ollie desperately tried not to let the feeling of disappointment seep down to his stomach. It did anyway, and Ollie squashed it flat and left the room.

* * * *

"I need me some hot pink choccie sugar." Taya skidded on her Crocs to slide up behind Ollie. "You game?"

It was currently approaching eight o'clock, their official off-duty time, and Ollie, desperate for the arrival of the day nurses to do his handover, wanted to disappear home and wrap himself in his duvet. After the important daily tasks, that was.

"Sure. But then I'm going to see my dad."

"I can come with if you like?" Taya offered. "Keep you company on the walk over?"

"No." Ollie shook his head, but the swinging doors burst open to drown out anything further and the same tip-tapping heels that had marched through twelve hours earlier came back in full force. Ollie's gaze followed Becky non-Monroe as she clonked her way to Room One. "It's okay. Need the alone time," he added to Taya while focusing on the silhouettes through the blind.

Becky shoved Jacob, who hadn't moved from the chair in three hours. Jacob leapt up and grabbed his coat while Becky flapped her hands in time with the muffled argument that bounded through the walls.

"Cute couple." Taya pointed the end of her pen across at Daisy Monroe's room.

"Yeah."

Jacob stomped out of the room, followed by Becky, and both nurses failed miserably at trying to look busy instead of watching the argument play out.

"I am still her father." Jacob gritted his teeth, attempting to keep his voice as low as possible at least. "You can't keep me away."

"Really?" Becky folded her arms, eyes wide. "It's a pity you didn't think about all this before, eh? Where were you when she first got sick? Where, Jacob?"

"That's not important now, Becky." Jacob swallowed, hard. And Ollie noted the change in the man's exterior. Like he'd been punched in the gut.

"You think you can be a father now?" Becky spat. "When you didn't want to be one before?"

"I was and will always be her father," Jacob snapped back. "And I am trying to prove that by being here. For her. And for you." His trembling finger made the statement that bit more poignant.

"I coped all those years when you weren't there for me. I don't need you here now."

"But she does."

Becky shuffled on her feet, arms falling from their fold, and glanced through the blinds.

"I will come back tonight, whether you need me to or not. And I'll wait. If you need me, I'll be waiting."

Becky narrowed her eyes, previous softening merging back to contempt. "Why don't you just post one of your online ads? Get yourself some company while you wait, hmm?"

"Fuck you, Becky," Jacob half yelled.

After exchanging concerned glances with Taya, Ollie rushed from behind the nurses' station and stood between the warring parents. He held up his hands in surrender.

"Hey, calm down, guys. This is a children's hospital."

Jacob hung his head. "Sorry, Ollie," he said, voice low. "My fault."

"*Ollie?*" Becky glared. "Is nowhere sacred to you, Jacob?"

"Becky," Jacob urged through a clenched jaw.

"Oh, piss off." Becky waved a hand. "Come back tonight, whatever. But I'm not staying when you are."

She stomped back into Daisy's room, slamming the door behind. It was a stroke of luck that the automatic lights switched on, signifying the start of daytime, and the usual hustle and bustle of breakfast trays and children running about in the corridors ensued. Jacob turned back to Ollie, his head still lowered.

"Can see where Daisy gets her firecracker from, huh?" Ollie smiled.

Jacob let out a shaky breath. "Becky's more than a firecracker. And she has her reasons."

Ollie nodded.

"Sorry for the commotion. It won't happen again."

Ollie waved him off as if it was nothing.

"Will you be working tonight?"

"Sure am," Ollie said. "Back on at eight."

Jacob adjusted his trench coat collar to stick up around his neck, bracing himself for the cold morning frost outside. "I guess I'll see you then?"

Ollie nodded, and he noticed the pause. Eventually Jacob spun on his heels and left, the doors flapping closed behind him.

* * * *

Ollie stood behind Taya in the usual long queue at the independent coffee shop situated on the corner of the street St. Cross stood on. It was always busy in this part of town. So near to Holborn and the financial district of London, this little High Street by the hospital was a mecca for those wanting good-quality coffee, decent independent health-food supermarkets and four-star restaurants. Most of it cost an absolute fortune, but those who worked in these parts could afford it. Luckily for Taya and Ollie, the local independents offered a twenty-five percent discount for all National Health Service staff, which meant that the queues held not only those wearing suits and carrying briefcases but also those with stethoscopes needing a caffeine fix after a twelve-hour night shift.

Taya reached the serving counter, ordered her rainbow hot chocolate monstrosity and raised an eyebrow at Ollie. He shook his head and glanced around the shop. His stomach did an unexpected flip at the hunched figure of a man on the tatty brown leather sofa stirring a spoon into a cup of perfectly constructed coffee. Ollie's whole body wanted to trot on over and offer his usual smile and idle chitchat, but something kept him where he was. Maybe the pull of the New Year's resolution?

"Want your usual?"

Ollie heard Taya's question, but his mind answered something else entirely.

"Ollie?"

Ollie snapped out of his staring, but not before Jacob lifted weary eyes from the coffee cup and met his.

"Um, no." Ollie shook his head. "I need caffeine. Get me a latte."

By the time Ollie shifted his gaze back, Jacob had stood and zipped up his coat. *Probably in a rush to get away from me.* Ollie couldn't blame the man. Twelve hours on a hospital night shift and the staff were just as eager for solitude. But Ollie's theory turned out false when Jacob meandered around the sofa and approached him.

"Ollie," he greeted.

"Jacob." Stunned, Ollie nodded back.

There was a brief pause, until Taya stuck her head between them. "Taya."

"Sorry, Taya, this is Jacob," Ollie waved a hand to Jacob and offered a welcoming smile. "Daisy Monroe, Room One, father."

"I know, honeybunch," Taya replied. "Work the same ward you do."

"Right, yeah, sorry," Ollie babbled, and the queue shuffled forward to receive its drinks from the end counter.

Jacob pointed to the takeout cup Ollie picked up. "If that's one of these lattes, you won't be sleeping anytime soon. The caffeine was especially rich."

"Yeah. They like to keep us nurses awake, no matter what time of day."

They staggered through the throng of customers toward the exit, Taya following behind licking up her mound of cream and chocolate candies.

"I'm off to see my dad now, so I need the pick-me-up."

Stepping down to the street, Jacob nodded. Taya licked more of the cream off, lifted up on tiptoes and kissed Ollie's cheek.

"Say hi to your dad for me," she said. "Bus is here." True, the 252 was pulling in on time for once, and Taya ran to hop on, leaving Ollie standing alone with Jacob.

"Whereabouts is your father?" Jacob asked.

"Oh, not far." Ollie nodded across the road, as if that helped explain the location of the nursing home in the whole capital city. "Fifteen-minute walk from here. Toward Angel."

"Want some company on the walk?"

"You going that way?"

"I can." Jacob smiled. "My flat's Shoreditch way, but I don't tend to live there much. It's not particularly welcoming. I could use the cold air to clear my head." Jacob suddenly paused. "Of course, don't think you have to. Totally understand if you'd rather be alone."

"I'd kill for some company." Ollie grinned. "With an axe."

While it should have been a pleasant stroll through the streets of London, it being early morning rush hour meant Ollie often had to hop behind or in front of Jacob to allow commuters to push past, so the conversation didn't flow freely. There was the odd droplet of information, pointing out of local pubs and recommended restaurants, places Ollie cycled on the days it wasn't freezing icy sleet on the roads. He talked about how he was making a playlist from all the old vinyl his father had loved in his youth and how he still needed to sort out all his father's keepsakes stored at his mother's place, his mother finding the task all too much to do herself. Ollie wasn't finding it awkward—rather oddly comfortable, like he had done this walk a thousand times with this man, whom he had only met a few hours ago, beside him.

Clutching his empty cup of latte in his thick-gloved hands, Ollie stopped at the gated entrance to the Acorn Nursing Home. A gleaming silver plaque on the gate announced it was privately run. No NHS here—this was top of the range. Only the wealthy afforded this type of final-destination place for their loved ones. Ollie wasn't wealthy. But the down payment from the doctor had helped secure his father's place, and the monthly installments he and his mother shared, contributions, along with his father's decent pension from the Royal Mail, meant they had been able to keep him there. Ollie wasn't sure for how long. Dementia could go on and on. His father could still be alive for another twenty years, and Ollie didn't want to work out how much money that would cost him and his mother. Not that he begrudged a penny. It was just a crying shame that it could see his mother destitute before she was able to retire herself.

"This is my stop." Ollie nodded at the gate.

"Right, yes." Jacob gave the place a once-over. He brushed his flowing hair away from his face with a gloved hand. "Want me to take that?" he asked, indicating Ollie's empty cup. "I'll shove it in the bin on the way to the station." He glanced around the road and scrunched his nose like a twitching bunny, obviously realizing there wasn't a trash can in the vicinity.

Ollie chuckled, handing over his cup. "Turn left at the end of the road. You'll see the Tube station sign. Not far."

Jacob nodded with a smile, and his fingers brushed Ollie's as he slipped the cup from Ollie's hands. Not that Ollie could feel any electricity from the touch—the thick wool of both their gloves prevented it. As did his New Year's resolution.

"Right, thanks." Jacob rooted around in his pocket. As he pulled out his Oyster card, it fell to the ground, and they both immediately crouched to pick it up. Each gripping an end, they stood in perfect unison, neither allowing their gaze to falter from the other. Ollie didn't want to let go. Even through Ollie's glove, Jacob's warmth drifted across the plastic wallet to him. By letting go, he would end all this nonsense.

Jacob tugged at the card, and Ollie was a little ashamed when he didn't let go. He offered a playful smile, masking his true reason for clinging on. Jacob breathed out a laugh and when he suddenly tugged again, a touch more forceful than previous, Ollie fell forward, crushing the card between his and Jacob's chests. Ollie dragged his hand down to his side on letting the card go, but he didn't move away. He couldn't. Jacob's breath warmed his otherwise freezing face and those piercing blue eyes delved into his soul. As the card fell to the ground once again, neither made a move to retrieve it and Ollie inhaled sharply when Jacob's gloved hand curled around his own.

"Jacob," Ollie whispered. It was meant to be an urging plea for him to stop. To move away because Ollie couldn't do either himself. Instead the word fell from his tongue like a teasing call.

Jacob responded to his name with a light press of his lips to Ollie's. Jacob's eyes closed, but Ollie's remained wide open, proving this wasn't all a dream. Jacob trembled against his mouth and Ollie's heart rate elevated to levels he couldn't count with his fob watch. Realizing he had to be the one to do the right thing, Ollie stepped back.

"Jacob," Ollie said again, his voice finding its vigor this time.

"Oh God, Ollie." Jacob shook his head and took a few steps back to increase the gap between them. "Shit. I don't—"

Ollie opened his mouth to speak, but it seemed Jacob was determined to bolt.

"No, Ollie, I'm so totally sorry." Jacob crouched down to pick up his card. As he stood, he locked eyes with Ollie. Regret. Fear. Remorse—they were all there in those baby blues. "I don't know why I did that."

"Right." Ollie kicked at the crunch of frozen moss between the paving slabs. "You're under a lot of stress right now," he said, finally looking at Jacob. "People do strange things when they're under stress. It's fine."

This time, Jacob opened his mouth to speak, but nothing came out, so Ollie squeezed his arm, nurse-style, and met his gaze.

"It's okay," Ollie said. "We'll forget it ever happened." Jacob didn't respond, so Ollie took his hand away and pressed the buzzer on the entrance gate. "Go get some sleep," he said over his shoulder. "Things'll look different in the morning. Or evening. Whatever. Time bears no relation when you work the night shift."

Jacob still didn't move, or say anything. The voice through the buzzer interrupted anything that could have been said, anyway.

"Ollie Warne," Ollie spoke through the speaker. "To see Gregory."

The gate unlocked and opened. Ollie threw Jacob a smile before walking through. The gates closed behind him on that moment, and on Jacob, and on any further feelings.

"Hey, Dad." Minutes later, Ollie was in his father's room, where he threw his bag down by the bed and scraped his coat off. "How you doing?"

His father sat on the comfy seat looking out of the window onto the private garden, tray table up to his chest bearing a cup filled with tea and leftover breakfast of toast and cereal. His father appeared the perfect picture of health. He was still solid, albeit with wrinkling skin, his hair a glorious shade of silver, and they always made sure he dressed impeccably well. Today was a white shirt with brown pinstripes, a red woolen sweater vest and a pair of dark-blue suit trousers. His brown slippers had the words *I heart Dad* on each foot, courtesy of Ollie's little sister. But it was what went on inside Gregory that had caused him to be ripped from his home and family.

"Very well, very well," Gregory Warne replied with a firm nod.

Ollie kissed his father on the cheek, then edged away and perched on the end of the bed.

"Although, the eggs weren't up to much today."

"It was toast and jam today, Pops," Ollie replied. "And cornflakes, by the looks of things."

"Right, right." His father gave a swift shake of his head.

Ollie hated that look in his father's eyes. The vacant expression where his father knew something was wrong but couldn't place it, so he sank back into the seat and avoided further conversation through fear he wouldn't be able to keep up.

Ollie picked at his nails, staring at the carpeted floor. He glanced up toward the door on seeing a nurse shuffle by. He offered up a smile and she returned it. The staff at the nursing home, too, had categories of smiles through which Ollie was able to decipher, without the use of accompanying words, the current status of his father's health. The nurse continued on her way, meaning there was no other news to report. There never really was, anymore. His father was in the mid-stages, rapidly increasing to the late.

"And how's that young man of yours?" Gregory asked out of nowhere. "Tell me all."

Ollie grabbed a leftover slice of toast from his father's tray and swallowed down the bite he'd taken. "No young men, Pops. Or old ones for that matter. Anymore."

"Oh." Gregory furrowed his brow once more and waved a hand at his bedside cabinet. "I'm sure…"

Ollie noted the diary on the side, the place Gregory stored photos and messages to help him remember who people were. Ollie jumped up and grabbed the book, handing it to his father. Gregory's shaky hands ruffled through the pages. Eventually, a glossy picture torn out of a magazine slipped out and he held it up to Ollie.

"They're the Vamps." Ollie chuckled at the red heart drawn with marker pen over one of the boys' faces. "Tilly's new obsession. They're a band, Pops."

"Right." Gregory nodded as if he understood.

Ollie knew he didn't, and it tore his heart in two.

"And your operation, it went well?"

Ollie hung his head. Of all the memories lost in his father's frazzled mind, the one thing that never faltered was of Tilly and her many hospital stays, operations and chemo that had controlled much of her infant life. It didn't matter that Ollie stood there, a full-grown man at twenty-four—his father could only see his little sister.

"Yes, Pops." Ollie resigned himself to the fact his father no longer remembered he had a son. "All went fine. She's healthy."

"Good." Gregory waggled a finger. "I will still walk you down that aisle."

Ollie slid the picture back into his father's diary and threw the slim book onto the bed. Lowering his backside onto the end once more, he dragged his feet on the soft fibers of the carpet while his father gave a tuneful hum. Ollie wasn't sure what song it was, but he hoped it was one his father and mother would have danced to during their early ballroom-evening courting days. If he could remember it, he would replicate it down the phone to his mother later in order to give her some renewed hope.

"Something bothering you?" Gregory asked.

Ollie snapped up to meet his father's eyes. For a moment, he thought he saw his father behind them. Like he could really *see* him. As if he knew it was Ollie there and not his precious miracle daughter.

"Can I tell you something?" Ollie asked.

"Yes, of course," Gregory replied. "You take this tray away. The smell of eggs is making me sick."

Ollie nodded and slid the tray from his father's table. He handed the uneaten breakfast to the nearest nurse out in the corridor and leaned back on the bed to face his father. Gregory sat forward, elbows resting on his knees and a smile on his face that warmed Ollie's heart. Whether he understood the conversation or even knew who he was having it with, the fact that Gregory looked interested was nothing short of a miracle.

"I kissed a patient's father today," Ollie blurted out. "Or, more, he kissed me. I stopped it before it went any further than a peck, but I didn't want to, Dad, I really didn't want to." Ollie sat up fully, dangling his legs down so his heels hit the bed's metal poles. "It's beyond unethical. I'm caring for his daughter after heart surgery. He's a father. I'm not even sure if he's gay. I mean, he's not with the mother. That clearly ended badly."

Ollie rolled his eyes and glanced away. On turning back to his father, he was stunned to notice that Gregory was still listening intently. Ollie couldn't be certain that his father had understood anything that he'd said. Not that Ollie minded so much. If he'd thought his father could understand, he probably wouldn't have been telling him. "I think the man, Jacob, is confused and scared and maybe I just offered him comfort? It can't be anything more than that. We just met. But, oh God, Pops, this heart"—he tapped his chest—"has never beat so fast before."

His father waved a hand, indicating Ollie should come to him. Ollie sank to his knees by his father's feet and squinted up at the man who had taught him everything. Compassion, ambition and how family and love came first, regardless. Memories flickered through Ollie's mind. All the memories his father had forgotten bit by bit. The memories Ollie now had to hold on to tightly for them both. Ollie's first time riding a bike, learning to swim, catching a ball. Moments that were soon clouded over and dulled after his sister had gotten so ill. Playtimes with Ollie had ceased to exist from the moment Tilly had been admitted to hospital. That was when his dad had taught him the most valuable lesson of all—accepting that Ollie's needs always came after his sister's.

He never failed to believe his father loved him. It was just that Tilly had needed their father so much more.

"When that heart beats," Gregory said, tapping a hand on Ollie's chest, "it means you are alive."

Ollie smiled, his eyes welling up behind his glasses. He tugged his father's hands to his lips and kissed them.

"Thanks, Pops."

Gregory ruffled Ollie's hair and sat back.

"You should get all your hair back soon, Tilly," he said. "It'll grow again and that man will love you."

Ollie bowed his head. Sniffing, he didn't notice the one tear escaping past his glasses lens until it reached his lips. He swiped it away with his tongue, tasting the bitter, salty residue.

Chapter Six

Play Therapy

"Good evening, sweetie pie, why the sad face?"

Ollie placed his tray on the table at the end of Daisy's bed the following night shift and snapped on his disposable gloves. Daisy shook her head and sniffed. Her mother, sitting next to her on the bed, had her arms around her daughter, comforting her as best she could. Ollie pouted at the pitiful look in the girl's eyes and Daisy reacted with a brief smile.

Ollie had multiple reactions to seeing Becky and not the man he'd been expecting in Room One. Slight relief washed over him, immediately interrupted by disappointment, leading on to concern and guilt. Overwhelming guilt that he had caused this girl's father to fear coming back onto the ward.

"She's upset about the scar," Becky explained.

Although she kept her voice light, Ollie could hear the hesitation and bitterness in it. Or was he overthinking things? He doubted she would know what had happened between him and her ex-partner earlier that morning.

"She was allowed to take a bath today and saw it in the mirror."

Ollie scooted around the bed and perched down in front of Daisy, startled to notice the similarities she bore to her father. Her long, thick brunette hair draped over her shoulders and those piercing blue eyes sparkled through her otherwise dark features.

"You mean your superhero zipper?" Ollie asked, pointing to Daisy's chest. "That's your superpower, girl. You do know how all those superheroes change into their costumes so quickly, don't you?"

Daisy shook her head, wiping her hand under her nose.

"They all have a zipper. Like yours. Except underneath your zipper might not be a Lycra costume you can use to fight crime, but there's a miracle underneath that."

Daisy seemed unconvinced. The itchy, burning red stitches traveling down from below her throat to her sternum certainly weren't going to feel like a miracle to her right then, and the incision would seem grotesque, not matching the beautiful images of Disney Princesses and pop stars displaying their perfectly sleek skin on the pages of the magazines spread out on her bed. But Ollie knew that underneath that scar a miracle had been performed. Even if it had been Dr. Rawlings who had performed it.

"And you know what else, sweet cheeks?" Ollie continued. "That's your trophy. How many other kids you know have a trophy they get to keep forever on their body, huh?"

Daisy shook her bowed head. The small smile curving her lips told Ollie he might be getting somewhere.

"You be proud of that." Ollie prodded her nose. "You're now special. So..." Ollie stood. "You turn that frown upside down, and I'll have a look-see if we have any extra special treats for a real-life Supergirl, huh?"

Daisy grinned and nodded. Becky offered a grateful smile in return, but it disappeared as her gaze slid over Ollie's shoulder. Ollie spun around and met Jacob's awed expression. Jacob clutched a plastic bag in one gloved hand, and snowflakes glittered on the shoulders of his black coat. His woolly hat covered most of his hair, but strands flicked out from underneath, and Ollie sucked in a breath when Jacob's blue eyes gleamed across the room.

"Daddy!" Daisy's smile grew wider.

"Hey, pumpkin."

Jacob's low voice made Ollie's stomach flip. It fluttered ever so much more when Jacob switched his gaze from his daughter to him.

"Hi."

"Hi." Ollie couldn't seem to make his legs move.

"Ollie says I'm a superhero." Daisy wriggled in the bed away from her mother's clutches.

"I heard," Jacob replied, and the gratitude in his eyes made Ollie shift his focus to the floor.

"Are you staying with me?" Daisy asked, oblivious to any unrest in the room.

"Sure am." Jacob stepped in farther.

Clearing his throat, Ollie finally made his jelly legs walk back to the foot of the bed and avoided any further eye contact by rechecking the items on his tray, pressing buttons on the obs machine, and anything else that would show his dedication to the job.

"Right." Becky stood. She leaned in and gave Daisy a quick hug and kiss. Gathering up her coat and bag from the sofa, she addressed Jacob. "I'll be back at eight."

Jacob nodded. "Anything I should know?"

"Why? Are we telling each other everything now?"

"Becky." Jacob sighed, his eyelids fluttering to a frustrated close.

"Mummy." Daisy sank back to rest on the mounds of pillows. "Please don't start shouting again."

Becky glanced down at her daughter and her toughened exterior softened.

"Sorry, honey." She gave her another quick peck on the forehead. "Be good. I'll see you in the morning. Get some sleep."

"Okay, Mummy."

Becky glided past Ollie and approached Jacob hovering by the door. Ollie couldn't help but watch out of the corners of his eyes.

"Actually, we should talk," Becky demanded.

"Okay," Jacob replied. "Right now?"

"No." Becky glanced back to Daisy idly flicking through the magazines littering her bed. "Not when she's around. I'll call you."

Becky brushed past him with her sharp, clomping shoes, the sound disappearing as the doors to the ward flapped shut. Jacob remained rooted to the spot. Ollie felt the awkwardness. So he did the only thing he could do, and got on with his job. After a few moments of collecting Daisy's obs and checking the bedsheets, Ollie finally acknowledged Jacob's presence with a reassuring smile. Jacob didn't return it, instead sauntering over to perch in Ollie's vacated seat.

"How're you feeling?" he asked his daughter.

"Okay," Daisy replied. "I'm not tired. Can we play?"

"Sure. Have you been sick today?"

Daisy shook her head, her long hair flapping around her shoulders.

"Can she eat?" Jacob asked.

Even though Jacob hadn't taken his eyes off his daughter, Ollie knew the question had been fired at him. His daughter's nurse.

"Yep." Ollie nodded. "Dinner's been and gone, though."

"Oh, right, no, I mean—" Jacob lifted up his plastic bag filled with the varieties of colorful foil and paper wrapping that indicated a child's dream was held within. "I brought her favorite snacks but wasn't sure if she could eat them."

"I see." Ollie winked at Daisy. "Well, I hear she's been a nurse's delight today, so I'm sure she deserves the odd snack or two."

Daisy cheered and Jacob gave a grateful smile. He rustled around in his bag and pulled out a share pack of Maltesers, making Daisy bounce up and down. Jacob laughed, and Daisy held out her hands for him to pour some of the chocolate balls in. She immediately popped four into her mouth, and Ollie chuckled at her puffed-out cheeks.

"Do you want some, Ollie?" she asked through her stuffed-full mouth.

"Oh, no. Thank you, though." Ollie nudged his head toward the door. "I have to get back to work, as all is in super order in here." He winked, and Daisy grinned with chocolate seeping through her teeth.

Jacob dropped the packet to his side, and Ollie swallowed down the guilt. He might have shared pizza in here last night, but he had to step back and reevaluate this situation before it got way out of hand.

He hadn't been able to sleep properly, thinking about Jacob, the kiss, and how he'd felt about it. He had never gotten the full eight hours' recommended sleep in the day, anyway, but he'd barely made four consecutive and was dog-tired standing on his feet with a full night shift to get through.

"I'll be back in four hours." Ollie wasn't sure which one he was addressing the statement to. "She's gone to four-hourly obs now. But if you need me—"

"Press the dress," Jacob finished for him.

Ollie breathed out a laugh. "Yeah," he agreed. "Take care of my little Supergirl here."

She waved and grabbed another handful of chocolates from the open packet in Jacob's hand. Outside, Ollie inhaled an anxious lungful of air and tucked himself firmly behind the nurses' station. This whole not-feeling-anything was harder than he'd first thought.

* * * *

"I did it." Taya grinned. "I actually did it. I did the friend-cull thing. Like everyone does in January, then by March, they've already started to friend-request you back."

"I always notice that," Ollie remarked. "You get a request from someone who you're totally sure you were already friends with. Turns out they cut your arse sometime back and now realize their Facebook feed doesn't take as long to procrastinate over and so come sneaking back with a thumbs-up at your new profile pic in the hope you won't notice they binned you."

"Exactly. So I cut about fifty people whose dinners I'm not interested in seeing and those who tag themselves at the gym or have their Runkeeper on their newsfeed, and those who write stuff like 'I'm so angry right now' then, when their friends ask 'why what's up, hun?', they say 'in-box you, don't want nosey parkers on here LOL'."

Ollie snorted in amusement.

"Leaves me with less, but, hey." Taya shrugged.

"Quality, not quantity," Ollie agreed and threw her a box of meds to add to the cabinet they were refilling.

"Exactly." Taya went back to sorting through the medication on the shelf. Night shifts meant more time to check the cupboards for supplies, and this night was turning out to be particularly quiet. No major upsets – most of the children on the ward were sleeping and having a night off medication and on four-hourly obs, meaning Ollie wasn't able to keep his mind off everything like he usually could. *Thank heaven for Taya and her incessant chatter.*

"I didn't cut you," she added, with a wink over her shoulder. "I have to say I like looking at your profile pic. Very sexy."

"Cheers." He handed over another box from the crate. "That selfie at the beach took at least eight goes to get right, and I still had to touch it up on the photo-editor app."

"Bullcrap."

"Seriously. I had this spot on my chin at the time, and nothing was getting rid of it. Turns out, you don't have to get rid of it in real life, because the photo editor thing does it for you. Oh, and my hair is not that blond, and my body is definitely four shades lighter."

"Not got on the sun beds recently?" Taya twisted around to close the cupboard now all the medical stock had been verified and refilled.

"Not over Christmas," Ollie said. "But I got a voucher for Sun Angel I plan to use ASAP because, seriously, I could be camouflaged by the frost outside with how pale I am. No one likes a pasty bod, and seeing as I've waxed all my hair off, it's on full view. You'd go blind from the reflective rays alone."

Taya laughed. "Give over," she said, hands on hips.

"Seriously." Ollie pushed the trolley crate to the side of the wall.

"Lemme see, then." Taya stepped forward to lift the bottom of Ollie's scrubs top.

"Oi, gerroff." Ollie tried to push her away, but she ducked under his outstretched arm and pulled his top farther up, revealing his slender, toned stomach. She gave a wolf-whistle, and Ollie nearly whacked her upside the head, until he froze to the spot on noticing Jacob peering down the corridor, clutching hold of Daisy's hand.

Ollie shoved Taya away and ruffled his top back down over the elastic waistband of his scrubs trousers. Taya stepped back, hand over her mouth, desperately trying to hold in her witch's cackle. Ollie subtly nudged her with his elbow before jogging up to Jacob and his patient. He smiled as if he hadn't just been caught with his top shoved up by a female nurse next to the secluded supply cupboard.

Jacob clearly tried to return the greeting, but no words came out. Ollie cocked his head and waited a little longer. It almost seemed Jacob was having a bit of a reaction to the scene he had witnessed. Ollie hoped it was a good reaction and not one that Jacob would dwell on at length on his parent feedback form or that would send him to the Patient Advice and Liaison Service to declare that the nurses tending to his daughter's care were juvenile cretins.

"I can't sleep," Daisy said, giving her father time to snap to and remove his stare from Ollie. Not that Ollie minded. With those piercing blues, Jacob could eye-fuck him as long as he wanted. Ollie immediately realized the total inappropriateness of that thought, shook his head to wave away anything further and turned his attention to the little girl.

"Oh dear." Ollie placed his hands on his hips. "We can't have that."

"She wanted to see if she could get into the playroom," Jacob said, having to clear his throat to do it. "It was locked."

Jacob still looked a little frazzled and Ollie was having all sorts of reactions to his blatant staring. One reaction he was going to have trouble covering up with the thin material of his scrubs alone. So he kneeled in front of Daisy and took her hand. *Focus on her and the job. Not her father and his eyes.*

"We have to lock the playroom at night as all the children are trying to sleep."

Daisy pouted, her bottom lip protruding out so far Ollie couldn't help but prod it with his finger.

"Can you not let her in there for a little while?" Jacob asked. "We'll be quiet."

Ollie swallowed. Saying no to Jacob, whatever his demands, seemed to be something he was finding impossible to do. "I'm so sorry." Ollie quickly turned back to Daisy. Refusing her access was so much easier. "If I let you in there, then everyone will ask me and by the time we know it, there'll be a party going on."

Daisy pouted again and looked up to her father, swinging his arm. Ollie checked his fob watch and ruffled a hand through his hair. "All right, look," he said. "I'm on my break in twenty. I have a pack of playing cards in my locker. How about, if I beat you at snap, you have to go to sleep? And if you beat me, I'll open the playroom."

"Okay!" Daisy nodded enthusiastically.

"Well, go on then." Ollie ushered her forward. "I'll meet you in your room."

Daisy twisted on her socked feet, and Ollie could tell she wanted to skip off back through the ward, but the little energy she had and the pain from her chest stitches meant she could only cautiously amble away.

"Thanks," Jacob said over his shoulder.

Daisy yanked his arm and Jacob stumbled to follow. Ollie waved him off, then turned to Taya, who stood some way behind him. She chewed on her thumbnail with wide, all-knowing eyes.

"What?" Ollie flared.

"Nothing."

"Good," Ollie countered and straightened out his scrubs before heading off to the break room.

* * * *

"So, are we all clear on the rules?" Ollie asked, eyeing Daisy, who sat propped up by pillows on her bed, covered by the mounds of blankets, Jacob perched forward in the comfy seat beside her. Ollie, one leg curled under the other, sat on the edge of her bed, the three of them making a perfect triangle of players. He shuffled the deck, expertly flicking the cards in each hand, and the breeze made Jacob's hair fly away from his face.

"Yes." Daisy giggled.

"Good. Jacob?"

"Yes," he said with a smile that lit up his face.

"Great." Ollie dealt the cards, using the mattress as a table. "Now, I don't want to get you all worried, here, but I'll have you know I am the snap champion of Bear Ward."

"Really?" Daisy sat forward with interest.

"Oh, yes," Ollie replied. "I have a trophy, too, y'know."

Daisy slapped a hand over her mouth and Jacob chuckled, shaking his head. Ollie took his share of the cards and shuffled farther up the bed. Daisy focused her attention on sorting her deck neatly in her dainty hand, so Ollie took the opportunity to wink at Jacob. Blushing beneath his dark stubble, Jacob smiled and Ollie straightened out his own cards with a minuscule sense of renewed triumph.

"Ladies first," Ollie offered. Daisy slid out her top card, but before she could turn it over on the mattress, Ollie held up his palm to stop her. "I'm giving you the opportunity to back out, now knowing you are playing against a champion."

Daisy snickered and shook her head. "No, I have my Daddy on my side, so you're playing against both of us."

"Oh, really, now?" Ollie cocked his head. "Well, I'd best be getting all my good moves out, if I'm to impress your father, here."

Jacob's eyes couldn't get any wider, or at least Ollie didn't think they could, and the fluttering in Ollie's stomach made it all the more worthwhile. He chuckled and waved for Daisy to continue. She shuffled forward and flipped over her card, placing it down on the mattress, revealing the ace of hearts. Ollie smiled.

"That's you, Princess." He nodded to the pack then turned to Jacob. "Give it your best shot, Jacob Monroe."

Jacob licked his lips. Eyes remaining on Ollie, he flipped over his card and slapped it on top. Eight of clubs.

"Ooooo." Ollie blew out between rounded lips. "Too bad." He threw his card on top and hovered his hand over it. Four of spades. He huffed and slumped back. Daisy giggled.

Ollie didn't let up his comedic narration of the game as it continued. He couldn't believe how much fun he was having, closed off in the room with Daisy and, he had to admit it, Jacob. He completely lost track of time, forgetting he was spending his break playing snap rather than eating like he should be. He didn't care—he could argue this was all part of the job. Daisy was smiling and giggling, and that was the best recovery medicine. The other nurses were all outside and would notify him of any alarms from his other patients. So he decided to finish the game, especially when he saw the yawn from Daisy. His plan was working. It was nearing one in the morning, and the girl was finally succumbing to her weariness. Playing snap with a deck of cards wasn't exactly the fast-paced noisy game it was when using the image cards in the playroom. The likelihood of matching a pair from a deck of playing cards was infinitely more difficult, making Daisy lose interest.

She flipped over her card and sank back onto the pillows, eyes drooping. The six of clubs sat on top of the six of hearts, and Ollie immediately whacked his hand on the pile. Jacob's slapped down on top. Ollie met his gaze and the crushing on his hand loosened for an imperceptible moment. Ollie was momentarily dumbstruck by the depths to Jacob's deep blue eyes, and he struggled to swallow the increased saliva in his mouth.

Stunned further, Ollie sucked in a light breath as Jacob glided his thumb along Ollie's hand, ghosting it across his skin. Without the thick gloves to mask it this time, electricity struck from the delicate touch. Ollie's heart pounded so hard his ears pumped with the flow. The room's surroundings blurred until Ollie could only see Jacob. His eyes. His lips.

Jacob slid his thumb over Ollie's skin in tender strokes, and Ollie tingled with every sweet caress. His skin numbed, along with his mind. Ollie didn't take his gaze from Jacob's, and his lips parted to make way for something to say, or do. The increasing heat from Jacob's palm formed a sheen of moisture over the back of Ollie's hand, and Jacob's fingertips trembled. All sense and reason left the room when Ollie slid his own thumb up to curl over Jacob's knuckle, an instinctive and involuntary movement Ollie couldn't control. He wanted to touch Jacob. He needed to. His beating heart was telling him to. Jacob's thumb hit parts of Ollie that had been suppressed for so long—his feelings.

"I think Ollie won that one, Daddy." Daisy yawned and rubbed her eyes.

Ollie had forgotten she was even in the room. Jacob snatched his hand away from Ollie's and bowed his head. Ollie's heart thumped, letting him know he was alive. Jacob had let him know he could still be alive.

"Ollie?"

Ollie whipped around at the sound of his name. Taya stood at the entrance to the room, having opened the door without him noticing. He widened his eyes in question and desperately tried to even out his elevated heart rate the echo of which had traveled up to his throat and wedged itself there. How much did she see?

"Room Four." Taya's gaze flickered from Ollie to Jacob. "Baby's NG tube has been ripped out. You have to come reinsert."

Ollie nodded at double speed. Jumping from the bed, he wiped his clammy hand down his scrubs then scampered to the door. Taya vacated the room without saying anything and Ollie glanced back at Jacob. He had his head bowed, twisting his hands in his lap.

"Snap," Ollie murmured.

Chapter Seven

Anatomy Lesson

Ollie bustled out of Room Four, leaving a screaming baby in the arms of his frantic mother after having had to insert the feeding tube through the poor little kid's nose, down his esophagus to his stomach. He stopped short when he nearly knocked into Jacob lurking outside.

"Is the baby okay?" Jacob's hands trembled as he swiped his hair away from his face.

Ollie glanced behind into the room. The baby had calmed considerably, and the mother was now lying on the bed with him. Closing the door, he turned to Jacob and nodded.

"Yeah. He can't feed orally, so we have to give him the tube. Obviously, he doesn't like it and pulls it out quite a bit. Can't blame him. I'd hate it, too."

Ollie swallowed and continued his walk to the nurses' station. He needed to get a handle on the rush of emotions surging through him. Jacob being there wreaked havoc on Ollie. A brief interlude and his mind back on the job had allowed Ollie to realize his stupidity. He couldn't let anything more happen. A kiss, a hand caress—they all spelled trouble. And gross misconduct. Even if his heart desired more of this man, it couldn't happen. *It shouldn't happen.*

Ollie scooted behind the desk for no other reason than to provide him with a protective barrier. He closed his eyes to regain some composure. When he opened them, Jacob stood right in front of the desk.

"I—" Jacob started.

"Jacob, please," Ollie replied, practically begging with his voice alone. "I can't—"

"I'm sorry," Jacob said and edged back. "I just wanted to say that."

He retreated toward his daughter's room, and Ollie's every impulse was to follow him. To hear more. To say more. But he'd already crossed the line more times than was acceptable with this man, and he couldn't put a finger on why. Even if his thumb had tried. There was something about Jacob Monroe that had cracked through Ollie's professional shell and seeped into his vulnerable side. Oh, not the way Dr. Rawlings had. He'd preyed on Ollie's vulnerability—Jacob was caressing it. With his damn thumb.

"Jacob," Ollie called before he could stop himself. "I'm sorry, too."

Jacob smiled, but it deteriorated as the ward doors flapped open and Dr. Rawlings marched in. Flipping his stethoscope to drape it around his neck, he approached Ollie at the desk. Ollie reluctantly tore his gaze from Jacob to address the doctor.

"How was your father?" The question came out mere chitchat, devoid of any real concern.

"Same," Ollie replied and shuffled around the desk for the files. He placed a few on the surface and slid them over.

Dr. Rawlings hummed in response and flicked open one of the patient folders. While he was busy checking the notes, Ollie took the opportunity to throw a glance Jacob's way. Jacob stood, leaning against the doorframe, arms folded. Ollie hated to admit the comfort he felt from that stance.

"Right." Dr. Rawlings slapped the first file shut. He tucked his hands into his chino pockets and pulled out a box. He slid it over the desk. "Replacement."

Ollie stared down at the leather casing and back up to the doctor.

"I don't want that," Ollie replied, his voice threateningly low.

Jacob had pushed away from the doorframe, arms now down by his side. Ollie blinked several times to refocus his attention where it was needed. "I want the one my father bought me."

Dr. Rawlings leaned over the counter, his face so close that Ollie could taste the espresso breath.

"Then don't leave it lying around in places my cleaner can find it." Dr. Rawlings voice sounded eerily quiet.

"Fuck," Ollie whispered through gritted teeth and edged out of the nurses' station, "you." He finished the sentence just that little bit louder.

Jacob cleared his throat, and Ollie whipped around to witness Jacob's eyebrows drawing in. Ollie swallowed down his resolve and stomped toward him. He had no idea why—Daisy wasn't due for obs, or anything else, and was sleeping soundly in her bed. But he had an overwhelming pull toward it. Or more accurately, to Jacob and the protective qualities he offered. It was a low move. Ollie knew that. But what choice did he have?

"Oliver," Dr. Rawlings called.

Ollie paused. Jacob's gaze flicked over Ollie's shoulder to the doctor.

"Some help in Room Seven, please."

"That's Taya's patient." Ollie didn't take his eyes off Jacob as he spoke. The disrespect was foolish.

"She's otherwise engaged."

Ollie threw a cantankerous glance over his shoulder. Dr. Rawlings gripped the file to his chest and arched an eyebrow.

"It's urgent. So I'll need you." The doctor lowered his voice. "Now."

Ollie turned back to Jacob. He blinked, fading out the concern in the blue eyes that stared across at him.

"I'll be right back, Mr. Monroe." Ollie straightened himself out before following Dr. Rawlings down the ward.

* * * *

Ollie tugged on his gloves, blew steam into the freezing morning air and shuffled on his feet outside the hospital exit. Dr. Rawlings had kept him by his side the rest of his shift, tending to tasks he was sure the other nurses could have fulfilled. It meant by the time he had made it back to Room One, Becky had returned and Jacob had been given his marching orders. Ollie hated to acknowledge the sinking feeling in his gut but he had to remind himself that Daisy would more than likely be discharged as an outpatient soon. Her recovery was all going to routine, and Jacob would no longer be in Room One, or any room in the hospital.

Tapping his coat pockets, he searched for his Oyster card to jump onto the first bus and go home to get some much-needed sleep. No dawdling this time for a drink with Taya, no visiting his dad—just straight to bed.

"Here."

Ollie looked up at the take-out coffee cup wafting under his nose, and his eyes widened in surprise.

"Latte, right?" Jacob asked.

Ollie smiled and wrapped his gloved hand around the cup. Returning the smile, Jacob let go.

"Thanks." Ollie took a sip through the hole in the lid.

The drink was perfect. And forbidden. Accepting gifts from patients was another no-no in the big nursing book of ethics. Nurses were meant to refuse all gifts, no matter how big or small the gesture. They could be deemed a way to receive favorable treatment and care. And this cup of coffee couldn't exactly be shared among his colleagues. Ollie guessed that was why it tasted that much sweeter.

"I thought you might need it." Jacob shrugged. "Busy night?"

"Yeah," Ollie agreed and avoided the worry seeping through Jacob's expression. "Home to bed. Sleep," he added by way of final confirmation. Jacob nodded, hanging his head to look at the floor.

"Oliver?"

That voice made Ollie's skin crawl but he didn't acknowledge the oncoming demand and idly sipped his coffee.

"I'll give you a lift to your father's." Dr. Rawlings approached Ollie's side. The man never let up, the main reason Ollie often gave in. But as Ollie flicked a glance at Jacob, he finally found his courage.

"Sorry, Dr. Rawlings." Ollie nodded to Jacob. "I promised to take Mr. Monroe here to the parent support group over at Heart Lake House." Ollie nudged Jacob's arm, making him twist on his heel to start walking up the High Street. "See you next shift, Doctor," he added over his shoulder.

Ollie gripped Jacob's elbow, steering him across the busy road and away from the hospital. Once out of sight of the adjacent buildings, Ollie finally released him and breathed out. "Sorry," he said. "And thanks."

Jacob nodded. "No problem. So, what's this parent support group?"

"Oh, something the Heart Lake charity lays on. Coffee, cakes and compassion for parents whose kids are undergoing heart surgery. Pretty sure Becky's been over." Ollie shot a worried glance at Jacob. "I mean, I can really take you, if you want?"

"No." Jacob shook his head. "No, it's okay. Becky's the one who needs the support."

Ollie nodded to let the statement not affect him either way. Fathers needed support just as much as mothers, and separated ones ever so much more. But Ollie guessed Jacob was trying to keep things on an even keel with his ex—their relationship was tempestuous, to say the least. No need for Ollie to go sticking his oar in. He'd done that too many times already these last twenty-four hours.

"So, you heading home?" Ollie asked, out of pure conversational habit rather than needing to know where Jacob sauntered off to during the day.

Jacob ruffled his hair. "Actually, I'm starving. Was thinking of getting some breakfast. Ever been to the Breakfast Club, Ollie?"

"The film?"

Jacob laughed. "No, it's a restaurant. Multitude of breakfasts from all over the globe served all day."

"Ah, I see." Ollie stroked his gloved thumb over the rim of his coffee cup and shook his head. "Then, no. Breakfast for me usually consists of the St. Cross canteen or whatever I have clogging up my cupboards in the way of cereal."

"Right, then." Jacob nudged Ollie's shoulder with his. "I'll treat you to one. Come on, there's one near my place that always saves a table for me when I'm in the area."

Ollie stopped in his tracks. Jacob hadn't noticed and trotted on ahead. He'd gone as far as the corner shop before he turned and cocked his head. Ollie should say no. There were a million reasons why having breakfast with this man was a no-no. If he whittled it down to its very simplicity, it was a matter of nursing ethics. But what really bothered Ollie were his increasing feelings for the complete stranger and how they could never be reciprocated. Jacob was under momentous stress and, whatever his reasons for clinging to Ollie, for the kiss, for the delicate hand stroking, it all boiled down to distraction. Jacob was using him as a distraction from his feelings toward his daughter and her mother. And that left a bitter taste in Ollie's mouth, and not from the latte. The latte was all sweet.

"You like pancakes, Ollie?" Jacob called.

Ollie breathed in. He nodded.

"Good. 'Cause theirs are to die for."

* * * *

The pancakes were particularly scrummy. And Ollie wolfed them down like he hadn't eaten in days. And now that he came to think of it, the last particularly substantial thing he had consumed had been Jacob's seafood pizza.

"So how come you have a table set aside for you here?" Ollie asked, wiping his mouth with the napkin after having dribbled maple syrup all down his chin.

Jacob breathed out a laugh and tapped his fingers along the cutlery next to his cleared plate.

"I'm a terrible cook," he admitted with a wince.

"Ha!" Ollie laughed. "Snap on that one, too."

Jacob blushed beneath his dark stubble.

"When I was at uni doing my nursing degree, I pretty much lived on noodles. Great hangover cure right there. And the student special canteen food. When I graduated and got the job at St. Cross, I vowed to learn and eat healthy." Ollie shoved his glasses up his nose. "Turns out, canteen food will forever be my staple diet. I throw in the odd smoothie for the five-a-day intake. We must practice what we preach, I suppose."

Jacob laughed, and the deep rumble undulated across the thick oak table.

"I'm always sent away for work," he explained, stroking back his hair. "I end up eating out on expenses. When I get home, I don't much fancy cooking for myself. This place"—he nodded over to the waiter at the front, who smiled and waved back—"became my go-to. Got to know the owners."

Ollie leaned back in his chair and rubbed his satisfied stomach. "Where is it you work?"

"It's a relatively new start-up company based on the new Silicon Roundabout. I used to work for a big corporate doing ethical hacking. After a while, the thought of wearing a suit all the time just to sit and tap at a computer in a closed-off booth took its toll. Found this new start-up that wanted to branch out. Decided to take a pay cut and have a go." Jacob shrugged. "They let me out into the world. Not only can I build the software that companies want and protect it for them, but I get to actually mingle with real life for a while."

"And I'll bet you're good at it."

"I'm no you when it comes to people, but the more I got out of the office, the more I enjoyed it. Meeting new faces." Jacob glanced out of the window at a passing unmarked police car with blue flashing lights racing by. "I didn't do much of that when I was with Becky."

Ollie didn't have time to respond as the waiter approached their table, interrupting his next question. Jacob rootled around in his back pocket.

"Wait." Ollie held up a hand. If he paid for this, it wasn't technically a gift offering. "Let me."

"I said I'd treat you, Ollie."

Ollie shrugged and handed over his card to the waiter. The man zapped it on the front for the contactless payment to whiz through and the subsequent high-pitched bleep made Ollie flinch.

The waiter winced. "Terribly sorry, sir, but the card has been declined."

Ollie's cheeks burned. He closed his eyes with the realization Christmas had sucked him dry and he had a whole three weeks to wait for his wages. Taking the card from the waiter, he made a mental note to go find a payday loan. He couldn't very well borrow money from his usual source. Certainly not now. Jacob said nothing more and handed over his card. Bleep. Accepted.

Ollie couldn't help the feeling of disappointment that it was all over as he followed Jacob to the exit with heavy steps. Jacob held the door open for him, and Ollie shuffled out onto the pavement. The restaurant was set away from the bustling Shoreditch High Street and located down a secluded alley where tourists would no doubt get lost trying to find the sought-after haunt with its four-star recommendation on TripAdvisor. It meant that when Jacob joined him on the path, they were alone.

"Thanks." Ollie bounced on his loafers and rubbed his hands together to stave off the chill. "For breakfast. That was really generous."

"No problem," Jacob replied. "The way you made Daisy giggle and what you did for her when she was upset, you deserve it."

Ollie shrugged and drifted his gaze down to the pavement. "All in the job."

Jacob held a finger under Ollie's chin and lifted his face to look deep into his eyes. Ollie exhaled a mouthful of steam and his lips trembled.

"I don't believe that," Jacob said. "I believe you're a miracle, too."

Ollie could do nothing more. Keeping his finger curled under Ollie's chin, Jacob coasted a thumb across his lips. Ollie needed to move away. He had to stop this before—

It was too late. Jacob leaned in and kissed him. This time, however, it wasn't an accident, a mistake, or immediately followed by remorse. Jacob's lips lingered on Ollie's, spreading warmth through his entire body. Ollie switched off his mind and could no longer hold the urge within. He parted his lips and kissed him back. That tiny reaction seemed to give Jacob all the encouragement he needed, and he deepened the kiss, spearing his tongue into Ollie's open mouth. With a sharp inhalation through his nose, Jacob pushed Ollie back against the restaurant wall with the force of his kiss alone. Ollie hit rough brick with a thump, but neither of them stopped, and Ollie slid his hands around Jacob's waist to squeeze him closer. Jacob moaned a deep rumble and responded with his tongue, demanding deeper access to Ollie's mouth with heated desire. After a brief moment of mouths crashing, heart rates elevating and hands roaming places they shouldn't in a daylight alley, Jacob pulled away, his chest heaving as he shivered.

"I should stop," Jacob muttered through deep breaths.

Ollie paused. He needed to think about this. He *should* think about this. He knew the correct response. Trouble was, he didn't like it. He needed to feel something, even if it was wrong. So he tugged Jacob closer, grinding his groin against his own. Jacob was already as hard as he was. Perhaps he needed this just as much. Which made Ollie respond the only way he would.

"Don't," Ollie whispered in his ear.

Jacob exhaled noisily and slapped his mouth onto Ollie's again, dragging a hand to the back of his neck. Ollie couldn't have stopped even if he'd tried. So entangled in the kiss that was sending shock waves through his entire body, he didn't even notice the shuffle of feet as another couple approached the door to the restaurant. It was Jacob who stopped. Averting his eyes from the disapproving couple, he tugged on Ollie's arm to walk farther up the alley.

"Where are we going?" Ollie asked.

Jacob didn't loosen his grip, eyes focused on the road, but his trembling hand over Ollie's biceps told Ollie a different story was going on in his head.

"My place." Jacob's reply came in a voice so seductively low that the vibrations went straight to Ollie's sparking groin.

Ollie didn't respond. He allowed himself to be dragged through the backstreets until they reached the entrance to a block of flats. Only then did Jacob take his hand away in order to search in his pocket. He pulled out a set of keys, shoved one into the lock and shoulder-boosted the communal entrance door open. He held it ajar with his back and turned to Ollie still hovering outside.

"You can say no." Jacob's eyes pierced into Ollie's twisted mind.

Can I?

"We can just talk. Or maybe, really, you should go home..." Jacob's confidence drained away.

Ollie swallowed. He was under no illusion that this moment, right then, right there, would forever be ingrained in his mind as the one in which he suspended all rational reasoning and responded only in the way he wanted.

He stepped forward and kissed Jacob. Softly at first, but slowly building up to a full-on mouth fuck with his tongue. Jacob countered that action by pushing Ollie into the building via a forceful hand to the small of his back. There were no stairs that Ollie could see, so Jacob slapped his palm on the lift's Call button. They stood side by side, watching the illuminating numbers detailing its gradual descent from floor ten to zero. Nothing further was said as they waited and Ollie feared that in the time it took for that lift to reach them, his conscience would eventually kick in.

The ding and slide of the lift doors indicated that his resolve had left him for good, and Jacob urged him in with another shove to his back. Ollie clambered into the small stainless-steel box and leaned against the far wall to regain some breath. As the doors glided closed, Jacob hit the button without Ollie even noticing which floor had been pressed. Damn. He couldn't prepare for how much time he had.

He sucked in a deep breath, and Jacob didn't break his penetrating eye contact as the lift shunted to an upward climb. Ollie thought he'd have a moment to breathe, to evaluate, to reconsider. But Jacob launched forward and rammed his mouth on top of his, kissing him with frantic urgency. Ollie returned the kiss, but he couldn't touch. Not then. His arms dangled by his side, waiting to be told what to do.

Without words, Jacob grabbed them with his sturdy hands and held them out against the back of the lift, making Ollie into a cross. Jacob pressed his entire body into him, sustaining his possession of Ollie's outstretched arms to grind against him.

"Oh God," Ollie groaned as Jacob nipped at his neck. He couldn't move. He was pinned to the back of the lift by a man who was proving he was more of a beast than Ollie had first thought.

Jacob pulled back from exploring Ollie's neck further and looked him in the eyes. He didn't let up his hold on Ollie's arms, or stop thrusting against him.

"You okay?" Jacob asked, voice barely audible but the concern starting to outweigh the lustful desire displayed moments ago. "I can stop."

"Can you?" Ollie surprised himself by how aggressive the statement came out. "'Cause I can't."

The flicker in Jacob's eyes made Ollie's stomach flutter. Jacob smacked his mouth back onto Ollie's and slid in with his tongue, immediately lapping and no doubt tasting the remnants of syrupy-sweet pancakes. Ollie sucked on Jacob's bottom lip like a starved animal and the rasping of his stubble made Ollie's lips sore. The lift suddenly jolted, but Jacob didn't stop his insatiable kissing. He released Ollie's arms and they flopped to his sides, but Ollie soon had to throw them around Jacob's neck when Jacob trailed his thick hands around Ollie's hips, sliding them down to his arse and lifting him clean off the ground.

Ollie was more than a little startled. He'd never been picked up before. This self-proclaimed nerd clearly worked out. He latched on to Jacob's neck and had to wrap his legs around Jacob's waist as Jacob lost his balance and staggered Ollie back against the wall. The doors slid open, and Jacob threw a glance out into the corridor. With a grunt, he set Ollie down on his feet, curled his fingers around the front of Ollie's puffer coat and yanked him forward out of the lift. The doors shut behind them and Jacob stopped at the first numbered flat, fishing around in his pocket again. Ollie stood behind him, his heart rate reaching new levels as he waited in anticipation.

The door along the corridor opened and Jacob quickly let go of Ollie's coat. A young blonde vacated the next flat along. Ollie offered one of his smiles but didn't have the brain capacity to think which category it came under. Nor did he really care at that point.

"Hey, Jake," the girl said.

Jacob offered over a brief nod of recognition as his key jangled in the lock and his door opened.

"I took in a parcel for you. Shall I go get it?"

"I'll get it later," Jacob rushed out as he held the door open and ushered Ollie in. "Thanks, Kelly."

Ollie didn't hear the response as it was muffled by the sound of the front door slamming. Ollie lingered, glancing around the open-plan flat, and Jacob hovered by the door, as if the interruption of his neighbor had made him rethink his actions. The hesitation made Ollie nervous. So used to waiting for instruction, he was unsure what to do. Throwing caution to the wind, Ollie pulled Jacob forward by the collar on his coat and kissed him. Jacob left his lips on his, previous franticness making way for a more subdued response. Ollie couldn't bear for it all to end. He ground closer to Jacob, hoping for the same reaction he'd gotten in the alley. When he did, Ollie smiled and kissed across Jacob's jawline along to his neck.

"Ollie, I don't think… We shouldn't, not with everything happening." Jacob breathed, then moaned. "Not like this, not with you—"

Ollie cut him off from saying anything more by nipping his neck and trailing his hand to unzip Jacob's fly. Jacob growled, pushed Ollie back against the door and covered his mouth with his. To say Ollie felt the impact of his head hitting solid metal was an understatement, but the tongue slipping into his mouth robbed him of his ability to complain about anything. Jacob scrabbled and found the zip to Ollie's coat, yanking it down to split the garment apart and drag it along his arms. Ollie flapped his hands and the coat trailed to the floor. He gasped as Jacob slipped his cold hands up his top and gave that the same attention, ripping his glasses from his face to the floor in the process. With Ollie's coat and top discarded, Jacob finally removed his mouth from Ollie's. The deep moans as Jacob trailed his neck, his collarbone, and licked across to his chest knocked Ollie back against the door with a quiver.

Jacob took particular time roaming his tongue around Ollie's hardened nipple. Ollie was relieved he'd done the wax job only a couple days back, or Jacob would have felt the prickles of stubble. He sucked in a further breath when Jacob scratched his thick, smooth fingers down Ollie's sides, finding the waistband of his jeans. Standing to his full height, Jacob rammed his mouth back onto Ollie's and kissed him while making light work of unclasping his belt and popping open his jeans button. The noises coming from Ollie's mouth as he entwined his tongue with Jacob's were ones he was sure he hadn't ever uttered before. Especially when Jacob tucked his hand into Ollie's jeans and wrapped tough fingers around his throbbing cock.

Jacob tugged Ollie's jeans and boxers farther down his thighs and stroked feverishly. Jacob let up on the kissing and bent. Was he watching the head of Ollie's cock disappear on every upstroke only to reappear with demanding vigor on every downslide?

"Ollie," Jacob breathed.

"Fuck," was Ollie's only reply. Forming words was increasingly difficult with the sensations of Jacob's hand pumping him, making his knees weak and his toes tingle.

Jacob looked back up, locking eyes with Ollie but refusing to stop his delectable hand job. Ollie was in danger of losing it there and then, with those piercing fuck-me eyes delving into his own, which were pretty much saying the same thing. Jacob leaned in for a softer kiss, tasting him with renewed diligence. Jacob planted gentle kisses down Ollie's neck, to his chest, and his tongue tasted skin as he went. Sinking to his knees, he tugged Ollie's jeans down farther to his ankles, and Ollie flicked both off with his, thankfully, slip-on loafers. Jacob took a deep breath, then sucked Ollie's cock to the back of his throat.

Ollie inhaled loudly. Not taking his eyes off the sight of his cock bobbing in and out of Jacob's mouth, he dragged his fingers through Jacob's shock of thick, luscious hair. At first he did it to slide away the locks that blocked his view, but as he held it bunched in clenched fists, he used it to control Jacob's depth and velocity. Ollie banged his head against the door once again, with real concern he was causing damage to his skull. His knees buckled and Jacob slurped his mouth off his cock, but still used his hand to stroke up and down.

"Can I get you off like this?" Jacob stared up with those absorbing blue eyes.

"If you do, I might not stay standing."

Jacob chuckled deeply. "I'll hold you," he said and again wrapped his lips around Ollie's cockhead and guzzled it with a groan.

It only took a few more sucks, and Ollie gripped Jacob's hair, scratching his fingernails into his scalp, growling out his name while coming down Jacob's throat. His legs trembled, and he released Jacob's hair to try to hold on to something to keep upright. He couldn't find anything and was in danger of collapsing to the floor. But as his cock fell from Jacob's mouth, Jacob stood and pinned Ollie to the door with a demanding kiss. Not giving Ollie any time to react, Jacob squeezed Ollie's arse and yanked him away from the door. He staggered backward along the corridor, his mouth not leaving Ollie's all the while. Tasting himself on Jacob's tongue was enough to make Ollie's desire increase. It hit further heights as Jacob banged open a door with his back, spun Ollie around and pushed him down onto a king-size bed.

Ollie sank into the soft white duvet and scrabbled up to reach the headboard. He stopped short when Jacob proceeded to strip out of his coat and remaining clothes. Ollie licked his lips. The man's body was certainly not what he would have expected of a computer geek. It was broad, tough and muscular, scattered with thick dark hair over his chest that snaked down to his firm stomach. And when Jacob shunted off his boxers, his thick, hard cock bobbed out of a further nest of dark curly hair. Ollie's eyes widened at the sight and he propped up on his elbows as Jacob crawled onto the bed on his knees.

"Oh fucking God, I want that," Ollie blurted out.

"Yeah?" Jacob replied with a slight chuckle. He edged closer on, flicking Ollie's legs open with his powerful hands to perch in between.

"Fuck, yes." The drool coming out of Ollie's mouth was enough to back the statement up.

Jacob smiled and leaned down to kiss him. Ollie wrapped a hand around Jacob's cock and slowly teased it up and down, gliding his thumb over the head as he kissed back.

"Can I…" Jacob gasped, brushing his lips with Ollie's, making them tingle. He trailed off and trembled, so Ollie encouraged him by speeding up the strokes on his cock. "Fuck you."

"You'd better," Ollie replied and crashed his mouth back onto Jacob's. He pulled away and pumped more vigorously, making Jacob's eyes roll to the back of his head. Jacob groaned and leaned over to reach the bedside cabinet. "But before that," Ollie said, and Jacob arched an eyebrow, kneeling back in front of him. "I need to taste this." And he needed the time to get back up to full capacity to take everything Jacob was offering him.

Ollie opened his mouth wide. Jacob thrust forward and his deep gasp as Ollie wrapped his mouth around Jacob's cock was breathtaking. Ollie curled his hands around Jacob's pert, rounded arse cheeks, encouraging Jacob to use Ollie's mouth to get himself at least halfway ready to spill. Ollie could take it and lapped it up with hunger.

Jacob stroked a hand through Ollie's hair. "Ollie," he urged, and his name being uttered so delicately made Ollie's chest tighten. He let Jacob's cock fall from his mouth and looked up with a smile—this one in the 'yes, please' category.

Jacob offered one last sloppy kiss before leaning over to pull open the drawer of the bedside unit. The ruffling of a condom wrapper and popping of a cap sent Ollie to renewed levels of eager anticipation, and he lay back on the soft mattress to offer himself up to this man who, forty-eight hours ago, hadn't known he existed. In real life or his dreams.

Jacob shuffled forward, having sheathed his pulsating cock and slicked it up with a handful of sweet-scented liquid. He paused, gazing at Ollie's naked body.

"You're so fucking beautiful." Jacob's soft deep voice quivered with the delivery, and Ollie's whole body felt the vibrations.

Ollie smiled and held out his arms. "Come here."

Jacob did. He leaned down to kiss him, and Ollie curled his legs around his back, digging his heels into solid muscle. Jacob trailed a hand over Ollie's leg to inside his thigh and began to push it back. Ollie knew what Jacob was about to do. But he didn't need it. He needed Jacob. In him. Now.

"Just fuck me, now," Ollie croaked. "Please." He was used to begging, but somehow this time it felt far more desperate. *Not lip service. Real.*

Jacob sucked in a lungful of air, nodded and shuffled back to line himself up. Ollie lifted his legs higher and wider, and once Jacob entered him with a fierce thrust of his hips, Ollie moaned. Jacob spread him, filled him and completed him.

Jacob garbled incoherently, slamming in and out of Ollie. The mattress shook and Ollie had to hold his arms up to the jarring headboard to prevent any further injuries as he was forced up the bed. Jacob grabbed one of Ollie's legs, bending it farther, and forced it across Ollie's body, making Ollie swivel onto his side. Jacob leaned down to spoon behind him and wrapped an arm around his midsection. He bit at Ollie's neck and thrust in harder, letting out one long rasping groan as his orgasm shot through into Ollie, to make his entire body tremble.

Ollie felt as though he was in a vise grip when Jacob's arm sank into his stomach. Jacob blew out a gush of air, and Ollie had to peer over his shoulder to see the hair wafting away from his sweaty face. Jacob used that opportunity to kiss his lips, then collapsed down beside him onto the mound of fluffy pillows, finally releasing Ollie and allowing him to breathe again.

Chapter Eight

Recovery Position

Ollie opened his eyes to darkness. Strong arms wrapped around him from behind and the warmth of the fluffy duvet mixed with the heat coming from Jacob had covered his body with a sheen of sweat. He blinked, trying to focus without his glasses through the hazy pitch-black, when suddenly it hit him.

Ripping free of the embrace, Ollie sat up and looked desperately around the room. It was dark. Too bloody dark. The full-length window at the far back had blinds designed to keep out any rare ray of sun, and there wasn't a single trail of light peeping out of anywhere. He started to panic, until a hand soothed up his bare back.

"You okay?" Jacob asked.

"It's dark," Ollie stated rather stupidly. "Time? Work." His throat was too hoarse and croaky to form any sentences.

The soothing hand slid away from the small of his back, and the mattress dipped as Jacob moved away. A low whir indicated the docking station to his side had been switched on, and a faint blue glow illuminated the numbers on the digital clock.

"It's okay. Eleven." Jacob rolled to face Ollie and placed a calming hand on the small of his back once more. "Those are blackout blinds. And my guess, it's probably snowing again."

Ollie rubbed his eyes. Considering it had only been an hour since he'd passed out in Jacob's bed, feeling ridiculously tired was justified. He'd have quite liked to curl up and get the much-needed, and recommended, seven additional hours before starting his next night shift, but the memories of what had happened came raging down on him and his stomach began to churn.

Jacob propped up on his elbow, his fingers brushing his skin. "Ollie?"

He couldn't avoid it any longer. Ollie locked eyes with Jacob now he could see in the dim blue lighting. His desperate anxiety soon merged into blissful fluttering. Jacob, even more arousing on first wake-up, ruffled his hair over his face and his lips were red and swollen, but his penetrating eyes seemed weary. Ollie swallowed.

"Sorry," Ollie said. "I must have fallen asleep. I should go home."

Jacob didn't break his intense gaze as he lifted to sit beside Ollie and kissed his shoulder. His hair tickled Ollie as it fell onto his skin and he sucked in a breath.

"Stay," Jacob replied softly. "I like having you to hold."

His voice was quiet, almost as though he was self-conscious about saying what he did. It only made the delivery that much more adorable, and Ollie finally relaxed after the abrupt wake-up.

"Come here," Jacob commanded and wrapped an arm around Ollie's chest to push them both down on the bed.

Ollie obliged, allowing himself to be caressed as Jacob rubbed the tip of his nose against his shoulder. Ollie wriggled, getting comfortable, and soon turned to catch Jacob's lazy gaze.

"I guess this was always going be the awkward part." Ollie might as well be honest. This whole thing was riddled with an anxious air.

Jacob kissed his shoulder again and breathed in deeply. "It doesn't have to be."

Ollie bit his bottom lip. "You know," he started and wondered how to put into words what he needed to explain. "I could be in serious trouble for this."

Jacob lingered on Ollie's shoulder and closed his eyes. He nodded and kissed him again.

"Because I'm a patient's father?"

"Yeah," Ollie agreed. "I mean, it's pretty much point one in the rule book of nursing. No fraternizing with patients or their families." Ollie swiped a hand through his hair. "That and don't kill your patient," he added. Jacob leaned away, and Ollie quickly turned back with wide eyes. "Sorry," he rushed out. "Sorry, that was totally inappropriate. And see? Another reason why, right there. Nurse sense of humor. Can be cutting sometimes. Sorry."

Ollie took another gulp of air. This was the second time he'd needed to shut his mouth around this man. He should have shut it two hours earlier when he'd said yes to all this. Jacob's eyes pierced through the hazy blue light and a small smile curved his lips. He leaned back to Ollie and ran a thumb across his cheek.

"It's okay," Jacob replied. "All of it."

Ollie chewed the inside of his cheek, wondering how that statement could even be true. Jacob must have noticed his unease and wrapped his arms around him once more in a tightening embrace.

"It's not like I'm going to tell anyone." Jacob rubbed his forehead on Ollie's shoulder. "I understand this is difficult for you. But, seriously, the last thing I need is to give Becky more ammunition to not let me see Daisy. So, you're safe. This won't go further than this room, I promise."

Ollie could see the sincerity in Jacob's eyes. He knew what Jacob had said was meant to reassure him, but something was niggling away at his mind. All the fear he'd had before leaping into bed with this stranger started to bubble back to the surface. He couldn't help but wonder if this was a reactive cathartic release for a man so pent-up with stress. *If I'm simply a distraction.* And if Jacob's promise of discretion meant that this was a one-time thing, to stay locked in this room forever, never to be reenacted. Ollie always fell for the wrong man. Which was why he wasn't supposed to be feeling anything.

"Well, I guess my pondering on whether you were actively gay was answered this morning." Ollie tried to tread carefully, but he needed to know.

Jacob's brow furrowed at the question and Ollie had difficulty in not laughing at it.

"You knew what you were doing," Ollie explained. "So I'm guessing this isn't some rebound from Becky?"

"Oh." Jacob stroked his feet under the duvet and found Ollie's. "I haven't been with Becky in coming on six years." He fondled his toe along Ollie's foot. "Met her at school. I was a complete nerd back then and a late bloomer, I should say. She was the first girl to show me any attention. The fact that she was stunningly attractive and popular made me think I'd be foolish not to take her up on her advances."

Jacob slid his hand down to Ollie's chest and tickled Ollie's smooth skin with his soft fingertips. Drawing little circles around Ollie's nipples, he propped himself up on his elbow for a better look while he did it. Ollie watched on in awe. The man clearly had more to say.

"We dated. I lost my virginity to her at eighteen, and she got pregnant soon after." Jacob sighed and splayed his hand out on Ollie's chest. "I knew there was something off about it all, but I didn't really know why. Once she was pregnant, I did the right thing. I got a job, we rented a flat and we lived as a family. The love I felt for Daisy was instant, and it'll never make me regret having her. But things with Becky were always...difficult."

Ollie hadn't realized he'd been holding his breath, and when he finally let out a lungful of air, Jacob rested his hand on Ollie's deflating chest. He smoothed it down to Ollie's stomach and over to his hip. Just the mere descent made Ollie's groin spark, and he desperately tried to calm it. This wasn't the time to get turned on.

"Couple of years after Daisy was born, I started to explore what I'd been hiding," Jacob continued, hopefully oblivious to Ollie's inner turmoil. He took a deep breath and leaned down to rest his chin on Ollie's chest. "I started the new job and was away a lot, so it was the perfect opportunity. I joined an online thing, posted an ad saying I wanted to explore my sexuality, which was responded to quite quickly—"

"I can imagine," Ollie cut in before he could stop himself. He bit his lip and shrugged. "Ultimate gay fantasy. Bend a straight man."

Jacob snorted, sliding the hand on Ollie's hip to his back and squeezing. "Yeah. Before I knew it, I was meeting men wherever I was away. But I was still trying to make it work with Becky. We were a family, and with Daisy being ill, I couldn't just walk away."

Ollie ran his fingers through the flowing locks of Jacob's hair. He understood. He did. Everyone had baggage. He shut his eyes at that thought.

"Becky found out," Jacob continued. "For an IT genius, I didn't encrypt my passwords too well. Left my laptop open one night, and she found the ad I'd posted."

"Shit," Ollie muttered.

"Yeah. Needless to say, she was a bit angry. She chucked me out and has tried to prevent me from seeing Daisy ever since. Using my 'promiscuity', as her solicitor called it, to say I was an unfit father. I stopped everything after that. Came offline. Never set up any meets. Concentrated on proving I was a decent man. That I could be a father. Damage was done, though, and Becky, as you may have noticed, is still bitter."

Ollie nodded, seeing Jacob's sincerity and thinking this was the end to the explanation. He wasn't sure how he really felt about it. So Jacob had used men to get off and discarded them, continuing his life. That bit stung. *But am I any better?* What he'd been doing with Dr. Rawlings was no different. There was no future in it, yet he did it anyway. *And why?* Because the doctor met his needs. He gave him what he craved. *Why should it be any different for Jacob?*

"I never wanted to bring Daisy into that life." Jacob lifted up from Ollie's chest, his face inches from Ollie's. "I never thought there would be a man worthy to risk that for." He breathed in and kissed Ollie's lips. "Then I met you."

Ollie erupted in goose pimples at that kiss and the words. Whether or not Ollie was a rebound or a distraction, he was sure Jacob really believed what he said. He knew men who lied. He knew men who cheated. And he knew players. Jacob didn't seem like any of those. Whatever he had done in the past could be explained by desperation at being trapped so young and not knowing the right thing to do. So Ollie reacted the only way he could—he kissed Jacob back, and, as the man melted into him, Ollie knew he was in serious danger.

"You really are beautiful, Ollie." Jacob nudged the tip of his nose against Ollie's. "And I know this was fast and can have bad repercussions for both of us." He kissed him again. "But I don't regret it. I don't know what's happening here, but I don't want it to stop."

Ollie smiled. He nodded and wrapped his arms around Jacob to pull him closer. Sliding his hands down Jacob's back, Ollie reached the curvature of Jacob's pert arse cheeks, forcing him to shuffle on top. After a while of exploring each other's mouths, Jacob pulled away and up onto his arms to look Ollie in the eye.

"Do you always do night shifts?"

"No," Ollie replied. "We're on a rota. Some nurses choose night shift only, and they get paid a little more for it. But I do the shift patterns. I switch to day next week, so I have four days off to recover and get my body clock back on track." Ollie cocked his head. "Why?"

"I just wondered when I'd get to see you after Daisy comes home," Jacob admitted with a slight tinge to his cheeks that the dim blue lighting couldn't shield. "If you work nights and I work days, that'll make it hard."

That mere sentence made Ollie grin. He ran his hands up Jacob's back to his hair and swiped it away from his face.

"We'll figure something out, I'm sure." Ollie kissed him.

Jacob smiled and released his arms to fall into Ollie and roam his body with his lips. He'd almost reached Ollie's fluttering stomach when a loud buzz echoed around the flat. Jacob lifted his head and sucked in a breath. Ollie peered down—his dick now fully up to start the day—and raised his eyebrows. Jacob waited a moment longer, and when no further buzz came, continued his kissing descent. His chin hit Ollie's eager cock, and Jacob hummed deeply. Ollie felt the vibrations in his groin and slid his fingers through Jacob's hair that blocked his view. But before Jacob could respond any further, another buzz blasted out. This time it didn't stop. Whoever was pushing that button didn't want to be ignored.

"Shit." Jacob kneeled in between Ollie's legs. He ran his hands up Ollie's thighs, the annoyance of the intrusion evident across his face. "Don't move," he ordered with a point of his finger.

Ollie nodded, happy to obey that order. Jacob rolled off the bed, grabbed a dressing gown from a hook behind the door and stomped out of the room. Ollie shut his eyes and allowed the ridiculous grin to spread.

His whole body convulsed in sheer delightful anticipation.

Until he heard Jacob's voice outside the door.

"No, you can't come up."

Ollie couldn't hear another voice so assumed Jacob was talking through a speaker to the other person standing outside on the pavement.

"No, Becky."

Ollie froze, his previous squirming delight instantly replaced with overriding fear. He pulled the duvet over his naked body to his chin and sat up against the headboard, listening. A muffled curse, followed by a loud thump, shook the walls. A few moments passed, and the front door opened.

"Luckily you have nice neighbors," Becky's voice rang out. "We need to talk."

"Couldn't you call me?" Jacob replied.

"I did. Several times already this morning, and you haven't answered," Becky said. "I told you we needed to talk. Leaves me no choice but to come seek you out in your bachelor pad."

The fierce clacking of her shoes rattled the bed as they stomped farther into the flat. The door slammed shut and Ollie began to tremble. Lifting his knees to his chest, he hugged them over the duvet and didn't know whether to stay there, hide in a cupboard like some sordid teenager, or attempt to get dressed. He glanced at the floor. His clothes weren't there. They were littering the floor of another room in Jacob's flat, along with his glasses—he would need to find somewhere to hide. He banged his head onto his knees.

"Jesus Christ, Jacob," Becky barked. "You're a fucking slob."

"What do you want, Becky?" Jacob's voice bellowed with annoyance and exasperation. "Why couldn't you wait till I was back at the hospital? And who's with Daisy?"

"My mum's sitting with her," Becky replied. "Why? Have I walked in on one of your rendezvous?"

The final z sound of that word was particularly hissed out. There was a pause and whatever face Jacob must have displayed made Becky snort violently.

"Is there a man in here?"

"No," Jacob replied far too abruptly.

"Christ!" Becky screamed. "You know what? I don't even care anymore."

Ollie heard more clomping, as if Becky was roaming the hardwood flooring of the open-plan flat. *The bedroom door. Damn.* Jacob hadn't shut it completely. The light from the main living space drifted in to make a yellow line across the bed, focusing on Ollie like a spotlight. The sweat dripping from his forehead trickled his skin for a whole different reason.

"I needed to tell you I'm taking Daisy to Ireland." Becky's voice vibrated along the walls.

"What? No, you can't!" Jacob declared.

"I think you'll find I can," Becky replied. "As soon as she's recovered, I'm taking her over there. Simon's family are all out there. They own a farm. It'll be good for her. Fresh air, out of the city."

"For a holiday?" Jacob's voice quivered.

"No, Jacob. We're moving there."

Ollie didn't hear much else—the blood rushing through his veins went straight to his eardrums. He heard further muffles from Jacob, whose voice had quietened in the revelation. Ollie wanted to rush to him, to comfort him and tell this bitch where she could stick her precious Simon. But he couldn't. He was stuck there, naked, in the man's bed, where he really shouldn't be. A few more tense moments of silence. Then the click of the door and clacking of heels indicated she had left. Ollie waited a few breaths more. If Jacob didn't come back in this room soon, Ollie would march out there with everything on display.

Luckily, the door clanged open and Jacob shuffled in, carrying Ollie's discarded clothes. Ollie slid his legs down to lie flat, and Jacob sat with a solemn sigh at the foot of the bed, dropping Ollie's clothes next to him. Ollie could have cut the silence with Dr. Rawlings' scalpel. Eventually, he slid out of the duvet and crawled over to Jacob, draping his arms around his shoulders and kissing his cheek.

"I'm so sorry," he whispered.

Jacob tapped Ollie's hands clutched together across his chest and leaned back into the embrace. It was short-lived, and he curled angry fists into the duvet. "How can she just take her?"

Ollie was sure the question was rhetorical and Jacob was merely mumbling the words rather than expecting a reply. Ollie squeezed him closer and stroked his forehead along the back of Jacob's shoulder. He felt for this man—he couldn't deny it anymore. To hell with not getting involved in patient-family conflict.

"You could get a doctor's declaration saying she isn't fit for traveling and has to remain near to her consultant," Ollie suggested, voice light and low, carefully treading a line he wasn't sure he should even be on.

Jacob twisted around to face Ollie, his eyes glistening. "I can do that?"

"It's a starting point. You'd need to speak to Daisy's doctor before Becky does. And as far as I am aware, she hasn't declared the intention yet, or it would be in his notes."

"Her doctor?" Jacob confirmed. "Dr. Rawlings, you mean? Your Dr. Rawlings."

Ollie sank back into the bed. He nodded, then shook his head. "He was never mine. He belongs to all his patients." He looked Jacob in the eye. "He's a narcissistic, emotionally inept sociopath. But he's a great doctor, and, if you want, I can talk to him for you."

"No." Jacob shook his head. "No," he stated again more firmly. "I'm not giving him another reason to use you."

The fluttering in Ollie's chest released something in him he couldn't quite place. Jacob leaned back and kissed him.

"I'll figure it out," he said, but the slope to his shoulders told Ollie he was defeated. "I'm going to take a shower. Place is yours." Jacob waved a hand and stood. Running a hand through his hair, he marched out of the bedroom.

Ollie fell facedown onto the bed and banged his forehead against the mattress. This was exactly the sort of thing his New Year's resolution had been meant to help him avoid! Baggage. Stuff that came before him. Getting involved with someone who had so much else going on that Ollie didn't know where he fitted. This year was meant to be Ollie, flying free, playing the field, becoming the player. He rolled onto his back and stared up at the ceiling. *Who am I kidding? I've never been like that.* He'd always been the one to be played because of his goddamn inability to not feel a fucking thing.

He heard the whirring of an electric shower and turned toward the bedroom door. He sighed. *Might as well go the whole way. What's the point otherwise?* He rolled off the bed and padded toward the noise, finding a slightly ajar door opposite the bedroom and pushing it open. Jacob, behind the splattering glass of a walk-in shower, scrubbed his hair underneath the waterfall spray. Ollie bit his lip and watched the outline of Jacob through the fuzzy glass. He really was a delight for any eye to see. Even eyes that were blurred without the use of prescription eyewear. Breaking his resolve once more, he walked farther into the glossy black-and-white bathroom and slid open the shower door.

Jacob turned on his heels and staggered a little in shock.

"Thought I'd save you some hot water," Ollie said.

Jacob launched in for a demanding kiss, slapping Ollie against the cool tiles, and Ollie was happy to be this man's distraction from torment for a while.

* * * *

Later, Ollie sorted through the clothes bunched up on the bed and checked the display on the docking station. He still had enough time to get home and at least sleep some of this off before his next shift. Jacob, towel hanging low on his hips, rummaged through his wardrobe. Ollie smiled and shook his head at the absurdity of the whole situation. Dropping yesterday's underwear onto the unmade sheets, he cocked his head.

"Any chance I can borrow some boxers?" he asked, scratching the back of his neck and trying desperately not to sound embarrassed about it.

Jacob peered around his wardrobe door, raked Ollie's naked frame with his gaze, and chuckled. "Sure." He pointed to a chest of drawers.

Ollie hobbled over to pull open the top one and rooted around for something that might fit him. Jacob was probably a couple sizes broader than him, so whatever he found in there would be too big. But he didn't have much of a choice. He pulled out a pair of black mesh Iso Chill boxers from Under Armour. They seemed like they should fit a little better, being more workout-style. He pulled them on, snapped the waistband across his hips and twisted to Jacob.

"So, you work out?" Ollie said.

Jacob popped his head through his sweater and Ollie laughed, waving a hand. "You don't really have a computer-nerd body."

"There's a gym here in the basement." Jacob secured his belt buckle on his dark-denim jeans. "And I ensure that whatever hotel I get holed up in for work has one too. What else is there to do when you live on your own?"

"Fair point." Ollie pulled on the rest of his clothes. Before he could tuck his foot into his jeans, Jacob clamped his arms around him from behind and tugged him close, nipping at his neck, and Ollie's grin hurt his jaw.

"How about you?" Jacob asked. "Or is this body all from being on your feet for those long shifts?"

Ollie snorted. "I cycle, mainly. Gyms are boring. Staring at the same wall for hours? No, ta. I need the air." He shrugged. "Or smog. I only use the gym for its sauna and steam room."

Jacob hummed against his shoulder blades. "I can get on board with that."

Ollie chuckled and wriggled his hips. "Now stop it, or I'll never make it home before work."

Jacob reluctantly let him go, and Ollie managed to dress without further harassment. Picking up his coat, he checked in the pockets for his phone. The display illuminated several missed calls and a voice mail message.

"Shit," he cursed on instantly recognizing the number.

"Everything okay?"

"It's the care home." Ollie tapped in his voice mail number and held the phone to his ear. Holding his breath, he listened to the message. Ollie's heart pounded, and he swallowed the lump forming in his throat. He shoved on his jacket.

"Ollie?"

Ollie turned, having forgotten Jacob was even there. "It's my dad. He's had a fall. I need to go to him."

* * * *

Ollie didn't refuse when Jacob came with him. He wasn't sure why. He didn't say anything when Jacob shoved on his coat, marched him along the bustling Shoreditch High Street still illuminated with twinkling Christmas lights, through the packed Urban Street Food Festival and bundled him on to the Overground. Ollie, mind elsewhere, didn't even think to ask if Jacob knew where he was going. Nor did he question it when they arrived at the gate of the care home and Jacob followed him in. It could have been that Ollie just focused on getting to his father. Or, perhaps in some small part of Ollie's frazzled subconscious, it felt comfortable. *Like, why wouldn't Jacob come with me for support?*

But as soon as he entered his father's room and saw the frail outline of his pops lying on the bed rather than in his usual chair, propped up by pillows and bearing a nasty bruise on his cheekbone, Ollie thought otherwise. Having Jacob there to witness his vulnerable side might not be such a good thing. It was, however, like everything else that had happened these last couple of nights—too late.

"Hey, Pops." Ollie rushed to perch on the edge of his father's bed.

Jacob hovered by the door, probably feeling the awkwardness just as much as Ollie.

"You been fighting again?" Ollie joked and stroked his fingers across the bruise on Gregory's cheekbone.

His father had tried to take a bath by himself, slipped and fallen, hitting his face on the sink. The task of bathing wasn't something his father was allowed to do by himself, but Ollie presumed his dad had wanted to regain some lost control and had attempted it regardless. Especially as he hated to be told what to do by 'pretty young things' who could be the same age as Ollie's sister. That was what his pops maintained, anyway. Ollie tried not to take offense. His father was of a generation where such derogatory terms to describe nurses were the norm. Before the second phase of dementia had hit, he had been nothing but supportive of Ollie's choice of profession.

"I gave him my best shot," Gregory croaked out.

Ollie laughed and curled his hand around his father's. He looked deep into his eyes, trying to find the man he knew behind them, but fell short as Gregory's vacant gaze flickered around the room as if he wasn't sure if there was anyone there, or if so, how many.

"Try not to get in trouble, here, Pops," Ollie said. "You'll get a bad rep with the nurses, and they might start leaving the sugar out of your tea."

"Yes, yes," Gregory replied with repeated nodding. "I'd really like a tea. Is it English breakfast, Doctor?"

Ollie hung his head and sighed. He glanced over at Jacob, who threw back a reassuring smile, one Ollie returned before addressing his father once more. Gregory turned his head on the pillow and caught sight of Jacob lingering by the doorway.

"Is that…" Gregory lifted a frail, trembling arm to point a finger. His brow furrowed and he swallowed uneasily.

"That's Jacob, Pops," Ollie replied. "From the hospital."

"Yes, yes," Gregory said. "And the operation went well?"

Jacob's brow furrowed much the same as Ollie's father's. Ollie shook his head, hoping to convey some silent message that his father wasn't really making much sense to him, either. And probably wasn't referring to Jacob's daughter's operation. Ollie doubted his father would have recalled their last conversation so easily.

"Yes," Ollie breathed and slid his hand from his father's. "Tilly is fine."

"Good, good," Gregory said. "But I am worried."

"What are you worried about? Everything is fine. Tilly is fine. You just rest yourself, you hear?"

"It's Oliver." Gregory shut his dry eyes.

Ollie grabbed Gregory's hand firmly.

"Yes, Pops." Ollie smiled. "It's me, Oliver."

Gregory stared vacantly at Ollie, as though he knew he was there but couldn't place him. He held his breath and his lips trembled. He gazed at Jacob.

"Jacob?" Gregory narrowed his eyes as if trying to recall a memory.

Ollie nodded in confirmation and was surprised his dad had even remembered the name. Dementia defied all logic.

"Yes, Pops, that's Jacob." Ollie was startled to see a welcoming grin on his old man's face.

"Oh, Jacob." Gregory nodded with an unusual knowing smile. He waggled his finger that barely left the mattress and chuckled, which was an odd sound Ollie hadn't heard in quite some time. "You better treat my Tilly right." He leaned back against the pillows, his eyes drifting closed. "She's got a protective older brother, you know." Gregory heaved a painful sigh.

Jacob's expression displayed his confusion. Ollie shrugged, and Gregory's head flopped to the side, a brief snore emanating from his lips. Ollie decided to leave it there and walked around the foot of the bed with a renewed feeling of calm. His father was okay, and Jacob was smiling at him like some dopey sod. Ollie returned the grin, but it slowly faded as Jacob was ushered aside by a hand curling round his arm.

"Oliver."

Ollie's eyes widened into saucers, and he swallowed. "What the hell are you doing here?" He silently begged Dr. Rawlings not to turn around or recognize the man he'd just shoved away.

"When there's an incident and they can't get hold of you or your mother, they call me." Dr. Rawlings glanced down at the bed, and Ollie shot a look over the doctor's shoulder in the hope that Jacob would understand to leave.

Again, like everything else in the last few hours, it was too late. Dr. Rawlings narrowed his eyes and glanced from Ollie to Jacob.

Chapter Nine

Discharge Note

Ollie kicked his loafers off against the wall and slammed his door shut. His jaw ached from grinding his teeth the whole bus journey home. He knew he was in for some serious trouble now that Dr. Rawlings had seen him with Jacob. The fact that the doctor hadn't said anything and had simply marched out of the care home was more unnerving than if he'd summoned Ollie to follow him. He hadn't. So Ollie had to await the inevitable repercussions that would no doubt come to him at work.

He stripped out of his clothes, throwing them around the flat without any care or attention to where they fell. All he wanted was his duvet and at least four hours of uninterrupted sleep. Thankfully, Jacob hadn't followed him there and instead had allowed Ollie to head home by himself, citing that Ollie needed sleep and Jacob had other things he needed to attend to. Possibly finding a solicitor and get the ball rolling with his custody battle for Daisy. Whatever it was, Jacob had seemed in a hurry to get away. Ollie couldn't blame him.

Leaving Jacob's boxers on, Ollie tore off his glasses and threw them onto the bedside table, then collapsed face-first onto the bed. He scrambled to find the ends of the duvet and wrap it around his body. He needed to block out the world for a few hours. All the fears, worries and weights on his shoulders could fly off to dreamland for a while. Then the scratching of a key in his front door lock, followed by the slamming of the door and muttered cursing as items were kicked against a wall after having been tripped over startled Ollie awake. He launched off his bed and jumped over to his open bedroom door. He squinted at the blurred figure staring back at him and swallowed down his fear. "Forget how to knock?"

"Why would I knock? You gave me a key."

"For emergencies. And you've never used it before."

"Well." Dr. Rawlings raised an eyebrow and clapped his dress shoes farther up the hallway to the main living space. "Perhaps I see this as an emergency."

Ollie thumped the doorframe and cursed under his breath. He slipped his glasses on and followed the doctor to the living-kitchen area. Ollie had a small flat. Not much space and cluttered. The brightly painted orange walls made it seem more closed-in somehow, but Ollie liked the garish color. It brightened his mood. Elliot's tall, dark and broad frame took up most of the room as he silently ran a finger along Ollie's worldly possessions displayed on his white shabby-chic wall unit. Ollie leaned against the doorframe and waited, folding his arms across his bare chest.

Picking up a couple of framed family photographs, Elliot gave a slight *humph* sound then replaced them. He moved on to the other items, mostly theater memorabilia Ollie cherished. Since moving to London,

Ollie had become an avid West End-goer and collected programs and other merchandise from each show he'd seen and loved. His mother and sister often accompanied him when they were down visiting, and each of those keepsakes told a story. Mostly they reminded Ollie of each stage of his father's deterioration.

The doctor clapped down a *Les Misérables* mug with a sigh and turned to face Ollie. He raked his gaze down Ollie's near-naked torso and stopped short at the boxers. His eyes narrowed. Ollie unfolded his arms and tugged at the tight material on each leg, then covered his arms over his bulge. The boxers could be easily explained away. It wasn't like the doctor knew all his underwear. Still, it made Ollie uncomfortable the more Elliot stared at his groin covered by Jacob's boxer-briefs.

"Shouldn't you be going to bed?" Ollie finally snapped.

Elliot dragged his gaze up to Ollie's. "Is that an offer?"

Ollie snorted, violently, to the point his throat scratched.

Elliot smiled. He rummaged around in his trouser pocket and pulled out a gift-wrapped box. He stepped forward. It only took one stride for the doctor to be a whisker away from Ollie. He leaned in to press his lips to Ollie's ear, tucking the box into Ollie's clamped hands. He made sure to brush against Ollie's flaccid cock beneath the thin material.

"For you."

Ollie closed his eyes as Elliot kissed his cheek. He inhaled, gripping the box-shaped present, and the familiar strong musky scent meshed with hospital-grade hand sanitizer washed over him. The doctor always smelled good, even without the expensive brand of aftershave he wore out of work hours. As Elliot brushed Ollie's cheek with his knuckles, Ollie came to his senses and turned his face away.

"Aren't you going to open it?"

Ollie glanced down at the gift. He ran his thumb over the elegantly wrapped jet-black paper with its thin red ribbon. He knew what it was without having to unwrap it. Givenchy. The brand of cologne Elliot always bought Ollie and insisted he wear for their liaisons. A completely opposing scent to that of the doctor. Ollie was required to smell sweet. Ollie hadn't used up the entire bottle Elliot had last bought him. He'd just taken to not wearing it so much anymore. His first act of defiance and self-preservation, he supposed.

Ollie shrugged. Elliot stepped away, tucked his hands into his pockets and sighed. His silent breath trickled Ollie's neck.

"I've found somewhere else for you to live."

"Excuse me?" Ollie pushed away from the wall.

"This flat is too far from the hospital."

"And from you," Ollie pointed out.

Elliot chuckled. He spun to once again roam the minimal surroundings. Ollie's heart thumped. How ironic of Ollie's father to claim the beat was to let him know he was alive, and yet he stood here with Elliot, Elliot once again planning his life for him.

"This place is rather poky, wouldn't you say?" Elliot slid his gaze from the wall-mounted picture of Ollie and his sister taken several years ago to stare back at Ollie.

"I like it." Ollie shrugged.

"It really isn't the sort of place you should be in." Elliot shook his head and continued his sideward slant through to the kitchen. He opened the fridge, slammed it shut and checked through the cupboards.

Ollie shivered. Not only did the fridge waft some of its cold air his way, but the doctor encroaching on his personal space was more than a little unnerving. He could only remember Elliot being in this flat once before. Possibly twice. Elliot had claimed to hate it then. There could only be one reason for his presence here now. Ollie needed him to cut to the chase. He still had three hours of sleep to fit in. So, for that matter, did the doctor.

"Why are you here, Elliot?"

"Hmm?" Elliot didn't even turn around from the open cupboard he was poking into.

"Why are you here?" Ollie repeated, enunciating the words just to be sure he couldn't be misheard.

Elliot picked up a bottle of half-drunk red wine left on the sideboard and read the label. His nose turned up and he slapped the bottle down. Ollie rolled his eyes as Elliot continued rummaging through another cupboard.

"What are you looking for?" Ollie asked, his exasperation seeping out of every pore of his near-naked body.

"Why do you ask?" Elliot slammed the door. "Would you be hiding something from me?"

Ollie flinched. Biting his lip, he slid a thumb along the silk ribbon of the gift box then shook his head. He daren't look the doctor in the eye.

"Good." Elliot stalked back to stand in front of Ollie. "I really would urge you against keeping secrets, Oliver. Especially ones that could be somewhat damaging to you." Elliot breathed in deeply. "And our relationship."

"Relationship?"

"Yes, Oliver. Relationship. And I do feel the need to ask if this is the first one."

Ollie rubbed a hand over his perspiring brow. The cold shivers were making way for clammy sweats.

"The first one what?"

"With whom you have cheated on me with."

Ollie couldn't hold in the laughter. "Are you kidding me?"

The stern expression the doctor gave him answered Ollie's rhetorical question.

"Do I often joke?" Elliot cocked his head.

"No," Ollie replied without any need for thinking that one through.

"Then answer the fucking question!" Elliot bellowed, striking a hand against the doorframe behind Ollie's head with a thud.

Ollie nearly jumped out of his skin, and his heart leapt into his throat. He was well aware of Elliot's angry side, but it didn't come out all that often. The doctor was usually neutral. No emotion either way. Steady. Even his climaxes weren't particularly earth-shattering. But the scarlet glow on the man's face right then was more than a little startling.

"I've not cheated on you," Ollie mumbled. "I believe you first need to have a normal functioning relationship in order for that to occur."

Elliot ran his fingers along the edge of the doorframe, then rubbed the dust away with his thumb. "And what is it you think we have?"

Ollie breathed out a laugh and shook his head. He was finding this whole conversation rather absurd. "An arrangement."

"Well, yes." Elliot scrubbed a hand under his chin, scratching at the stubble. "And that arrangement expects certain standards."

"By me?" Ollie confirmed more than questioned.

Elliot laughed. "You think I am sleeping with anyone else, Oliver?"

Ollie shrugged. "Probably."

The eerie smile evaporated from Elliot's face as he stared at Ollie. The intensity of that gaze unnerved him, and he rather wished the previous unfathomable reaction would return. The elongated silence became unbearable.

Ollie hated silence. It reminded him too much of the hospital bays when his sister was out of surgery and his parents would sit by her side, not knowing what to do or say. Ollie had learned his incessant babbling and artful conversation skills from there alone. He was able to mask the fear, pain and misery, to avoid having to think about what was really happening by simply talking to his parents about mundane things that filled his brain. He knew that was what made him a popular nurse among the children and the other staff. If there was a difficult situation to address, Ollie could always bring light relief in the form of his chatter. *Never underestimate the power of idle chitchat.*

But right then, as Elliot continued to stare uneasily at him, Ollie lost his ability to talk. Instead, he squared his shoulders.

"I am rather tired, Elliot," Ollie said. "So..." He waved toward the front door.

That seemed to snap the doctor from his thoughts.

"Becoming involved, sexually, with patients' family members could destroy your career, Oliver."

"I am aware," Ollie replied. "I am not involved, sexually or otherwise, with anyone. Jacob Monroe was with me at the nursing home as I had agreed take him to the support group place when I had the call about my father." Ollie shuffled on his feet and glanced down at the floor. He was walking a thin line. "I didn't expect the man to come with me, but I am sure you can understand my mind wasn't thinking of work at that point."

Elliot hummed. "Well, I wouldn't want this 'mistake' to cost you your job. I know how important, and vital, it is to you."

"Is that a threat, Elliot?"

"Not at all. You are a fantastic nurse. A valuable asset to my team."

Although the delivery of the doctor's words sounded genuine, and were ones he had uttered many times previously, Ollie couldn't miss the flicker of deviousness in Elliot's eyes. Especially after he leaned in and ghosted his lips along Ollie's cheek.

"I need you."

Ollie shuddered. Those words. The ones that had also been used countless times before. Ollie froze, clutching so hard at the box in his hands that the paper crumpled.

Elliot tucked his hands into his trouser pockets and sauntered down the hallway.

"Before shift," Elliot said, his eyes on the door. "You should head to the sexual health clinic."

Ollie twisted around. "Excuse me?"

"Test yourself for everything. I'll have the report sent to me."

"I do hope this is one of your really bad jokes, Elliot."

Elliot shot a look over his shoulder. "No, Nurse Oliver Warne. I have to know that my staff are clean when working with patients. And I wouldn't want anything passed on to me."

"I am clean," Ollie replied through gritted teeth. "I don't recall a time you didn't wrap your sordid penis in an extra-thick, extra-safe condom." Ollie shuddered at the memory. "Would you like me to note that on the form they ask me to fill in, Doctor?"

Elliot chuckled. "You can write anything you like on that form. Perhaps even the list of current partners. I think that would make an interesting read."

Ollie closed his eyes only to hear the door being yanked open.

"And, Oliver?" Elliot barked. "You will come back to my place when I ask. We will discuss where you are to live and what's to happen next in our arrangement."

"And if I say no?"

"I'm sure you already know the answer to that one."

The slam of the door was exceptionally loud, and Ollie was rather surprised Elliot didn't succeed in making the walls tumble down upon him. But that would have been all too convenient.

* * * *

Seven-thirty p.m. and the already freezing temperatures in the city had plummeted drastically. Frost had already settled along the pavement, the parked cars and yellow ambulances clogging up the High Street. Ollie jumped off the 252 bus, whipped up his coat collar to stave off the chill and waved at the server clearing the bistro tables outside the café. Checking for any speeding taxis, Ollie scurried across the mini-roundabout, passed the corner pub steadily filling up with the after-work business crowd and trudged through the sleet to the glass-fronted hospital. The huge poster displays of children smiled out at him, but Ollie didn't feel the usual pride he'd grown accustomed to. He suspected the blood running through his veins lacked any warmth for him, either.

The automatic doors slid open, and even though general appointment hours had finished for the day, the reception still swarmed with families dotted around the brightly colored seating area. Children giggled and ran over the rock-pool projection on the floor, chasing the animated fishes off the picture and creating pretend bubbles in the simulated water. Ollie nodded a greeting to the purple-T-shirt-wearing volunteer at the entrance and followed the whitewashed walls decorated with brightly painted animals indicating each separate wing. His freshly sanitized loafers squeaked with every vexing step toward the staff lifts, and he almost ran on the spot waiting for the doors to open and take him to the third-floor Bear Ward. His incessant trembling couldn't be put down to the temperature alone. And he wasn't sure what was making him more nervous, the fact that Elliot had gotten under his skin—again—or that Jacob could be waiting for him in that ward.

He changed into his scrubs in the staff locker room, his neck hurting from twisting around at every entrance. He sighed and flattened down his hair, adjusted his glasses and tucked the fob watch onto its clip. He looked at his reflection and tried to see if there was anything off about his appearance. Nothing obvious to scream out what he'd been doing that day. He was still shivering as he gave his hands and lower arms a thorough clean under the warm taps then walked to the ward.

He slapped through the swinging double doors to the cardiology wing and acknowledged Taya behind the nurses' station. She grinned and held up a pack of nicotine chewing gum. Ollie snorted. At least she was trying, which was more than he could say for himself. He gave her a peck on the cheek.

"Not a single cig all day." Taya beamed.

"Wow. Well done."

"Thank you." Taya nodded. "I've had about a million of these, though." She threw the pack of gum onto the desk. "Plus, I'm wearing the patches."

Ollie chuckled, skimming through the files laid in his in-tray.

"And I bought one of those vapers. Strawberry-flavored. Quite nice."

Shaking his head, Ollie opened Daisy Monroe's file and rolled his finger down the day notes, scanning each compartment for anything he hadn't seen from last night's checks. There was no letter or note to say the mother planned to take the patient on a flight, so Ollie slapped it shut.

"Where's Patty?" he asked. "She's meant to give the handover."

Taya waved a hand over to Daisy's room. She'd sneaked in another stick of gum and couldn't speak through the amount she tried to chew. Ollie squinted to see through the gaps in the blinds of Room One. Daisy sat up on the bed, her mother by her side and Patty, her day nurse, clearing up around her bed.

"What happened?"

"Been sick a few times today. She's off all meds, apparently," Taya continued through a muffled mouth, clearly not picking up on Ollie's unusual concern. Not that he wasn't always concerned about patients, but this one had a tug on his heart. Or more accurately her father did. "Patty'll explain. She told me to send you in as soon as you got here."

Ollie pulled his scrubs top down, took a deep breath and sauntered over to Room One. Just like any other shift. Any other patient. Any other family to deal with. He swallowed as he pushed the door open.

"Hey there, Supergirl," Ollie said with a beaming smile.

Daisy didn't return it. She didn't even try. She slumped back on the mounds of pillows and groaned. Ollie peered over at Becky, who looked right through him as if he wasn't there. Ollie figured that was the best response he could get right then.

Patty held a mound of wipes, blankets and whatnot, all reeking of vomit. She, however, did offer Ollie a smile. She angled her head, and Ollie followed her to the doorway where she proceeded to tell him that Daisy's recovery had taken a turn for the worse. Sickness and diarrhea, dizzy spells, no energy. She was off all meds until the doctor could assess her, and Ollie was to do to fifteen-minute obs while sharing his patient load with Taya and the other night nurses. Ollie nodded. Patty squeezed his shoulder, offered a wave over to Daisy and trudged out of the room to go home and probably get her eight hours of recommended sleep.

"Right." Ollie stepped back into the room. He walked to the side of the bed and perched to sit down, checking her face. "Are you just trying to stay here because you don't want to go back to school? Having too much fun on Bear Ward, eh?"

Daisy shook her solemn head. The poor girl looked exhausted. Eyes bloodshot and droopy, skin pale, her long dark hair like rats' tails dangling around her shoulders. Her lips were dry with cracked skin from all the dehydration. And when Ollie placed a palm to her forehead, she was clammy and hot to the touch.

"When will the doctor get here?" Becky asked.

Becky, just as weary as her daughter, folded her arms. Her hair grabbed back into a greasy ponytail made the lines of concern on her forehead more noticeable, along with the fear behind her eyes. Ollie had to swallow down his personal guilt and slap on his professional demeanor to acknowledge the woman.

"I'll have to check," Ollie replied. "I'm sure he knows what's happening and will make it his priority to get to her."

"I've been waiting a while to talk to him. I have other things to discuss too. Can you call him?"

Ollie stood and wandered over to the sink by the wall, pushing down the soap holder and washing his hands thoroughly. "I'll go check."

His stomach flipped like a spin wash as Jacob approached the door. He gave a brief nod and Jacob returned it before walking past and fully into the room.

"How is she?" Jacob asked.

Ollie was about to answer before he realized the question had been addressed to Becky and quickly shut his mouth.

"Sick," Becky snapped. "She's had fucking heart surgery, Jacob."

Jacob sighed and perched on Daisy's bed. Her eyes were flickering shut and he stroked a hand down her cheek. Ollie could feel those fingertips. He knew those fingertips.

"I know, Becky," Jacob replied, exasperation in his voice. "Can we keep this civil, please?"

Ollie did his best to ignore the domestic scene that he was already far too involved in and tried to maintain his professional status. He picked up the clip-file at the end of the bed to read through all the obs and check what needed to be done.

Becky slammed her hands down to her sides and made a noise in her throat Ollie couldn't describe. As though she was hacking up, Daisy-style. "Who was he?"

"Who was who?" Jacob replied, calmly.

"The man you were fucking while your daughter lay in a hospital bed and threw her guts up," Becky hissed, leaning threateningly forward.

Jacob stood and pointed a trembling finger across the bed. "You weren't here either," he managed through gritted teeth. "You came to me. Who was with her then? Who was with her last night? And the night before?" Jacob ran a hand through his hair. "Don't judge me, Becky. I'm doing the best I can under the circumstances you put me in."

"You put yourself in those," Becky snapped back. "You don't get to play the wounded party here. It's unfair. To me. To her. You can't be all Fathers 4 Justice when you weren't a fucking father to begin with."

"I have, and always will be, Daisy's father." Jacob clenched his fists, and Ollie was sure he would launch across that bed and ram them into the woman. "My relationship with you has nothing to do with her. Is it him? Is this everything Simon has been telling you to say? Try to make me give up? Let you take her away from me? So *he* can play Dad?"

"At least he wants to be a father! And not just a fu—"

"Don't you dare!" Jacob jammed a finger in the air, his face scorching red. "Not ever in front of her!"

Ollie rushed forward. "Please," he begged, looking from one to the other. "If you want to argue, you'll have to take it outside the hospital. This is Daisy's room. Daisy's recovery. This is completely unacceptable."

"Do *you* think he's a good father?" Becky asked, waving a trembling hand over the bed at Jacob but addressing Ollie. "I'll bet you see tons of decent fathers in here. How does he measure up to you?"

"I'm not answering that," Ollie replied. What he should have said was that he wasn't going to get involved in domestic disputes. Trouble was, he already *was* involved. *Too involved.* "Now you have to calm down, or I'll need to call security to take you out."

Becky snorted, refolding her arms and stood her ground. Ollie took the opportunity to throw a brief reassuring smile Jacob's way. Jacob nodded in response.

"You can go," Jacob said.

"I'm not leaving until I see the doctor," Becky replied. "You leave."

"I'm not going, either." Jacob unzipped his coat to throw it on the chair. "Looks like we might have to try and get along."

Both parents glared at each other across the mattress. Ollie had seen parents of sick children arguing and taking their stress out on each other countless times. He remembered his own parents' battles when Tilly was undergoing her chemo and surgeries. But this stare-off was making him even more uncomfortable than it had in those days. And that was simply to do with how close he was to the situation. Yet another reason to explain why not getting involved in patient-family conflict was a rule he should have stuck to.

Ollie slapped on a pair of disposable gloves and moved around to Becky's side of the bed to check all Daisy's obs via the machine. Becky stepped back to let him pass, and as Ollie brushed the hair away from Daisy's face, he locked eyes with Jacob hovering over the other side. Jacob smiled and Ollie couldn't help but return it. The machine bleeped, and Jacob's eyes grew wide. Becky started forward, and Ollie checked the readings. Dropping to sit on the bed, he tugged open one of Daisy's eyelids.

"What is it?" Jacob asked.

"She's passed out," Ollie replied. "She's too hot."

Ollie shoved down Daisy's bedcovers and removed pillows to get her some air. His fingers brushed Jacob's and Ollie felt the electricity. He wanted to reach out for more but Becky stopped all chances, hovering by his side.

"She's done that already today," Becky said, biting her shaking thumb nail. "The other nurse says we need to keep her hydrated."

"Yep," Ollie replied over his shoulder, laying Daisy flat on the mattress. "I'll get a drip put in." He glanced up to Jacob, whose fear was evident. "She's okay," Ollie reassured him.

Jacob nodded. All was quiet while Ollie checked the ratings on the obs machine. Becky hovered, eyes on her daughter with a noticeable shake on her shoulders. Until she stilled, staring hard at Ollie, more precisely at his pristine white loafers with the red stripe along the rubber sole

"Nice shoes."

Her hard, tight voice breaking the silence made Ollie jump. "Thanks?" He waggled one. "Nurse standard."

"I've seen a pair like them, just recently actually." Becky glared at Ollie. "And those glasses."

Ollie swallowed. He paused, not having anything he could say. Frozen like a statue, Ollie avoided looking at anything other than Daisy, now sleeping soundly and far more peaceful than the atmosphere in the room. *Focus on the job, like I should have been doing all along.*

"You disgust me," Becky spat, her fierce glare now locked onto Jacob. "Not even his daughter's hospital is safe from Jacob and his need to get his cock sucked. I've had enough. All that crap about being a father! It means nothing to you, does it? Get the fuck out!"

"Becky—"

"Don't." Trembling with rage, Becky shook her head. "I cannot do this again! Not now. Not with Daisy like this."

Ollie stood and held out a hand to each of them. "This is not the time."

"Never a truer statement, Nurse," Becky sneered. "Leave, Jacob! Before I get really fucking angry."

Jacob opened his mouth, about to retaliate. Ollie couldn't allow Jacob to speak. Whatever he said, confirmation or denial, it wouldn't make the situation any better. Ollie needed to stop this quick before it went any further and ruined everything he had worked so hard for. "Maybe it's for the best." He addressed Jacob.

"Ollie—"

"There's a parents' lounge, Mr. Monroe." Ollie cut him off. "Perhaps you could wait there?"

He heard the snort of disdain coming from Becky and guessed it was her way of letting him know that, regardless of his use of Jacob's full title, she wasn't convinced they weren't on more than first-name terms. Ollie raised his eyebrows, urging Jacob to let this be. Heaving a heavy sigh, Jacob grabbed his coat from the chair, leaned forward to kiss his daughter's cheek and stroked his hand down her face. He then turned and stomped out of the room without a second glance at Ollie. The flapping of the ward doors echoed after.

Becky gave Ollie a once-over. Ollie stared back, unflinching. The silence dragged on with neither removing their gaze from one another, until Ollie remembered he had a job to do. He cleared his throat.

"I don't know what you think you're insinuating, here, Ms...." Ollie hoped she would complete the rest.

Becky folded her arms. "Miss Daley."

He could see now why she kept Daisy's name as Monroe. He shook his head. "Miss Daley – "

"Did he say you were beautiful?"

Ollie's throat stuck. He wanted to refute the accusation. He needed to. He had to find some way of convincing both this woman and his patient's doctor that they had got it wrong. But as he stared up at Becky, his heart hammering and chest tightening, her expression said it all. He'd never seen a woman so full of hurt and anguish.

"Did he stroke your face and whisper sweet nothings?" Becky's voice was light now, almost as though she was simply detailing facts. "Did he ask, ever so politely, if he could fuck you, but he was already halfway there anyway, making it impossible for you to refuse?"

Ollie sucked in a breath, his nostrils flaring through the tremble. *How could she even know any of that?* The bleeping of the machine evened out, Daisy's fragile body returning to normality, and, ignoring the fear bubbling in his stomach, he ruffled the sheets to drape them back up to her chest.

"Did he say he wanted to see you again but couldn't say when, then, ever so conveniently, forget to give you his number?" Becky stepped forward, lingering at Ollie's back. "I've lived this, Nurse. I know. A leopard doesn't change his spots and a cheater will always be a cheater."

"Miss—"

"I've heard it before. From the ones he left behind. From the messages they've sent. You're definitely his type. He likes the ones he can manipulate. The ones with a kind heart who'll fall for his sob story and be suckered into thinking he's a decent man, with morals. When really? He's got a dozen of you. In every fucking city."

"Miss Daley, I urge you to stop." The tremble in Ollie's delivery overwhelmed him. He couldn't look the woman in the eye. It would only give him away. And what hurt more than anything was that everything she had said was true.

"I don't blame you." Becky lowered onto the bed beside Daisy and stroked her daughter's hand, her previous anger dissipating to make way for a woman beaten by life's circumstances. At that moment, Ollie couldn't blame her either. Not for the anger, or the contempt, or her brash and hurtful words. If anyone knew how Becky felt, it was Ollie.

"Can we focus on Daisy, here, please?" Ollie's professional tone kicked in for one last time.

Becky's eyes glazed over. "That's what I've been trying to do. For years. Keeping Daisy away from all of that. And yet, here I am. Again. I've picked up the pieces more times than you'll ever know. Back during the days when he said he'd stop. When he said it was a phase, a fling, it had all meant nothing. We've all been sucked in by Jacob Monroe. I have been. I fell for his lies." She stepped back and sized Ollie up from head to toe. "You're not the first one, Ollie. And by far you won't be the last."

Ollie couldn't respond. Not to anything. There was no point denying anything or defending his or Jacob's actions. The less he did or said, the better his position would be. But the blood that ran through his veins was like ice on his skin. The plummeting in his stomach made him want to reach for one of the cardboard pots and hurl his guts into it. Instead, he checked all the wires leading to the obs machine, pushed his glasses farther up his nose and inched around the bed for the exit.

"Just so you know, the only one who'll ever be in his heart," Becky said before Ollie reached the door, "is this little one."

* * * *

Jacob's head shot up when Ollie opened the door of the parents' lounge. He was the only one in there, with it not really being used all that much during the evening. It was a simple room, neutral shades and soft furnishings, innocuous pictures on the wall, comfy chairs set in a circle so parents could talk, a kitchenette equipped with kettle, fridge, and microwave. It was a space for parents to escape the bustle of the ward and give themselves quiet time to reflect and recuperate.

And as Ollie walked in, Jacob's wide pleading eyes ripped him in two.

"How is she?" Jacob asked.

"Stable. Sleeping. No signs of stress. The doctor will see her soon."

Jacob nodded. "I'm so sorry about Becky." He closed his eyes tight.

Ollie slipped down on the seat next to him and inhaled a deep breath. "Maybe you should stay away." The words stung Ollie's tongue as he said them.

Jacob opened his eyes. "What?"

"I'm just thinking what's best for Daisy, and having two parents at each other's throats in her room will not aid her recovery. Maybe it's best, all round, if you were to leave."

"What did she say to you?"

Ollie tucked his hands under his legs. "Nothing I didn't already know."

Jacob snorted. "Just sounds much worse coming from her, though, right?"

Ollie met Jacob's eyes, and that penetrating blue sliced him like a knife. He knew it had been foolish to get involved. He knew it was ridiculous to believe anything the man said. Ollie didn't know him. He didn't know who he really was. He'd gone on face value and that could never lead to a good thing. He also knew he couldn't listen to the scorned ex either. All he could listen to was his heart. But it was beating so fast he wasn't sure what it was trying to tell him.

"Ollie." Jacob uttered his name so softly that Ollie couldn't help but tingle.

"Jacob." Ollie was sterner with his delivery. "I can't, right now. I can't. I've had my fill of being second." He sucked in a deep breath and licked his lips. "I know I'll never be first for Elliot. He'll never take care of me like he does his patients. I know I'll never be first to my father, or my mother. They'll always have Tilly, or each other, to focus their attention on. And I'll never be first to any of those little kids out there I spend twelve hours a day making my main priority, just so I don't have to think about how I'm always cast aside. But, God, Jacob." Ollie slid his hands out from under his legs and wiped them down his trousers, ridding them of the clammy sweat. "I'm not sure I can be another afterthought."

Jacob laid a trembling hand down on top of Ollie's, making him look up and finally face him. "Everything I told you is true," Jacob said. "I'm no saint, Ollie. Neither are you. Yes, I was dishonest with Becky. And, yes, I haven't been truthful with many of the men I've been with. I've left a trail of destruction behind me and I'm not proud of it. But it's in the past. And this" —Jacob gripped Ollie's hand tighter— "*this* I feel. I really do. For the first time, I'm being completely honest." He stroked a thumb in smooth circles over Ollie's skin. "I know you feel something, too."

The door to the parents' lounge clanged open, and another parent walked in. Snatching his hand from under Jacob's, Ollie stood. The mother, who Ollie only recognized from Taya's patient load, went into the kitchen and the kettle flicked on to boil soon after.

"Feel free to stay here, Mr. Monroe," Ollie said. "I'll ensure you are informed of your daughter's progress."

With that, Ollie flattened down his scrubs and headed for the door.

"Ollie," Jacob called after him.

But Ollie couldn't do it. If he turned right then, he'd most definitely feel not just something, but too much.

Chapter Ten

Rapid Response

"So, I'm meeting him as soon as I switch back to days. He seems nice. Which is a real change from the usual weirdos on POF."

Ollie nodded, biting his lip while checking through the noticeboard at the nurses' station and zoning out Taya's incessant babbling. He appreciated the background noise and didn't really want her to stop. Adding a few hums of agreement or snorts of amusement encouraged her to continue. All his mind wandered to was the time and how this night shift seemed to be whizzing by rather than being its usual dreary slog. *Time flies when we're having fun? It also goes on warp speed when there's a looming undesirable deadline.*

He'd gotten through last night's shift relatively unscathed. Jacob had taken his advice and left. Becky had remained by Daisy's side alone. He'd only seen the doctor on patient duties. But on returning home and falling into his bed, solo this time, his landline answering machine had bellowed out a message from Elliot that the following shift, he would be taking Ollie back to his house for their discussion. Ollie had been thankful Jacob wouldn't be there to witness his demise back to being Oliver. And Ollie feared that Jacob's presence would provide him with a backbone he couldn't afford. And without Jacob there now, Becky's words seeped through his mind and colored his judgment. It hurt, but Ollie did his best to get back to what was important. *My job. Keeping my job.*

"At least he said more than just 'hi, you're nice,'" Taya continued. "He put thought and effort into the message."

Ollie hummed again and glanced over at Room One. Daisy was asleep, recovery back to normal, and her mother curled up in the chair Jacob had occupied on the previous night shifts. She had clearly passed out too. He looked up at the clock. He needed to go in there and check the girl's last set of obs before day shift. He really didn't want to and was very close to asking Taya to do it for him, but she had powers of deduction similar to those of Sherlock Holmes, and he thought better than to have another person in on his dirty secret.

"What's happened?" Taya declared, slapping her boxes of medicine onto the desk and ramming her hands on her hips.

Ollie shot a confused look her way. "Huh?"

"You're quiet," Taya stated. "Exceptionally quiet for Ollie Warne. You were yesterday too. Come on!" Taya snapped her fingers. "I've told you I'm going to meet a guy from Plenty of Fish and you haven't insisted you either come with me or stock me up with neuromuscular-blocking drugs just in case."

"Sorry, T." Ollie sighed. "I'm just preoccupied. My dad and that. Sorry."

"Okay, sweets." Taya tilted her head. "As long as that's all it is? Because if a certain doctor has anything to do with it—"

"No, no, nope." Picking up his tray, Ollie suddenly thought he would be better off in Daisy's room rather than out here to end up spilling anything he really shouldn't. And he didn't just mean the mounds of medicines Taya was currently slotting away.

Taya narrowed unconvinced eyes, but Ollie was saved by the bell, or rather the clanging open of the ward doors. As Ollie glanced up to see who had entered, saved didn't seem such an appropriate word any longer. Jacob marched into the ward, ignoring the nurses' station, and more poignantly Ollie, heading straight for his daughter's room.

"Shit." Ollie bolted out from behind the desk, skidding on his shoes to reach him. He clamped a palm on Jacob's chest, gently shoving him back and away from the open door. "Hey."

Jacob looked down at the hand splayed across his chest and back up to meet Ollie's eyes behind his glasses. Ollie's hand felt as if it was on fire, his entire being rushing through to his palm in some silent plea to touch more of the man in front of him. So Ollie whipped it away and pushed his glasses up his nose.

"Move aside, Ollie," Jacob practically growled.

"Jacob—"

"You cannot keep me from seeing my daughter. And neither can she." Jacob waved a frustrated hand toward the door. "Not this time. I was forced out of here yesterday like some criminal. I'm no criminal, Ollie. That's my daughter in there." Jacob stepped forward to lower his voice into Ollie's ear. "You can push me away from you, because you're scared of feeling something or whatever, but you cannot push me away from my daughter. I don't know how long I've got with her."

The glisten in Jacob's eyes wrenched Ollie's gut. He sneaked a glance over at Taya, who watched on in grotesque fascination. He avoided her mouthed question in order to address Jacob.

"Call security if you have to," Jacob said. "But I'm going in there."

He tried to move past, but Ollie squared up in front of him once more. Both Room One occupants were asleep, undisturbed by the commotion outside their shared space. Ollie's garbled mind went into overdrive. What Jacob had just said rang through him. Had Jacob only left yesterday because Ollie had asked him to? That hit him where it hurt. He'd kept a father away from his daughter for no other reason than selfish fear.

"Okay, wait," Ollie breathed. "Let me get this sorted, and I'll let you in."

Jacob stepped back. Ollie indicated for him to follow, and, on reaching the nurses' station, saw Taya's gaping mouth hadn't closed yet.

"Taya." Ollie kept his voice low, almost pleading. "Can you do Daisy Monroe's obs for me? And while you're in there, encourage mum to move over to the sofa bed and draw the curtains."

"*Ollie,*" Taya warned, tilting her head.

"Please, T." Ollie did beg that time.

Taya sighed, glancing from one man to the other. Eventually she nodded and picked up Ollie's tray. Ollie watched through the gaps in the blinds for a moment to see Taya gently nudging Becky, ushering her toward the sofa bed. Once Taya started on the obs, he turned back to Jacob.

"I'm sorry," Ollie said. "I shouldn't have made you leave. That wasn't fair."

Jacob nodded but didn't look Ollie in the eye.

"She's okay," Ollie reassured. "Back to normal readings the last twenty-four hours. The doctor is pleased with her recovery."

Jacob nodded again, chewing on his bottom lip. Ollie couldn't help it any longer and did his usual nurse squeeze to Jacob's arm. Jacob flicked his solemn gaze to Ollie, making Ollie's breath catch.

"I'll help you." The words slipped from Ollie's tongue before he could change his mind. "I will."

"What does that mean, exactly?"

Ollie released his grip and drummed his fingers on the countertop. Now it was his turn to avoid eye contact.

"I'll speak with the doctor. I think I can get this sorted. I can get confirmation that Daisy can't leave the country for the time being."

Jacob cocked his head. "Does that mean—"

"It means, I can get you what you want," Ollie cut him off, unwilling and unable to admit what that potentially entailed.

Jacob didn't say anything further, although Ollie could tell he wanted to. He did appreciate the silence then. Nothing could be said to make this situation any better for either of them, so Taya's return was a welcome distraction.

"All done." Taya slapped the tray back down on the desk. "Mum asleep, curtains drawn."

She gave Ollie a stern eyeball, which he ignored in order to usher Jacob to Room One. Jacob immediately rushed over to Daisy's bed, sat on the edge and leaned in for a brush of his lips to his daughter's forehead.

Ollie did his hardest to bite down on the envy he felt of that little girl. It was like the painful bouts of unhinged jealousy he used to get when his parents would kiss his sister. Back then, he'd been a child, unable to control his emotive response to being cast aside time and time again as his sister had bathed in his parents' attention. He still felt it now whenever his father called him Tilly and forgot who he was. His sister was always at the forefront of his father's mind and Ollie was a mere afterthought. His harrowing envy was always replaced with overwhelming guilt. He was sure Tilly would have swapped places with him in a heartbeat, and Ollie was proud to admit he would have done too. Not only to be the one to take on his baby sister's pain and suffering, but also to have an inch of his parents' love and attention.

"Thank you, Ollie," Jacob whispered.

Ollie nodded in response, then curled his fingers around the door handle and closed that one ever so much more delicately. When Becky woke up, Jacob would just have to deal with the consequences. Ollie would hopefully be long gone and dealing with his own torment back at Dr. Rawlings' town house. He stepped with heavy shoulders over to the nurses' station where Taya stood waiting, arms folded.

"Do I want to know?" she asked.

Ollie shook his head and cleared up around the desk ready for Patty's return.

"I'm not sure they do patches for feelings," Taya mused. *The sleuth strikes again.* "Or gum." She pulled out a pack from her pocket and crinkled the foil to pop a stick into her mouth. "I'm thinking of going to the cinema later. Fancy coming? It's quiet first thing in the morning."

"Sorry," Ollie grumbled. "I have to be somewhere else."

"Your dad?" She tucked the gum back into her pocket.

Ollie shook his head and didn't respond further as the doors clanged open and a few of the day nurses, including Patty, arrived half an hour early for the handover. Dr. Rawlings swanned in at the back, stethoscope dangling around his neck, laughing and joking with those who fell to his every whim yet didn't know the real truth of what that meant. Ollie swallowed.

"Oliver." Dr. Rawlings greeting was firmly back to his usual one.

"Doctor," Ollie replied in his just-as-practiced delivery.

"Shall we go see to Daisy Monroe? You can hand over to Patty while you're there." The doctor placed his hand on the veteran nurse's back and steered her toward the room.

Ollie followed, glancing over his shoulder at Taya who stuck a finger in her mouth and mimicked throwing up. Ollie snorted and took a deep breath as they entered the room. Jacob shot up off the bed.

"Mr. Monroe." Dr. Rawlings picked up the clipboard at the end of the bed. "Welcome back."

Jacob flickered from Ollie to the doctor and the day nurse. "How is she?"

"Responding well. No further complications. She'll be on course for discharge shortly." The doctor glanced up from the clipboard, stern eyes on Jacob. "You'll be delighted to see the back of this hospital, and my staff, I'm sure."

Ollie begged whoever was listening for Jacob not to retaliate to such disdainful words. Maybe he wouldn't pick up on the double meaning.

"I'm not so sure, Doctor. This hospital will forever have a place in my heart."

Shit! Ollie could do nothing. He wanted to return a smile of some description from his myriad categories but couldn't seem to locate one that would portray what he felt. Dr. Rawlings' penetrating stare was on him anyway. So he stood straighter and awaited the next part.

"Patty?" Dr. Rawlings glared through Ollie.

"Yes, Doctor?" Patty responded with distinct efficiency and years of training.

"Daisy Monroe can go back to three-hourly obs. We can take her off nil by mouth, and Dr. Khan has been brought up to speed on her nightly care, and he will be on the ward in the next two hours."

"Yes, Doctor." Patty nodded.

Dr. Rawlings turned back to Jacob and opened his mouth to speak when the curtain separating the room from the parent sleep bay was ripped open.

"What the hell are you doing in here?" Becky's fierce glare turned on each of the room's occupants but settled on Jacob.

"I'm seeing to my daughter, Becky," Jacob replied. "Let's keep calm until we know all is right. Then we'll talk."

"Let's leave the family to it, shall we?" Dr. Rawlings gestured for Ollie and Patty to leave the room.

Patty made her way out, but Ollie shuddered at the clamp of Dr. Rawlings' hand on his shoulder.

"Nurse. We have an appointment."

Jacob ripped his glare from Becky to Ollie.

"Yes, Doctor," Ollie replied.

Dr. Rawlings marched out, straight over to the nurses' station to sign out with his other patients, and Ollie slumped off.

"Ollie?" The desperation in Jacob's voice caught not only Ollie but Becky, as her narrowed glare proved.

Ollie didn't know what he could offer in consolation. He couldn't quash his hope that Jacob was going to rush forward and rescue him. Put him first. For once.

"Daddy?" Daisy's little voice croaked out. "Where were you?"

Jacob's gaze shifted at once to his daughter, and that was all Ollie needed to leave the room.

Chapter Eleven

Pain Relief

The keys clanging down on the glistening black-glass coffee table sent shivers up Ollie's spine. He flinched as Elliot slid off his leather jacket, fluffing it out and hanging it on the back of one of the breakfast bar stools that divided the living space from the kitchen. Dr. Rawlings' Victorian town house was a fully refurbished, modern, open-plan home set over three floors in one of the leafier parts of London. Only a consultant's salary could have afforded the type of luxury he lived in. Ollie had been on floors one and two, the third floor had always remained off-limits. Ollie often wondered if that was where the doctor hid his secret family. He fully expected the doctor to emerge one day with a wife and three kids who had been locked up there in the attic until he'd seen fit they could roam in his world. Perhaps they were granted access to rest of the house when Elliot, and of course Ollie, wasn't there? And that was the reason Ollie was never allowed to leave anything behind!

Two years Ollie had been in and out of this house. Or, more accurately, the master bedroom. The first time, Ollie had thought he'd struck gold. A doctor, a good-looking and well-mannered cardiology consultant and surgeon, had invited him back for dinner after having met him during one of Ollie's student placements. The dinner had been candlelit, the conversation fascinating, the table manners impeccable. And while Ollie couldn't honestly admit that the act of falling into bed with someone on a first date was out of character for him, he was rather surprised that Elliot had wanted it to end that way too. Back then, if either of them had been in more trouble for what they'd done, it would have been the doctor. Ollie had been a mere student nurse. Easily led, easily manipulated, and easily prone to listen to a sob story.

And, boy, did Dr. Rawlings have one. He'd laid it on thick that night too, no-holds-barred as they lay together in the aftermath on his luxurious cashmere pocket-sprung mattress of the king-size bed, engulfed in the goose-feather duvet deep enough for Ollie to bury his misdeeds in. The doctor was married to his job. The children in his care needed him far more than anyone else. He didn't have time for relationships as no one could accept him for who he was and the hours he put into his work saving the lives of children on a daily basis. His parents hadn't accepted his homosexuality, and so he lived a lie to keep them happy and their heads held high at Sunday Mass. After they'd died, Dr. Rawlings had found he didn't know how to live the life he'd buried for so long.

Ollie had fallen a little bit in love with him under the heat of the covers and the passion in his words. He'd accepted what the doctor said wholeheartedly. Who wouldn't? The man was a hero. He had pumped with his bare hands the hearts of little children who would have otherwise succumbed to the harsh fate of disease and congenital defects. And Ollie could understand wanting to please his family, even if it had meant hiding who he really was. Luckily, his own coming-out story had been rather uneventful. Perhaps his parents had already had far too much tragedy and misfortune to really care all that much, but he knew his mother and father were wholeheartedly accepting, although he had heard his mother's sobbing coming from her bedroom after his announcement. Tilly couldn't have children due to the cancer having attacked most of her body, so with Ollie being gay, any hope of biological grandchildren had been thwarted.

Elliot had convinced Ollie that what they had was special. He showered Ollie with gifts and declared time again that he needed time, patience and understanding. Along with that came the secrets, the denial and the agreement that what they did was between them. Ollie couldn't leave any trace of his visits because the doctor often brought other consultants back to the house—offering a place to stay for out-of-town doctors who might be supporting him in a newly developed operating procedure or a particularly challenging patient diagnosis or, more often, to learn from one of the best pediatric cardiologists in the country. Ollie had accepted that. For a while.

Roughly a year in, when Ollie's father's signs of dementia were getting progressively worse and his mother had been struggling to cope with both him and Tilly at home, Ollie had called it a day. He needed to support his mother, he needed a job and he needed no complications. Moving back home to Hertfordshire on finishing his London-based university course meant he would need a job out of the city. Therefore, his arrangement with Dr. Rawlings had to come to an end. And he'd been rather relieved at the fact. Having a secret boyfriend had taken its toll.

It was Elliot who had suggested the care home. The best in London, its price tag evidence of its status. There had been a job vacancy in the St. Cross cardiology ward, and Ollie, if he applied, would be more or less guaranteed the position. Elliot had an enormous amount of sway among the hospital higher-ups. He was well regarded, practically the face of St. Cross. His efforts for the hospital didn't stop at saving children's lives. Dr. Rawlings had raised much-needed funds for the refurbishment of several wings over the years. His annual fundraisers were the highlight of the hospital calendar. He was chair of several committees—about many of which Ollie had no idea what they did or serviced. Dr. Rawlings was everywhere, known by everyone, with a huge influence and an all-powerful status. Ollie couldn't really have ever said no. *Unless I was told to.*

Elliot had offered to make the down payment on the care home, which, being a short stroll from the hospital, meant Ollie could see his father daily. Elliott would act as guarantor if Ollie and his mother could keep up the monthly payments between them. It had all sounded a little too perfect. And on agreeing to the proposal, Ollie had had no idea what he was really letting himself in for. Relieving his mother of all the torment and struggle she had hoped she'd left behind when receiving the news of his sister's remission didn't seem that much of a burden for Ollie to shoulder. Until the arrangement had become less about romantic dinner dates and more about simply bending over.

He had tried to put an end to it more times than the most recent. Each time, he was reminded that he couldn't afford the care home without a guarantor and making his father move to somewhere else would only bring on further illness, not to mention anxiety for his mother. So, each time, Ollie caved. He got sex, so what was the big deal?

But now there was Jacob.

"You can take your coat off, Oliver," Elliot said over his shoulder, crouching at his built-in wine rack. He slid out a bottle of red wine and popped it onto the breakfast bar counter.

Ollie unzipped his puffer jacket and slipped it down his arms. He looked around for somewhere to throw it, hoping to find a valuable antique or expensive art sculpture he could knock over in the process. Giving up, he draped it over the leather chair adjacent to the coffee table.

"Wine?" Elliot held up a crystal goblet.

"No, thanks."

Elliot clapped the bottle down and poured two glasses anyway. Maybe his imprisoned wife upstairs would drink it once Ollie had gone. Because there was no way he was spending the night. The day. Whatever. Elliot picked up both glasses, and his heavy intake of breath bounced off the white walls as he sniffed at the striking deep-purple contents. He held out a full glass to Ollie, then leaned in and kissed his neck. Ollie closed his eyes. He took the glass only because it was in danger of spilling over him with how lecherous Elliot was being, and leaving yet another impossible-to-wash-out stain on his T-shirt. As soon as the doctor's coarse tongue began to lick up his neck, Ollie shuddered.

"You smell divine," Elliot whispered into his ear.

Ollie cursed himself that he'd instinctively dabbed the Givenchy cologne on his neck when he'd changed back at the hospital.

"Live to serve." He'd meant it to come out as facetious, but the words were true. It was why Ollie was there, after all.

Elliot chuckled, a deep sound that resonated along Ollie's spine. The hairs on Ollie's arms and the back of his neck stood to attention. But it wasn't the same pleasurable reaction he'd gotten the previous day when Jacob's breath had made him tingle. The doctor's heavy breathing felt more bristling, and Ollie's skin crawled, the hairs aiding its leap away from his body.

Elliot trailed his lips across Ollie's ear, to his cheek, and eventually found his mouth. He tried sliding in with his tongue, but Ollie backed away, shaking his head.

"I thought we were talking." Ollie wiped his mouth with the back of his hand.

"Fine." Elliot waved his glass, gesturing toward the black leather sofas surrounding the coffee table. He strolled over to one, sat with a heavy slump and took a sip of his wine. He waved an impatient hand to one of the other seats.

Ollie edged around the one he'd hung his coat over and sat. Placing his wineglass on the table, he eyed the doctor.

"I knew this day would eventually come upon us," Elliot said with a smile. He swished his glass before taking another mouthful.

"What day is that?" Ollie tapped his fingers on the hard armrests. He never did understand why the sofas in this place were so damn uncomfortable. They'd probably cost a fortune, and, yeah, they looked sophisticated enough and matched the black-and-white decor, but they weren't the sort of sofa where one could kick back and indulge in a movie on the ridiculously large plasma screen hanging on the wall. They also weren't that comfortable to be naked on when the leather stuck to sweaty flesh. Ollie shook his head to mask the second shudder of the morning.

"The day you found someone else and wanted to end this union we have." Elliot tapped a shoe against the glass tabletop.

"I haven't found anyone else, Elliot," Ollie lied through gritted teeth. "I've just had enough. I had enough months ago, but you blackmailed me back then. If you're going to do it again, can we cut to the chase? I'm rather tired."

"There's a perfectly good bed upstairs should you want to relax."

Ollie slammed back in his chair with a snort. Shaking his head, he took in all the sculptures and artwork, the only details that prevented the house from being an empty shell. On his first visit to this place, Ollie had thought they were quirky and rather elegant—artefacts that he'd thought might help explain the doctor's interests outside the hospital. Ollie had hoped to use them to delve into the man's mind a little. He'd soon found they were items picked up at random in some boutique shop recommended by whoever did Elliot's interior design. Elliot didn't have attachments to possessions—not like Ollie and his watch. People were also part of that category.

"I love you."

Ollie snapped his gaze from the brushstrokes of the latest painting on the wall to the doctor. Elliot remained in his poised position—legs crossed, wineglass clutched in an outstretched hand perching on the armrest and the other hand splayed on the sofa cushion beside him. His eyes were eerily still for a man who had just uttered those unmistakable three words.

"I beg your pardon?" Ollie replied.

"Oh, come off it, Oliver." Elliot uncrossed his legs and leaned forward to rest his elbows on his knees. "I love you. Isn't it obvious?"

"Erm, no." Ollie shook his head at the absurdity.

"I've been sleeping with you for two years," Elliot stated. "I do not sleep with anyone else. And I am rather disturbed by the fact that you have been."

Ollie stood in involuntary protest. "I haven't."

He wasn't sure how convincing the statement came across, especially with the tremble in his voice, which, if he could feel, Elliot could probably hear. Apart from Jacob, it was true. Ollie hadn't been with anyone else. He'd had opportunities, sure. He'd had the odd cheeky kiss or two in a nightclub or bar, but he'd always known better than to follow through with anything more. Jacob had been an exception to that. And Ollie wasn't sure if that hadn't been a really bad judgment call. Like the one he'd made in this house two years ago.

"Sit down, Oliver," Elliot demanded, waving his glass before taking another lingering gulp.

Ollie sat and gripped the armrests once more, digging his nails into hard leather. His heart hammered, tightening his chest with every breath. He was having difficulty understanding where this conversation could be heading.

"Do you love me?" Elliot asked, plainly.

Ollie met his stern glower across the coffee table. Elliot raised his eyebrows with the question and his perfect poise didn't falter, as if he had simply inquired if Ollie took milk with his tea. Ollie swallowed and licked his drying lips. The silence was unbearable. Ollie rather wished he had the bleeping of machines to drown it out. All he could hear was Elliot's breathing and the occasional bubbles popping in his glass of red wine. The fact the wine wasn't sparkling went some way to prove how deathly quiet it really was.

"I probably did once," Ollie offered. "But I'm afraid it was chipped away every time you sent me from this house like a low-rent whore. Until, eventually, all I had was indifference. Which has now merged effortlessly into contempt."

Elliot's sharp intake of breath and the increased tapping of his foot was the only indication that those words had affected the man. His face remained as blank as ever. He finished his glass and set it on the coffee table. A last drip of liquid slithered from the rim and over the bowl, making its final descent down the stem to land with a circular splodge on the black glass. Ollie wondered whether to go tell the man to get a coaster. Red wine circles were a bitch to get out. He knew that.

"So, what do we do?" Elliot finally asked. The question and its delivery reminded Ollie of when the doctor would ask his fellow medical professionals about a patient's perplexing adverse reaction to standard medication. It didn't seem an appropriate response from someone who had just been told he was hated by the man he was supposedly in love with.

"I'm not sure I know what you mean," Ollie said.

"I shall rephrase." Elliot slipped his foot to the floor and leaned forward. "What do you want from me, Oliver?"

Ollie took a deep breath. He was still riddled with unease at this conversation. He supposed what Elliot expected him to say was Ollie wanted them to be finally be out in the open—to declare their love to the world, to act as a proper couple. To stop being sent from this house as nothing and to be allowed, at least, to keep hold of his possessions should he accidentally leave them in the bathroom after a shower. Trouble was, Ollie didn't want any of that. What he wanted was to feel something. *Resolutions never work out, anyway, do they?*

"I want you to leave me alone." Ollie's heart hammered with the fear of it all, once again reminding him how alive he was. But after what he was going to say, he wondered for how long. If ever there was a man who knew how to cause death in the most accidental of ways, it would be a heart doctor. "I want you to sign off from being the guarantor on my father's care home. I want to switch shifts so we never have to work alongside each other. And I don't want you to ever touch me again."

Ollie paused and waited for any type of reaction. When there was only a stone-cold stare, Ollie thought he might as well go the whole hog.

"And I want you to compose a letter stating Daisy Monroe mustn't leave the country until she becomes a legal adult to switch care to a standard hospital."

Silence.

Ollie grabbed the wine he hadn't planned on drinking and guzzled the lot. He gripped the glass to give him something to use as a weapon should he need it.

"Well, then." Elliot finally stood, curling his fingers into the knot on his tie and ripping it apart. "I guess you'd best be going upstairs."

* * * *

Ollie kicked the front door to his flat shut, threw his loafers off to bounce against the wall and dragged his coat down his arms, dumping it on the floor with a huff. He marched with heavy steps through his flat and straight to the bathroom, where he stripped out of his clothes and avoided checking his reflection in the mirror. Placing his glasses on the windowsill, he switched the shower on to maximum heat and stepped in to scald his skin.

His body was red raw when he emerged. The hot water and excessive scrubbing at least added some color to his pasty complexion. Perhaps he'd leave it a few days before cashing in his tanning voucher. He collapsed onto the bed and wrapped the duvet around him to turn himself into his usual human sausage roll and shut his eyes, attempting to block out the images assaulting his mind. He'd made many mistakes in his life. But the past couple of days had hit his all-time top worst-moments list. And it was only the second week of January. Lucky he wasn't going to be feeling a thing, not anymore.

He snorted at his own stupidity and tried to wriggle under the pillow when his house phone's shrill carried down the corridor. His carefree voice that didn't know the torment of time to come rang out its usual cheery message, and Ollie awaited the beep.

Silence. Click off. Long bleep. Thank fuck.

Ollie closed his eyes once more and started to count down from one hundred—a surefire way to get ridiculously bored and eventually switch off. He'd got to eighty-seven when the flat's buzzer interrupted his descent. He held his breath. Whatever parcel was being delivered to another recipient in the block could be answered by someone else. But the buzzing continued on a relentless loop. Ollie exhaled heavily, dragging himself out from the bed. He jumped along the corridor, still wrapped in his duvet, and hit the Answer button.

"What?"

"Ollie?"

That voice was unmistakable and more than a little unexpected. Ollie's voice caught in his throat and he shook his head, believing he must have dozed off some several numbers back. Until the second uttering of his name rung out with renewed urgency.

"Jacob?" Ollie finally questioned into the speaker.

"Yeah," came the reply. "I—"

"How the hell do you know where I live?" Ollie shrilled, realizing he was now most definitely awake.

"I'm a hacker, Ollie," Jacob replied, deadpan.

Ollie narrowed his eyes and muttered under his breath. Jacob's spelling of *Budgie* had obviously been the correct one.

"You hacked into my bank account?" Ollie's voice was now so ridiculously high-pitched he was sure downstairs' breaking-their-tenancy-agreement dog would think Ollie was calling to him.

"No. That's overstepping the mark. Although it might have been easier."

"Then wh—"

"You might want to set your Facebook to private," Jacob said. "Nice picture, by the way."

Ollie shook his head fiercely. "My address isn't on that, Jacob."

"I know, but when you didn't answer your mobile number—that's on full view for anyone, FYI—I got your dad's name and hacked the care home," Jacob replied. "I've called all the numbers on their list. No answer, except for the one I think may have been your mum, but I hung up. So this was my only option. Can I come up?"

Ollie hung his head and pinched the bridge of his nose. He had no idea what to say. He wasn't exactly in the best condition, body and mind, for guests. Especially Jacob. He'd hoped he wouldn't have to face the man to be despised so soon, or have to lose everything, including his self-respect, in one fell swoop. The entrance buzzer rung out again—Jacob obviously believing Ollie to have either fainted or legged it. Ollie lifted a trembling finger and hit the button to unlock the main door.

"I take it you know which flat?" Ollie called into the speaker.

The slamming of the downstairs entrance door shook the entire building in an affirmative answer to his rhetorical question. He cursed under his breath and ran back into his bedroom, throwing off the duvet and scrabbling for something to put on his naked body. Hopping into a pair of boxers, he heard a light tap on his flat door and gave up on finding anything else. He jogged out to the hallway and unlocked the multiple catches and chain to yank it open.

Jacob's penetrating blue eyes caught him first. They widened in surprise and scanned his entire frame.

"What?" Ollie grumbled. "It's technically my bedtime."

"Sorry." Jacob shook his head, his hair falling in tufts around his face. He swiped it back, and Ollie noted the effort it took him to keep his eyes fixed on Ollie's face. "It's just..."

Jacob gave up on saying anything further, and evidently abandoned trying to keep his eyes northward. He stepped in the door, slid a freezing-cold hand onto Ollie's bare hip and kissed him. He dug his fingertips into Ollie's skin, deepening the frenzied kiss. Ollie was squeezed against Jacob's fully winter-wrapped warm body as he stumbled into the flat and the door clicked shut behind him.

Ollie kissed back for a brief moment, reveling in the sweet taste of Jacob's mouth and the firm grip the man had on him. Jacob roamed both hands around to his arse, but before Ollie could allow himself to be picked up again, he wriggled free and stepped back, slapping a hand to Jacob's chest.

"Calm your shit," Ollie demanded.

Jacob stepped back. "Sorry," he mumbled. "It's just, you, I don't know, I can't—"

Ollie couldn't help but smile. Whether or not the guy was a player, he was bloody good at making Ollie feel number one when in his presence. He just had to remember there could well be a string of number ones.

"Go sit your arse in there." Ollie waved toward the lounge area. "I'll get some clothes on."

Jacob trundled off toward the living room, not before giving Ollie a not so subtle once-over. Ollie shook his head and shot back into his bedroom. He rooted around in his drawers and settled for a loose pair of joggers and a T-shirt. He didn't mean to go for the tightest one he owned…it just happened to be the one on top of his pile. He padded barefoot out to the living room and continued on to the adjacent kitchenette.

"Coffee?"

Jacob sat hunched over on his fabric sofa. Ollie only had the one sofa—a second-hand two-seater at that. But at least his was infinitely more comfortable to lounge on. He'd not had sex on it before and cocked his head in thought as Jacob nodded, then shook it off and focused on making the coffee. Mugs in hand, he inched around the small living space and handed one to Jacob. He sat beside him and blew into the hot liquid. Jacob twisted in his seat and placed his mug on the coffee table.

"What happened with the doctor?"

Ollie shrugged and took a large gulp of coffee. Having caffeine this late in the day wasn't going to help him get his much-needed sleep before his next shift. Now running on empty, he counted the hours until his four days off where he could get his body clock back on track.

"Are you in trouble?"

"No more than usual," Ollie replied, doing his best to not let anything that would give him away seep through his features.

Jacob placed a hand on Ollie's knee and slid it up to his thigh. The heat from Jacob's hands through the thick cotton of Ollie's jogging bottoms felt as though his skin was on fire. Perhaps it still was due to the scalding-hot shower.

"Ollie." Jacob's penetrating blue eyes were filled with deep remorse. "I'm sorry if my actions have caused you hassle. I'm sorry for putting your job at risk. I'm sorry for everything Becky said to you."

Ollie exhaled a weary breath. He placed his mug down on the floor beside him and slipped a hand onto Jacob's.

"It's not your fault," Ollie said. "I'm a big boy. No one makes me do the things I do." Ollie paused, knowing that wasn't strictly true. The past few hours were evidence of that.

"Becky won't be saying anything about it. I can assure you. I've convinced her it wasn't you."

Ollie glanced away and bit his thumbnail, undecided on how he felt about that. Relieved that the mother wouldn't be filing a complaint about her daughter's nurse but wounded that she could so easily accept Jacob had been sleeping with another random man. And that was exactly what he was. A random man.

"I guess I'm the one who's sorry, then."

Jacob frowned, and Ollie let out a long sigh, wiping the clammy sweat over his forehead. He really didn't want to elaborate any further. Even admitting his failure to himself was hard enough. But as Jacob sat there waiting for him to explain, Ollie knew he had to give something. "I can't help you."

The look in Jacob's deep blue eyes made Ollie regret what he had to say. He could do it for his mother and he could do it for himself. But something made him unable to go through with it for the man in front of him. And he couldn't help wonder why that was.

"I couldn't get Elliot to write the letter for Daisy. And I'm pretty sure, after today, I may be under a disciplinary, anyway. Regardless of you sacrificing your custody position for Daisy."

Jacob sucked in a breath, emotions playing out across his face—him trying to fit all the pieces together. Jacob couldn't know what all that really meant, and so Ollie needed to give him something more.

"Elliot likes favors in return," Ollie said. "Normally, I've obliged. Today, however, I struggled to go through with it. I doubt my departure from his house will go unpunished. So, I really am deeply sorry, Jacob, but I can't help you keep Daisy here."

Ollie swallowed, suddenly realizing what that could all mean. Jacob losing Daisy to Ireland would leave him home and heartbroken, and Ollie would be there to pick up the pieces. No longer having to play second fiddle to Jacob's daughter, Ollie could be his number one. The blood drained from Ollie's face. *That wasn't the reason I was finally able to say no to Elliot, was it?*

"Is that why you think I'm here?" Jacob asked, his voice low and quiet. "Because I want you to get me the damn letter?"

The hurt in his eyes fired on all cylinders. Ollie shrugged. He didn't really know what to think anymore. His mind was mush.

"Ollie. I want you. I came here for you. And you know what? I'm so glad you didn't go through with anything that doctor asked. Jesus Christ, Ollie! Is that what's been happening?"

"Jacob—"

"You are worth more than that. And you were right. You do deserve to be treated as number one. I only wish I could do that for you." Jacob shifted to lock his gaze onto Ollie. "I know Becky made you think otherwise about this. I don't blame her. Everything I did to her was unforgivable. I don't expect her to get over it. I can only do what I can now to prove I'm a decent father. A decent man. I haven't been with anyone else in a really long time, Ollie. So if you want assurances on that front,

I can give you it. I know this is fast, I know this is unexpected, but I feel something here. The question is, do you?"

Chapter Twelve

Surgically Removed

"No."

He meant it. It was only one syllable to answer Jacob's question, yet it held a multitude of meaning. Emotions surged through Ollie. Stuff he'd buried long deep. How he felt about being pushed aside time and time again. How he felt about stamping on his own feelings in order to give his family what they needed. How he felt about Elliot. But most of all, how he was feeling about the man moving steadily away from him.

Ollie grabbed Jacob's hand, squeezing his fingers together in a tight grip. Jacob gazed down with those consuming, almost metallic blue eyes of his, and Ollie drew in his own breath.

"I don't feel something," Ollie muttered, his voice hoarse with the admission.

He couldn't believe he was saying anything at all. He wanted to leave it at no. It wasn't a lie. But the look on Jacob's face made Ollie continue. He had no idea if what Jacob had stated was even real. Ollie had fallen into bed with many men in his past, wanting to drown out the heartbreak from his life, from his work. Elliot had arrived at the right time—Ollie's sister had been in remission, yet his father had taken a turn for the worse. Sleeping with a man so emotionally inept had enabled Ollie to switch off, mind and soul, and allow his body to take over. Jacob had all but admitted he had done the same, in different ways perhaps. The real fear that Ollie was a distraction for Jacob still consumed him. *I've always been a distraction. For my parents, when Tilly was sick. For the children I care for daily. For Elliot. I'm really good at being a welcome recreational relief for others.*

He might have wanted to leave it at no, but his mouth continued on relentlessly.

"I feel so fucking much I'm frightened."

The silence dragged on, but Ollie didn't look up. He couldn't. He'd spectacularly ruined his New Year's pledge by letting out his vulnerable side. *And to a stranger, no less.* His heart pounded in a desperate attempt to prove it was still there. That he was alive, and no matter what happened from here on in, his heart would always remind him of such things. It wasn't until Jacob sank to his knees, gripping Ollie's hand and curling a finger under his chin that the tug made Ollie lift up to face him. Those blue eyes delved right into his soul and scooped out his resolve.

"Me too," Jacob admitted in a whisper.

Ollie wanted to believe him. He did. In a way. Just because there was so much doubt, it didn't mean what was felt now was going to last. *Nothing lasts. There's always an end in sight. Whether it's an end paved with sunlight and laughter or an end engulfed by darkness and sorrow. There's always a final goodbye.*

"I want to promise you things." Jacob's voice cracked. "I want to take your fear away. I want to take you to bed and hold you." He leaned forward and kissed Ollie's lips. "But I'm scared that I'll break your heart in the end. Whether I mean to or not. I don't know how to do this either."

Ollie needed to push this man away. Nothing good could come of a fling that had begun in such dire circumstances, regardless of what feelings were being bandied around with no care or attention. Ollie was already halfway to losing his job, which would mean losing his father's care home. And Jacob was halfway to losing his daughter. Everything about the situation screamed that it couldn't work. Trust didn't come easily to Ollie as it was. He'd learned not to trust anything. He was a witness on a daily basis to so much pain and sorrow that happened to people who didn't deserve it. How could he trust fate or feelings when they would always be crushed?

He'd never trusted Elliot. It made it easier to keep doing what he did. He'd used the man as much as Elliot had used him. A mutual benefit. But, after the declaration earlier... *Is it me who has the problem?* He had been the one to take all Elliot offered and yet keep the distance he needed. Ollie inhaled, his chest rising with the realization, right then, that he wasn't exactly the expert in normal functioning relationships either.

"I'm a bit messed up," Ollie finally admitted.

Jacob snorted. "Aren't we all?"

Ollie shut his eyes. It made it easier to utter the next words he needed to. Without having to look at Jacob's expression full of anxiety that would no doubt sear through to his heart, he could be honest.

"I think, though," Ollie muttered, "you should go."

The silence lingered once again. Eventually, feeling Jacob move away, Ollie opened his eyes. Jacob stood and nodded.

"You're right. We need to park this and revisit when Daisy's out of hospital and once you've sorted things with the doctor."

Ollie bit his bottom lip and looked away, nodding. It hadn't really been the reaction he had expected. With the way things had been with Jacob before, he had expected the man to fight to stay. To reenact their previous, and undeniable, passion. That he'd so easily stood and accepted Ollie's request made Ollie's chest tighten. He knew it was stupid. What he had said, he meant. It was just that his heart had obviously wanted a different sequence of events.

"I'll see you later, then," Jacob mumbled and zipped up the jacket he hadn't bothered taking off. "At the hospital."

Ollie nodded. Again. He stayed where he was, listening out for the front door handle twisting. As it opened, Ollie shot up. He hurtled down the corridor and grabbed Jacob's arm to yank him back, pull him closer and kiss him. Messily.

He couldn't deny the overriding heat that surged through him. He'd never felt such longing before, especially when Jacob returned the kiss with equal fervor. Slamming Ollie against the adjacent wall, Jacob dived in to taste him and slid his hands up the tight-fitting material of Ollie's top, ruffling it up to grapple at the skin beneath. Ollie was sure neither of them was even breathing at this point. Jacob crushed his groin against Ollie's, letting him feel the increased hardness concealed within. Ollie groaned. He shouldn't do this. He couldn't do this. Not again. So used to making the same mistake again and again, Ollie began to regain some composure.

He rammed his palms into Jacob's chest and urged him away. Jacob staggered back, and no more words were needed. A small smile formed on Ollie's lips, and he wiped away the saliva slathering them. Their eyes did the talking for a moment, until Ollie realized he did need to speak. To explain, perhaps. The mixed messages he was giving this man weren't going unnoticed. By either of them, he presumed.

"I'm sorry." Ollie pushed away from having been pinned up against the wall. Again. "I do want you. I do. But let's go slow."

It was Jacob's turn to nod. He slid his hand onto Ollie's cheek, rubbing a thumb along the stubble. Leaning farther in, Jacob kissed his forehead, and Ollie's eyes fluttered to a close at the sweet, intimate gesture. Ollie smiled, as was natural, and Jacob returned it awkwardly before exiting. Ollie banged his temple against the hard wood of the door, attempting to knock his sense back in.

He got back into the living area in time to see the leftover coffee vibrate with the slamming of the heavy entrance doors below. Ollie rushed over to his balcony window. Sliding it carefully apart, he peered down at the waves of dark hair below battling with the heavy gust of wind. Ollie sucked in a breath. He wanted to call out, tell the man to come back, forget the right thing to do and let their hearts rule. The way they had done before. Until Jacob pulled out his mobile phone, scrolled a few times and lifted it to his ear. Ollie told his heart to stop hammering so he could listen.

"You there?"

They were the only words Ollie could hear as Jacob nodded and trotted across the road, narrowly missing a passing car, and heading toward the Tube station. Ollie shut his window, along with his eyes. He wished his heart would shut the fuck up too.

Because he really didn't want to feel it.

* * * *

"I'm not sure about the lemon one, but the mint is almost like the menthols."

Ollie nodded idly—his neck was starting to get repetitive strain injury from it. He stopped on approaching the entrance to the hospital, having not had any sleep whatsoever that day. He'd decided to meet Taya for a chat in the hope that she would take his mind off things and they had walked through the freezing rain to work, fitting snugly under one umbrella. It had mainly been Taya doing all the talking, though. But that wasn't particularly unusual.

She blew out a different set of smoke, or steam, or whatever the hell it was from her pink vaper, grimaced and waggled her tongue.

"Makes your tongue go funny," she said with a pout.

"Why don't you just go the whole hog?" Ollie suggested. "Cut it all. The gum, the patches and the vapes?"

"Because I need something, Ollie darling. Not all of us can shut off our needs so easily."

She prodded him in the chest and sucked up another lungful with the bubbles gurgling through the fluorescent plastic tube, then wafted the sweeter-smelling exhalation into the rain.

"So, anyway." She tucked the contraption into her oversized bag held on her shoulder and snapped shut their shared umbrella, shaking out the droplets to join the puddles on the pavement. "Are we expecting Doctor Dick to make a scene here today?"

Ollie glanced through the automatic sliding doors. The hospital had always been his mecca. The welcoming glass frontage and brightly decorated reception area, the smiles on arrival, and the sounds of children playing to drown out their fear—it had all contributed to him loving and feeling a proud part of the iconic London landmark. Now, though, his stripped-raw nerves made it difficult to set foot inside. He hadn't told Taya everything, although she was figuring stuff out all by herself. She did that. *Bitch.*

"I don't know. I'm hoping he can't. I mean, we're both at fault here, right?"

"It's not against the rules to date a doctor." Taya tapped her pink Crocs on the pavement, shoving the umbrella into her bag. She glanced back up to catch Ollie's eye. "But a patient? Well, that's different."

"He's not a patient," Ollie grumbled. "Obviously."

"Okay." Taya rooted around in her bag for a pack of nicotine gum. She popped one out of the foil pack and shoved it into her mouth. "A patient's father is also on the don't-touch list."

Ollie hung his head and scratched the nape of his neck.

"Isn't it lucky?" Taya continued, almost a little too chipper, and slapped Ollie on the arm to shove him nearer to the automatic doors. "That you don't have any feelings?"

"No."

The reception area seemed different, somehow. Quieter than usual. Only a few straggler mums with children in buggies or wheelchairs queued at the dispensing chemist to the left, and one lone child sat on the rock pool projection clapping his hands to catch the animated fish. The purple-T-shirt-wearing volunteer once again welcomed them in with her practiced smile.

"Like you, my resolution just merged into a different vice."

"Oh, yeah?" Taya slammed her palm on the lift's Call button. "What's that?"

"Instead of not feeling a thing, I decided to just feel everything."

Taya snorted. "TMI, hun."

Ollie pushed the back of her head, and she staggered into the lift with a chuckle. As Ollie joined her, all he could think about was the time he had spent in just such a space with Jacob. He shut his eyes to block out the memory of being pinned to a wall.

The doors slid open and he and Taya hopped out. Taya bounded off to get changed in the female staff room, and Ollie trudged on toward the men's, his heartbeat on overdrive. He had a sudden urge to hook it up to one of the obs machines just to hear the incessant shrill it would no doubt give off. Taking a few deep breaths in the hope of calming himself, he pulled down his scrubs top and stuck his smile back on his face. This smile was an all-new category. It came under a new column—the forgotten-how-to-smile smile.

Slamming open the doors to the cardiology ward, he desperately tried to keep his facial greeting fixed on his lips for the day nurses who would all welcome his arrival. Not because of him, exactly, but more because it meant they could bugger off home. At the nurses' station Patty greeted him with a nod and handed over a mound of blue card files. Ollie skimmed through them, checking the names on the front to see if there were any changes or new ones added. A loud thump of cotton sheets being discarded outside the door to Room One made Ollie jump. He adjusted his glasses on his nose and squinted to look through the darkness between the closed blinds. Whipping around, he flicked through the files once more and swallowed. "What happened to Daisy Monroe?"

Patty slipped her arms through her rain mac and zipped the knee-length coat right up to the collar. "Discharged. One less patient tonight. You'll be pleased."

Ollie swallowed fiercely. He spun on his heel, his soft pumps squeaking on the freshly washed floor. "Patty?" he called, before she had a chance to escape. "Were both sets of parents informed?"

Patty nodded and pushed open the swinging doors. "Yes, dear," she replied. "Mother was here, and I called the father. Had to leave a message as he didn't answer. Her file has gone to outpatients."

Ollie nodded gratefully, and the searing pain made its way down his neck and across his tense shoulders. He smiled, the unnerving one, and slammed the files down onto the counter.

So that was that.

Chapter Thirteen

Congenital Deficiency

"Was it you?"

Dr. Rawlings peered over the card file he was flicking through at the nurses' station and his glasses edged down his nose as his dark eyes met Ollie's.

"Was what 'me,' Nurse Warne?" He didn't mask his annoyance and his voice was loud enough to be heard by all the other staff dotting around on their nightly duties.

Ollie's blood ran cold. He shivered. *Is this where I commit career suicide?* Strangely, he didn't care. Glancing over his shoulder, he checked the coast was clear before leaning forward over the desk and gritting his chattering teeth.

"You know what. Daisy Monroe. Discharged? She was sick the other day. Forty-eight-hour incubation period?"

Dr. Rawlings stood, not moving a muscle except the ones that allowed his gaze to scan the ward. He slapped down the file he'd been perusing and unhooked his glasses from his ears, tucking them into his top shirt pocket. He cleared his throat. Calm and collected. The same exterior Ollie had come to despise.

It was nearing ten p.m. on the night shift, and Daisy's fate had had Ollie stewing for the first few hours on duty. He didn't have his phone on him and hadn't had the time to go back to the lockers to check for any messages from Jacob. No one who had worked the day shift was left on the ward, and it wasn't as though he could ask any questions about his discharged patient without raising eyebrows. Normally, a patient went, a new one arrived, and work continued on relentlessly. This time, however, Ollie was finding it hard to move on. He cursed his crippling nurse ethics that it wasn't so much the girl he was concerned about.

So, as soon as Elliot had made his appearance into cardiology recovery for his nightly rounds, Ollie hadn't been able to keep his mouth shut.

The doctor's voice was gut-wrenching loud. "Are you insinuating, Nurse, that I have not upheld my professional duty of care to my patient?"

Ollie didn't reply. But nor did he break his penetrating glare of accusation, because that was exactly what he'd been thinking. There were only two consultants in the entire hospital who could sign Daisy off to outpatients, and one was standing in front of him. And this one had a vendetta. A reason to perform such a shameful act of unprofessional misconduct.

Ollie stepped back, folded his arms, and entered into a stare-off he was none too sure he would win.

Dr. Rawlings laughed. Belly laughed. Guffawed might have been a more accurate word to describe the sound coming from the doctor's haughty mouth. Ollie lost a bit of his resolve. And the stare-off. A few of the other nurses had stopped whatever that kept them occupied on a closed-off quiet ward and were sneaking peeks his way. Taya stood from crouching by the supply cupboard and mouthed at him. Ollie couldn't make out what she was saying. But he could guess.

"I forgot how romantic you were." Dr. Rawlings' laughter subsided enough for him to say that with a sinister undertone.

"Excuse me?"

"You believe I would jeopardize my professional status over a lovers' spat?"

The doctor adjusted the stethoscope around his neck, and Ollie had a sudden urge to squeeze the ends together to choke the bastard. *Lovers' spat?* It wasn't a spat. It was the end to his temporary self-destruction—at least, that was the only way he could fathom having been with the doctor so long, torturing himself over again. And, yes, he believed wholeheartedly that Elliot would use what he had in his arsenal to get back at Ollie. The man always had. He had used his father's illness and Ollie's need for a job to be close to him, not to mention the need for someone to take care of him when he had been at his most vulnerable. Elliot had used anything and everything. Using a patient wouldn't have come as a great surprise, although it did pain Ollie to really believe it.

"When you complete your five-year degree in medicine—" Dr. Rawlings once again raised his voice enough so the colleagues, patients and visiting relatives could hear every damning word. "Followed by two years of general medical training, then a further two years' acute care common stem, then the six years continued specialist training in pediatric cardiology, perhaps then, Nurse Warne..." He casually tucked his tight-fitting shirt into his chinos' waistband. "Perhaps then we can discuss your opinion on my treatment of my patients."

Ollie winced at every intonation in the doctor's voice. The ward had quietened enough for them to have heard all of that. Not that it was ever particularly noisy at this time of night. Ollie's arms unfolded to flop at his sides in defeat. He had no comeback. He could never argue his way out of it, no matter if he tried. He scanned Elliot's face for a glimmer of the man he thought he knew, daring him to let it show.

Elliot's penetrating eyes were drilling holes through to Ollie's brain, and Ollie had to look away. Get away. He shuffled out from behind the nurses' station to go find something—anything—else to do. Changing sick and shit-stained bedsheets would be a darn sight better than trying to decipher the inner mind of Dr. Rawlings.

In a way, Ollie needed to believe Elliot hadn't done this out of pure spite. Ollie's overriding concern for a man he had only met a couple of days ago was wreaking havoc with his rationality. Elliot was a good doctor—a great doctor. Ollie had told Jacob as much. He had to cling on to the hope that Elliot wouldn't have sacrificed a little girl's recovery to simply prove the point that Ollie couldn't ever win, or ever be free of how he made him feel.

Without seeing Daisy's notes, Ollie couldn't find out how her recovery had been going through the day shifts. Nor would he be able to find out where she had been discharged to, or find out any parental consent or forwarding address. Now he was officially released from being Daisy Monroe's carer, Ollie had no authority there. Dr. Rawlings was the authority. As he always was.

"Nurse?"

Ollie turned. Elliot slammed his hand onto the desk, then ran it down his tie.

"I suggest, should you have any further complaints about my work, you bring it up with HR." He dipped his chin. "As shall I."

Something snapped. Ollie's patience, maybe. And not the patients he headed toward. His mouth spat out the words that had been on his mind for quite some time.

"You are a narcissistic piece of shit."

The gasps around the ward were evidence that Ollie hadn't said that as under his breath as perhaps he'd meant to. Or not meant to. He wasn't sure. He was so wound up he had an urge to let everyone know that he wasn't a lovesick nurse like all the others who ogled the hospital's most eligible bachelor on a daily, and nightly, basis.

The sudden twitch in Elliot's jaw caught Ollie off guard. He still believed the doctor had used him, but for the life of him, he couldn't understand why. What had Ollie provided for so long that any other vulnerable nurse couldn't have? Everything that had happened between the two of them wasn't all Elliot's fault. Ollie knew it deep down. He could have ended things. If anything, it was Ollie who had been in the driving seat for a while. The doctor risked more than Ollie did in having maintained their 'relationship' the way they had. There was only one person to blame. As always, it was Ollie's blatant inability to accept his goddamn feelings.

"Ollie."

Taya came to his aid, gripping the top of his arm. Ollie shook his head, brushing her off, and stomped toward the supply cupboard. Anger had never been an emotion Ollie accepted well. There was never any point getting angry at things he couldn't control. Perhaps that was why he felt it so badly right then. This was something he could have prevented. It was all his fucking fault, for believing he could shut off. Not just with Elliot, but with Jacob.

"Taya." The doctor's voice poleaxed him like a stab in the back. "I believe Nurse Warne may need a break."

That did it. Ollie did an immediate one-eighty and marched back to the nurses' station, making Taya stumble as he brushed past her. Slapping his palms onto the doctor's hard chest, Ollie pushed him with a force he didn't know he possessed.

"You're damn right I need a break!" Ollie yelled. "From you. Maybe everyone here should know how you use people for your gain." He waved a hand at all the other nurses who had shunted forward to watch the commotion, along with a few of the parents who were still up. "How you manipulate young nurses into your bed then control every aspect of their lives so they can't escape."

"Oliver." The doctor's voice as low as his temperament. "I manipulate no one. I offer. If you take, you take. That's not my doing." He cocked his head. "I offered you love. You took my offer, and you screwed on it. I'm unsure why you would think you are the abused party here."

Ollie laughed, and he wasn't sure what was so damn funny. Elliot raised his eyebrows, staring at Ollie in a way he had only ever seen in the bedroom.

"Love?" Ollie snorted with disdain. "You love me?" Ollie wanted to hear it. He wanted the whole goddamn hospital to hear it.

"Yes."

Ollie stumbled back. *Wow. Didn't expect that.*

"I told you I did."

Ollie shook with an emotion he couldn't place.

"Oliver—"

"Ollie!"

"Ollie." Elliot stroked a thumb across Ollie's cheek.

Ollie's skin didn't know whether to crawl, shudder or lean into the familiar soft touch for a comfort he continually craved. He backed away in case he made the wrong choice, and Elliot's hand dropped to his side.

"I am willing to put this behind us." The statement was delivered in Dr. Rawlings' usual professional tone. "We can work together. We are both professionals. If you no longer want my company outside of this hospital, I am adult enough to accept that." Stepping forward, he pointed a finger in Ollie's face, mere inches from his nose. "But if you accuse me of anything untoward to do with my patient care, I will report this, and we will have to go through the whole ugly process. Together." Elliot narrowed his eyes. "Are you willing to put on the official record as to why you might think I would have discharged a Miss Daisy Monroe ahead of schedule?"

With absolutely nothing further to add, Ollie thought an early break was a fucking fantastic idea.

* * * *

"Come on, Ollie, you're a nurse."

"I'm not sure what that has to do with this utterly fucked-up situation of mine."

"Hmm."

Taya made a face at the clump of soggy canteen food being spooned into a plastic take-out container. The server handed it over, and they slid along the breakfast offerings that were shriveling under the fluorescent light in the St. Cross canteen until they reached the payment till at the end. Ollie held up his bowl of cereal that he wasn't sure he could even stomach, but Taya had insisted they try to at least consume some breakfast. She had offered to pay, so Ollie had gone along against his better judgment. He had wanted to get the hell out of the hospital at the end of shift, but he owed Taya an explanation for everything that had gone on.

"Think of it like all the times you ripped off the bandages, or plucked stitches out from your patients." Taya slalomed through the plastic tables filling up with various hospital staff and exhausted family members stocking up on calories for the next day by their child's bed, and found a vacant table at the back by the pop-up charity auction.

Ollie slipped into the bright orange sponge seat and smiled over at the charity worker. Teenage Cancer Trust this week, and Ollie had already put most of his wages into the collection tins around the hospital—possibly why he was now flat broke—but he dug deep into his coat pocket and pulled out some more coins, clanging them on the table to add to the tin later.

The whole night shift had carried on relentlessly. Ollie had successfully managed to avoid Dr. Rawlings for most of the twelve hours from hell. He'd successfully avoided talking to any of the other nurses, who had all given him a multitude of different looks throughout the shift, not to mention categories of smiles. He'd also managed to successfully avoid hearing from Jacob.

Without his number, Ollie was scuppered. He had checked his phone so many times during his shift the blasted thing had run out of battery and his charger was at home. He'd come to the conclusion that if Jacob wanted to contact him, he could have. He knew Ollie's number. He knew where Ollie worked. Hell, he now even knew where he lived. Ollie couldn't help but think twelve hours had been enough time for Jacob to have packed and caught a flight to Ireland. Maybe the man even had another Ollie over the water. Becky had insinuated as much.

Ollie clung to the hope that Becky wouldn't be so stupid as to take her just-out-of-heart-surgery daughter on a flight so soon. Or that Jacob would have left without so much as a goodbye. Neither of which he was completely convinced of. He wasn't sure of anything anymore.

"Are you talking about my public separation from Dr. Rawlings or my private separation from Jacob?" Ollie had finally given Taya all the information for her to digest along with her mound of scrambled eggs.

"Both," Taya replied, scraping her plastic fork against the sides of the polystyrene container in order to get every minuscule speck of food. "It's done now." She shoveled the last of the breakfast.

Ollie dabbed his lip in indication, and Taya wiped her mouth with a napkin.

"You said you wanted to end it." She shrugged. "Now it's ended. You've done the hard part. It's gonna sting like buggery for a while, but now the wound can heal without the preventative pressure wrap."

Ollie glanced down, twisting his cereal bowl around in his hands. At least they were sitting inside this time for their usual morning catch-up—Taya mainly chugging on vapors and keeping up her New Year's resolution meant they didn't have to freeze their arses off outside the corner café. Which would also save him a fair bit of money. St. Cross canteen food was heavily subsidized. More for him to give to the charity tins. "You saying that I need to heal first?"

"That's usually how it works." Taya fished her phone out of her pocket. She swiped through her endless notifications, chuckling at a few before squinting over the screen to Ollie. "Don't we tell our patients all the time to get back on the horse, football pitch, dance floor, whatever, only once they've fully recovered?"

"I'm not sure this is the same thing."

Taya reached over and rubbed her fingers down Ollie's knuckles, trying to catch Ollie's gaze. "It's all matters of the heart. Apparently, our specialism."

Ollie sighed. He knew she was right. He'd done the right thing by confronting Dr. Rawlings and finally putting an end to their years of toxicity. Elliot wasn't going to be chasing Ollie back now, that was for sure. Even if Elliot tried, Ollie was fairly certain he was now strong enough not to cave. There wasn't anything more Elliot could bribe him with, or offer him, if he wanted to use the doctor's words. He'd spent his twelve-hour shift of avoidance tactics mulling over what Elliot had insinuated. That Ollie had taken everything that had been 'offered'.

Maybe the man was in love with him. But it was some twisted kind of love that Elliot needed to make him feel superior. A doctor trait? Needing to feel like a god even outside the hospital where he saved countless lives? Ollie had all but succumbed to doing that for him. Fuck, the more he thought about it, the more he feared he'd been acting out some daddy complex. He shuddered at the revelation.

But then there was Jacob. Ripping that bandage off was going to cause a deeper sting, a lingering one he wasn't sure would heal quickly.

"Give yourself time, Ollie." Taya broke into his silence. "He was one man who, yeah, came around at the right time. But there'll be others, and you'll be ready for them next time."

Ollie nodded. She was right. She was absolutely right. He picked up the plastic spoon and chomped through the granola cereal to settle his churning stomach.

"He was hot, though," Taya mused with a sly grin.

Ollie snorted. Which probably wasn't the best thing to do, as it made milk fly out from his nostrils. Taya laughed and handed over her napkin. Ollie wiped his nose and sighed.

"Yeah," he finally agreed. "So fucking hot. Could give your pink hot chocolate shit a run for its M&Ms."

Taya pouted and folded her arms. "I'd just convinced myself I didn't need that this morning. So, anyway, are we keeping to these New Year's resolutions? Y'know, momentary lapses, but now we'll try it for sure?"

Ollie wriggled his hand out of his jacket sleeve and offered it over the table to Taya. She smiled and slipped her hand into his, giving it the one solid shake.

"Not feeling anything," Ollie confirmed. "I'm done. Exchanging the Band-Aids for a brick wall."

Taya laughed, albeit unconvinced. As her laughter subsided, a shadow loomed over the table.

"Ollie?"

Chapter Fourteen

Misdiagnosis

"Hey, Kwesi, how's it going?"

Ollie couldn't mask his disappointment. Of course the shadow wouldn't belong to Jacob. Kwesi was at least four inches shorter, less broad in the shoulders, and his skin was markedly darker. Jacob was long gone, and Ollie was probably a mere distant memory already. Like all the others were. Ollie put on his welcoming smile to greet Kwesi, the hospital's cardiology secretary.

"Good, thanks, Ollie." Kwesi returned the smile, but, as an office worker, his wasn't so bright, and apprehension glimmered behind it, especially when he scrubbed a hand through his closely cropped black hair.

"You getting breakfast before work?" Ollie asked. "Might want to get in the queue before Taya goes up for her second lot."

Taya stuck out her tongue.

"Ah, no."

Kwesi rummaged through the satchel slung over his shoulder. He produced a white envelope, the hospital stamp mark evident on the top corner and Ollie's name scrawled on the front. His full name. *Mr. Oliver Warne.*

"Sorry, Ollie. I was told I had to give you this before you went off for your four-day break between shifts."

Ollie nodded. He slipped the envelope from Kwesi's hand. He bit his lip on recognizing the messy handwriting. Why was it doctors had to be so illegible? It was just another arrogant trait. Like they didn't need anyone to have to read their words. No one would understand them other than doctors, anyway. Dr. Rawlings could still show his superiority and dominance over Ollie merely in writing his name on a damn envelope. An official envelope. For an official letter.

Ollie folded it in half and tucked it into his puffer jacket. "Thanks."

Kwesi nodded, looking as though he'd rather not have been that messenger service. So, Ollie, good old people-pleasing Ollie, had to do something to prove he didn't blame the guy.

"How's that man of yours?"

Kwesi's smile grew wider. It almost rivaled Ollie's. Actually, it did—it was genuine.

"Yeah, pretty good, thanks. Should be back from the charity drive soon."

"That's great. Looking forward to finally meeting him."

Kwesi nodded, his grin not fading, then made his way out of the canteen. Ollie caught Taya's arched eyebrow.

"What, you didn't know he was gay?"

"I didn't know the whole damn hospital was. No wonder I can't get a date around here."

"You fancied Kwesi?"

Taya shrugged. "He may have been on my list. Which I will now delete." She pointed. "What's the letter?"

Ollie sighed. "I'm pretty certain that it is my written warning of gross misconduct."

"Fuck. Would he really have done that?"

Ollie nodded. "Yeah. I believe he really would."

"You can fight it. Tell them about Elliot and you."

"No point. It's fine. Maybe I can get a job at my dad's nursing home or something. Kill two birds with one stone."

Taya gave him one of those looks. The one she gave to soothe parents in the ward. The one that Ollie gave his patients, too. The one that signified she knew this was awful bad news, but that she had to maintain a brave face in order to not have to deal with the aftermath of a breakdown. It was amazing how much could be communicated in just one look. Not just categories of smiles within nursing, but also an array of expressions all really doing one thing—providing sympathy.

"Bus." Taya looked down at her wristwatch and scraped back her chair.

Ollie gathered up the rubbish from the table, along with the loose change, and jogged over to the bin to dump the containers. He dropped the coins into the charity pot. Taya linked her arm with his and practically dragged him out of the canteen and through the now bustling corridors of the hospital.

With day shift starting, appointment queues filled every wing and orderlies rushed beds and wheelchairs to different parts of the hospital. St. Cross continued on regardless, and Ollie's stomach plummeted—he might not be part of it much longer.

Outside, Ollie shivered. The snowfall had made way for rain, and Taya squealed as they pelted across the road toward the bus stop where for once the red Routemaster was pulling in on time. Ollie paused.

"You coming?" Taya asked.

"Think I might head to my dad's." Ollie freed Taya's arm and tucked his hands into his coat pockets, his fingers brushing the envelope within. "Might as well get the ball rolling on that one."

"Go get some sleep first, Ollie." Taya tapped her card on the reader. "Things might look different in the morning." She shrugged. "Evening, whatever."

"I don't think I could sleep right now, anyway."

He waved her off and followed her walk along the row of seats. She kissed her fingers, sticking them to the window after, and Ollie tapped them back through the glass. The bus pulled out of the stop and Ollie was left alone to walk to the nursing home. He recalled every step of these paths with Jacob. He'd done the walk many more times alone, but somehow that one time with Jacob would now make him feel forever isolated.

He was so engulfed in his own bubble, he couldn't even move out of the way of rushing commuters. His shoulder was bumped a few times, but he could not muster the ability to apologize or offer a smile. This New Year had only been a couple of weeks, and yet he'd spectacularly lost everything within the short space of time. Some of it had been needed. But never had he thought that removing Elliot from his life would be followed up by losing his job. Which, now, would lose his father his care home.

Funny, though, how none of that compared to losing a man he hadn't even known before this week. Jacob had such presence it seemed he'd been in Ollie's life forever. Perhaps he had. In Ollie's dreams. Ollie scrubbed a hand over his face. *Fucking hell, what a complete sap.* Ollie had lost any belief over the years that romance even existed. Of course, Elliot hadn't allowed for romanticism. Unless it had been part of his game.

Ollie laughed at the absurdity as he arrived at the gates of the care home. Even that spot as he rang the buzzer made his stomach flutter—the place he and Jacob had shared their first kiss. Ultimately starting the decline of Ollie Warne. Did Jacob even know what Ollie had sacrificed by allowing his advances? Would he even care if he did? Jacob's thoughts were for his daughter. Where they should be. Not with some stranger.

It had started snowing, but Ollie didn't even feel the flakes landing on his shoulders and hair. He was numb to everything around him. Well, he'd certainly fall back down to earth with a bump when he had to explain that he could no longer keep his father in the care home and needed to find an alternative, or even take him in himself. He was a nurse—he supposed he should use his compulsory training to look after his father at home. A carer's allowance certainly wasn't much, but Ollie couldn't think about his own money just then.

"Morning, Ollie."

Ollie managed to put on a smile to greet Claudine, the manager, at the front desk.

"He's just had breakfast—feel free to go through."

His father sat in his usual seat, headphones on and eyes closed. But the slight tapping of his fingers on his thighs and the brief elevation of his lips indicated that he was happy listening to one of his favorite CDs. So Ollie thought perhaps it was best to get the awkward business over with first.

"Actually, Claudine, could I speak with you first?"

"Everything okay, Ollie?" Claudine dropped her paper file to the desk and tilted her head.

Ollie scrubbed a hand along his forehead. He swallowed. Doing this was going to lose the deposit. Not to mention he'd have to pay a penalty of some description, sending his limited overdraft further into the red. There was simply no way he would ask his mother to contribute. This had to be his failing to deal with. The only way his mother would be able to afford to keep his father here would be to sell their family home. Ollie couldn't allow that.

"Can we talk?" Ollie glanced around the busy lounge filled with residents on various sofas and high-back chairs, either reading or playing various card or board games. Most, though, stared vacantly into space. "Privately?"

Claudine ushered Ollie over to the manager's office. Ollie sat with a heavy sigh while Claudine perched on the edge of her desk. She was a nice lady. Ollie liked her. She had a tough job, with all the recent funding cuts to social care, but her heart was in the right place. That didn't mean, however, she was going to take losing a hefty lot of income any easier.

"I'm afraid I can't keep my father here any longer." Ollie scratched at the denim on his jeans.

"Right." Claudine shuffled up on the desk to cross her legs and fold her arms. "Are you not happy with his care here?"

"No, no, nothing like that." Ollie adjusted his glasses. "His care has been first-rate. And I thank you and all your staff for taking such good care of him. I really couldn't have asked for a better place for him to be. Which is why this is really a difficult decision, but one I unfortunately have to make."

Claudine nodded. "May I ask why? And where you plan to place him next?"

"I'll take him in."

"Ollie, I know you're a nurse, but caring for someone with your father's condition, twenty-four-seven, is actually a lot harder than when it's your chosen job. For which you're paid."

"I'm aware of that."

"Caring for relatives," Claudine continued, "while admirable and sometimes the best thing for the patient, can have a huge impact on those doing the caring. It will drain you. Some days he may be perfectly fine, but others he will be extremely difficult to handle. I have to warn you that those days will be especially hard for you to witness. Without support, it can be very isolating and may have repercussions on your own health and well-being."

"I am aware of all those things. Believe me."

"Right, well, I am sorry to hear you can no longer keep him here." Claudine stood and walked to the back of her desk, wiggling the mouse on her laptop when she got there. "When will you be taking him?"

"How long is he paid up until?"

"I'll have to check the finances." Claudine sat in her leather swivel chair and spun it around to face Ollie. Her features softened. "Are you sure, Ollie? Is there something we can do to help?"

Ollie shook his head. "I have no other option. But thank you. I appreciate your concern."

Ollie felt as though Claudine wanted to say something further. Perhaps another lecture on how much of a burden his father was going to be. Ollie didn't want to hear it. This was his father. He had to take care of him. Like Gregory had Tilly for all those years. *It's what families do.* Ollie hung his head with the sudden realization. That was what Jacob had to do. Ollie sighed and nodded a grateful thanks to Claudine.

"I'll check your father's account." Claudine swung back to the computer screen. "You go visit him. I'll let you know the outcome before you leave."

His father, still listening to his CD, had his eyes closed. Ollie decided to just let him be. He busied himself around the bed, plugging his phone into his dad's charging station and reorganizing the items displayed on his cabinet. Checking each photo in the frame, he smiled. He folded the pajamas laid out on the bed and tucked in the corners of the sheets more securely. *Nurse habit.*

His chest tightened. How could he explain all this to his father? He wouldn't understand, even if he was of completely sound mind. What could he say? That Ollie had spectacularly managed to destroy not only his professional career but his father's stability by being a poor judge of character? Giving bad news wasn't something he had ever gotten used to. Giving awful news to parents who weren't his own seemed so much easier. He could remain distanced from it all. He could act as the shoulder to cry on. Whose shoulder could Ollie cry on now? Certainly not Gregory Warne's.

Ollie paced over to his father's chair and sank to his knees. Sliding a hand on top of Gregory's, Ollie breathed in.

"Pops?"

Gregory opened his eyes, shock and confusion spreading across his face. Ollie slipped the headphones off for him and placed them on the tray table next to the old-style CD player.

"How you doing, Pops?"

Gregory beamed. His smile lifted his drooping skin and brightened his blue eyes behind the dark-rimmed glasses.

"Oliver." Gregory slid his other hand on top of Ollie's, his voice cracking. "What a lovely surprise."

The blood rushed through Ollie at hearing his name uttered from his father's lips. For a brief moment, Ollie was transported back to earlier times. Back when he'd been this man's son.

"What were you listening to?"

Gregory turned his head toward the CD player. His brow furrowed. Ollie bit his lip. He needed to stop asking the man questions. Even simple ones.

"I don't remember."

"That's okay. You looked happy, so I'll bet it was one of those old dance-hall numbers, right? Where you were serenading Mum? Did she look beautiful?"

"She's always beautiful." Gregory dipped his head. "Everyone is rather jealous of me."

"I don't doubt it, Pops. But I also bet that the girls were all jealous of Mum, too."

Gregory tapped his fingers on Ollie's hand. Ollie took a deep breath and steadied himself from wobbling on his feet.

"I'm taking you home, Dad."

Gregory's eyes widened.

"I'll be taking care of you from now on."

"I'm going home?"

Ollie nodded. "Yes. We can listen to those CDs all day long. You can teach me how to dance properly."

Gregory squeezed Ollie's hand tightly. His eyes glistened beneath his thick glass lenses. "I'll teach you to dance, and you'll be snapped up by all the girls." Gregory smiled. "Young and oldies."

Ollie snorted a laugh. Biting down on his lost resolve, he decided to let that one lie there. He wasn't going to relive that conversation again. Not that it had been a bad one. More nonchalant, really. His parents had been dealing with Tilly when he'd finally admitted to them he was gay. *I guess they didn't have the brain space to process the information.* Maybe, now, in hindsight, his father had pushed that knowledge down into the depths of his memory to never recall. Was that why whenever Ollie mentioned a man in his life, Gregory automatically assumed he was talking with Tilly? It hurt. But Ollie had more pressing matters to attend to than his own feelings.

"What about your job?" Gregory asked, and concern flickered behind his watery eyes. His father was having one of his good days.

"I've decided to quit." It wasn't a complete lie. "I'm going to take care of you instead."

"What?"

Ollie whipped around at the female voice from the open doorway. He stood.

His mother's bright-blue eyes were wide with horror. His sister gave Ollie a softer look from beneath her pink-rimmed glasses that matched the clip she wore to hold back her short pixie-style blonde hair. She mouthed something to Ollie he couldn't decipher. Not over his heart hammering too loudly at his mother's stern expression.

"Ma, you don't usually visit this early."

"Tilly had a day off from school. Teacher training. Now don't change the subject, Oliver, what is going on?"

"Vera?" Gregory's voice, although confused, elevated hopefully.

Ollie's mother planted a kiss on her husband's cheek and he gripped her hand, tugging on it.

"Did the operation go well?"

Ollie hung his head and shut his eyes. His mother perched on the edge of Gregory's seat.

"Yes, dear, all went fine."

"Oh, that is good news. We should get Tilly that new My Little Pony she's always asking for. A bravery gift."

"Pops." Tilly crouched where Ollie had been. "I like the Vamps now."

Gregory ruffled his daughter's hair, making the clip slide away. She readjusted it to pin back her fringe.

"And how is that young man?" Gregory asked. "I hope he is treating you well."

Tilly peered up to meet Ollie's gaze. Ollie shrugged.

"What young man, Pops?" she asked.

"What was his name, Oliver?" Gregory tapped his knees, and Ollie could almost hear the creaking cogs of his father's mind working overtime. "Ah, yes, Jacob."

Ollie caught the looks of confusion spreading from his mother and sister. The mention of Jacob's name had Ollie's stomach fluttering. This time, however, it wasn't with excitement. Jacob's name was now ingrained in his father's messed mind, like it was on his own. *How can one man have made this much of an impact on my life in such a short space of time?* Ollie almost despised him for it. It had been years since his father had remembered anything about Ollie's life or the visitors he had brought to the care home. That had only been Taya and Elliot. Yet it was Jacob who had become so important. Even if his father did think Jacob belonged to Tilly.

"I think Jacob might be Ollie's man, Pops." Tilly smiled and winked up at Ollie.

"Well, I have told Ollie he must do the big-brother talk with him. We want our Tils treated like a princess." Gregory glanced up to Ollie. "Right, Oliver?"

"Right, Pops," Ollie mumbled.

His mother stood from her perch, hands on hips. "Now would you like to explain what is going on here? You've quit?"

"Yes," Ollie lied again. He shrugged. "Sort of. I'm going to take Dad home. I'll take care of him."

His mother's voice rose. "In a third-floor flat?"

Ollie hadn't thought that bit through. He was about to say he would be coming home to his mother's until he saw the look in her eyes. She'd like nothing more than to have her husband home. But Gregory wasn't exactly the man she had married. And while the love would always be there, his mother couldn't cope with Gregory's erratic mind, sudden outbursts and unexpected wanderings in the night. She had tried. She had tried for years. Her pained expression as she raised her eyebrows at her son communicated all that history.

"I'll get a ground-floor flat," Ollie replied.

"Like it's that easy." Vera clamped her fingers to her mouth. "Why?"

"We can't afford it, Mum." Ollie lowered his voice, doing his best to keep it light and not scare his father, who hummed while stroking Tilly's hair. "It was probably foolish of me to think we could keep him here."

"But what about the guarantor?" Vera's voice trembled. "You said the hospital was supporting this."

Ollie closed his eyes. *Moment of truth.* "I'm afraid that has now fallen through."

Vera frowned. Tilly stood and reached out to curl her hand in Ollie's. Ollie squeezed it back for the limited comfort it gave and inhaled a weary breath.

"I think perhaps there's some things I need to tell you."

* * * *

Ollie zipped up his coat and sat with a heavy sigh on the bench outside in the nursing home's front courtyard. He glanced up at the sky, which was heavy and thick with dark clouds. The bench was frozen. Icicles hung from the windows that looked into the communal lounge. But Ollie didn't care that the freezing water seeped through his trousers to coat his arse.

All he could see was his mother's face as he recounted to her everything that had happened. Not just the last few days, but the years he'd been secretly seeing the doctor. He hadn't bothered with an edited or revised version. He'd just decided to let it all out like some therapeutic counseling session. He guessed his mother was finding it difficult to come to terms with Ollie's spectacular misjudgment and failures—she hadn't said a word and had allowed Ollie to walk out so he could sob in private. Ollie had always been the stable one in their family unit. Vera had never needed to worry about him before. Well, Ollie had now added a bunch of shit for his mother to stress about, along with her husband's care and her daughter's health.

Ollie felt like crap. But it wasn't anything he didn't deserve.

"Want some company?"

His sister handed down Ollie's phone to him, wrapped her thick cardigan around her and scooted to sit beside him. Her skin was so pale her face appeared almost blue against the outside security light. Ollie wrapped an arm around her shoulders and squeezed her in. She rested her head on his chest and he kissed her temple.

"Mum'll get over it," she mumbled into his puffer jacket.

"I know."

"She's just angry."

"I know."

"Not with you. With the world, I think."

"I think, this time, it might be a little to do with me." Ollie rubbed her arm and rested his chin on the top of her head. "And the disappointment is much harder to take than the anger."

Tilly didn't say anything, so Ollie closed his eyes. It pained him to think his sister might now think differently of him. There always came a point where once idealistic views of older siblings and parents were quashed, making way for seeing them as humans. Real people who made real mistakes. Ollie had seen his parents' flaws early on when discovering they weren't superheroes hadn't been able to stop Tilly's pain.

"Well, if you ask me," Tilly finally said, breaking the silence, "this doctor sounds like a right arsehole."

Ollie laughed. "Yeah. He can be. But he's also helped Dad, and it's my fault he won't be doing that anymore."

Tilly slipped out from under his arm and looked him the eye. "That's bullshit."

"Tils, your potty mouth has gotten worse since you went back to that school."

"Don't patronize me, Ollie." She slapped his leg. "I saw and heard a lot while stuck in a hospital bed, y'know. When people think I'm not listening, they say stuff. I heard more than my fair share of curse words from Pops, from Mum." She pointed a finger. "From you."

"All right, all right. Keep your hair on."

Tilly slapped him hard on the chest with the back of her hand. Ollie recoiled and rubbed through his puffer coat. After a while, Tilly snorted with laughter. Just hearing that sound made Ollie smile.

"It sounds to me like this doctor was a bit of a user," Tilly stated, matter-of-factly. "He used your vulnerability to get what he wanted. Like on *Real Housewives* the other day."

"Tilly, please don't watch that absolute trash."

"Why not? It's got some cute blokes in it. You'd like it. If this doctor really loved you, I don't think he would have fired you. He certainly wouldn't see our dad chucked out of here, and he wouldn't put a mark on your record. So…" Tilly ruffled Ollie's hair. "Did he really love you?"

Ollie paused for a moment. Such maturity on sixteen-year-old shoulders. It was a shame his sister knew how the world worked even though, for most of her childhood and adolescence, she hadn't really been able to be a part of it. Ollie tucked his hands into his pockets, hitting the envelope still scrunched inside. He pulled it out, staring at the scrawled handwriting for a moment. Had Elliot loved him? He wasn't sure the man had been capable of it.

Sighing, Ollie flipped the envelope around to tear through the gummed-down fold. He slipped the letter from inside and sucked in a breath. He didn't want to open it. Nor to read the sordid words.

Tilly snatched it from his hand and unfolded the paper. Ollie was about to protest before he realized it was probably better to hear it from someone else.

"Who's Rebecca Daley?"

Ollie furrowed his brow. He shook his head, confused. Until it slowly dawned on him. He hadn't remembered her surname. He just knew it wasn't Monroe. He'd been made aware of that. Loud and clear.

"Becky."

"With the good hair?"

"What?"

"Nothing. Who's Becky?"

"Jacob's ex. Daisy—the child I was caring for—her mother."

"Oh." Tilly bit her lip, her gaze darting across the page. "This makes sense then."

"Christ." Ollie rubbed his thumbs into his eyes. "Has he written absolutely everything?"

Tilly met Ollie's gaze. She held it, face expressionless. Then she smiled and whipped the letter around. Ollie snatched it from her and speed-read the words. There was no mention of gross misconduct. There was no mention of any type of misconduct at all. In fact, there was no mention of Ollie's name anywhere. The letter wasn't even addressed to him. It was addressed to Ms. Rebecca Daley. And cc'd at the bottom was Mr. Jacob Monroe, with a note explaining there was no forwarding address for the father and that this was a copy of the original letter.

"It's to prevent her leaving the country."

Tilly nodded. "I can see that, dummy."

"Do you think he's given me this to pass it to Jacob?"

"Erm, ya-ha." Tilly whacked his leg. "So you better go find him. Like, now."

Ollie stood, folding the letter to tuck it back into his pocket with hands that shook. "Go!" Tilly pushed him away. "Quick. Run for the airport like some cheesy chick flick!"

Ollie laughed, nodded, and was about to do just that when he glanced through the window of the nursing home. His mother lowered his father into one of the chairs in the communal area and met his gaze through the glass.

"Shit," Ollie cursed.

"Language, Ollie."

Ollie shook his head. "What about Dad?"

"Ollie?" Claudine, arms wrapped around herself to stave off the cold, headed toward him. "Glad I caught you."

"Problem?"

"No, no problem. You asked how long he's paid up until? Well, we had a payment accepted yesterday. Full year."

"What?"

"Full fees for a year up-front. He can remain here until then. I mean, you are welcome to discharge him into your own care, but we wouldn't return the payment. It's nonrefundable, I'm afraid. But if you decide to keep him here, then we will need the name of your next guarantor once the funds have run out."

Ollie scratched the back of his neck. "I don't understand."

"Dr. Elliot Rawlings submitted the funds for one year but asked for his name to be removed from the account.

It means if you don't have the funds by this time next year, we would need another name to secure his care." Claudine shivered as the snow began to fall more heavily from the sky. "Or, by then, your income may be enough to cover it. I'm sure you'll have reached senior nurse status by then."

Ollie's mouth hung open. He was frozen to the spot, and it wasn't the snowfall that was doing it. He shook his head, trying to take in everything that had happened. Until Tilly kicked his leg.

"Go, you wally!"

Ollie snapped out of his trance. He yanked his sister up from the bench and hugged her fiercely. Then, without any further ado, Ollie dashed toward the exit gates before he could realize he had no clue where Jacob would be or how to contact him.

Chapter Fifteen

Belief in Recovery

Ollie's legs took over. He pelted out into the street and headed directly for the Tube station. He was certain he could find the restaurant he and Jacob had had breakfast in a couple of days back. But the delirious haze he'd been in when he'd been dragged from the Breakfast Club to Jacob's flat meant he wasn't sure he could retrace those steps. He had no other option but to try.

Jumping onto the first Tube that shunted into the station, Ollie grabbed the pole and took a deep breath. It gave him a moment to compose his thoughts, piece together all that had happened. Elliot had written the letter to keep Daisy in the country until her recovery was complete. The original letter had been posted to Becky's home address. That address was on the top of his copy. But there was no forwarding address for Jacob. That meant Jacob couldn't have seen it. Yet.

Jacob could have immediately headed home, thinking that Daisy was off to Ireland. Or maybe Jacob had gone directly to Becky's to try to stop her. Ollie looked at his wrist, then slapped his hand to his thigh in frustration. *Still no fucking watch.* He hazarded a guess that it'd been fourteen hours since he had started work. And pretty much twenty-odd hours since Jacob had left his flat. Ollie decided not to dwell on the fact Jacob hadn't called him. There could be a million and one reasons. But as the Tube edged closer to the station where he needed to alight, Ollie's brain went into overdrive.

Would the letter even make a difference to Jacob when it came to Ollie? Yes, it would mean Daisy could, and should, remain there for the time being. But in no way was this letter going to mean Jacob wanted a relationship with Ollie. If anything, that letter proved Ollie still had ties to the doctor.

Shit. Ollie hadn't even thought about Elliot. It had all been about Jacob. But everything Dr. Rawlings had done—the letter, his father's nursing home—had that been because he really was in love with Ollie? Or was it simply to draw a line under everything without harming both of their careers? Whatever it was, Ollie started to feel like a piece of shit. And guilty. All-consuming guilt. But wasn't that what narcissistic sociopaths did? Made their victims feel guilty while they perched on their pedestals and peered down at their mere subordinates? At least, that was what all the Pinterest snippets Taya sent him nonstop indicated.

The train stopped, its doors whooshing open, and Ollie jumped down and legged it up the steps. Heading out into daylight, Ollie pulled his phone out of his jeans pocket. He held it up to the sky, waving it around in some absurd attempt to grab the signal faster. Half bars shot up, after that part charge in the care home, but nothing popped through. Ollie ruffled his hair, growled silently under his breath, and scrolled through his contacts. Closing his eyes, he hit the Call button.

The voice that answered was tight, crackly, as though he had just been woken. Ollie bit his lip—he probably had.

"Thank you," Ollie said.

Silence on the other end, just breathing. Ollie decided he'd just leave it at that and went to put the phone away.

"Oliver?"

"Yes?"

"You called my house phone."

Ollie pulled the phone away and checked the display. He bit his lip and his stomach plummeted. Until he remembered he didn't have to care about the rules. Not anymore.

"I just called to say thank you for paying for my dad's care. That was generous."

"Not generous. It was a peace offering."

"Then peace has been accepted."

"You'll need another guarantor."

"I know. I'll find one."

There was yet more heavy breathing down the phone and a few crackles that Ollie believed was the old-style wire being stretched from the main port.

"I have your watch."

"What? I thought you said you'd chucked it out?"

"I did. But I retrieved it. I'm afraid the glass has been cracked. But it's fixable. I guess I had hoped you would wear the one I bought for you."

Ollie rubbed his temple and couldn't help the laughter. "Like I'm some possession of yours."

"No, not at all. Oliver."

"Ollie!"

"Ollie, I know you find this ridiculously hard to believe, but I do care for you. I'm just from a different generation. I wish I could be as carefree as you are."

"You can be. You don't have to hide who you are, Elliot. Not from your staff, not from your fellow consultants, and certainly not from your family."

More silence. Ollie glanced around at the bustling Shoreditch High Street and decided to head on up to find the restaurant. He was just about to say goodbye when the doctor caught him off guard and he nearly fell off the curb onto the busy road to be knocked down by a passing bus.

"Give me another chance."

"Elliot—"

"I'll try. Why don't you come to the annual consultants' charity dinner with me? As my…"

Ollie stopped, steadying himself on the path. He waited, until it became all too awkward.

"As your what?"

"Guest."

Ollie barked a laugh. "If you can't even say it when it's just me and you, then you'll never be able to say it in company. I'm done hiding, Elliot. I'm done being cast aside. I'm done with being second choice."

"You think you'll be first choice to a man whose daughter has a lifelong heart condition?"

Ollie gripped the phone so tightly he feared the glass would crack. "At least that's a more worthwhile second place. And not just to his precious reputation."

"Ollie—"

"No, Elliot. Listen, please." Ollie pinched the bridge of his nose. He was tired and emotionally drained and this conversation wasn't helping. "Thank you. Thank you for what you have done. But nothing has changed to do with my feelings toward you. It could have been great. I tried to make you happy. I couldn't. Maybe one day you'll find that person to serenade at your doctor parties, to show off to your consultants, to shout it from the hilltops that you are in love. But that person wasn't me. And if I'm honest with myself, I always knew it. And I always knew you weren't that person for me, either. It's been years, Elliot, and I've only just told my family about you." Ollie took a deep breath. "I need to put myself first for a change, and find that someone." He rubbed his loafer on the concrete pavement. "Whoever he may be."

More silence dragged on down the phone.

"You think you'll get all that from him?"

"I don't know," Ollie admitted. "Maybe not. But I have to try. Because if I don't, I'll forever wonder. Even if I were with you."

Ollie's chest tightened. The first time in his life he could put himself first. That was a massive step. He wasn't even sure it would bring him the happiness he craved. Perhaps it would bring further pain. But whatever it brought, Ollie was going to feel every damn thing.

"I wish you well, Oliver." The doctor's voice was more distant. "You've always had a mature head on your shoulders even though you pretend otherwise. Especially with that ridiculous answerphone message you have and your insane cheeriness."

Ollie snorted.

"I'll request you work under a different consultant from now on."

"Wait, Elliot."

"Yes?"

"You don't need to do that. Like you say, I can be mature. I'm sorry for what happened at the ward today. Shouting at you. I was angry. It won't happen again." Ollie chewed on his bottom lip. "Let's just let bygones be bygones and move on. It doesn't have to affect our working relationship."

"That may be, Oliver." The doctor inhaled and there was further crackling. "But I'm unsure I could see you each shift, knowing another man has had his arms around you."

Fucking hell, that was emoshi. And completely unexpected. Ollie didn't know what to say. He stood there, in the middle of the street, mouth hanging open and his heart in overdrive, letting him know he hadn't been pummeled by that damn bus.

"One day," Ollie started, "you'll have someone's arms around you who does it because they want to and not because you ask them to. Just open up a bit more."

"Goodbye, Oliver."

The click and whir drowned out Ollie's next thoughts. He tucked his phone back into his pocket and took a deep breath, inhaling the exhaust fumes and cigarette smoke wafting by from the corner office block where the employees got their five minutes of freedom. He couldn't feel guilt. He shouldn't. That was exactly what Elliot had been great at. Making him feel ten dozen emotions all at once, ranging from infatuation to hatred. He was done with that rollercoaster of a life. He was ready to feel something different. For someone different. Even if it wasn't reciprocated.

He glanced up the busy High Street, trying to remember which way to go. He trudged on and stopped by a homeless man with his dog sitting outside the cashpoint machine stuck on the wall next to the

Tesco Metro. Ollie searched his pockets, found a few coins and a scrunched-up fiver. He crouched and handed the guy the money.

"Bless you." The man ruffled his dog's ears. "Have a wonderful day."

Ollie smiled. "Thanks." He squinted up along the road. "Hey, you know where the Breakfast Club is?"

The man pointed a dirty finger up the street. "Chuck a left at the next junction. Then down the alley. Nice grub in there."

Ollie stood, then peered back down.

"That's a nasty rash." Ollie nodded at the man's hands, which were riddled with a red and flaky skin blemish. "You should get that seen to."

The man shrugged. Ollie's instinct took over and he walked straight into the shop to find what he needed, then jogged back out. He handed down the man a pot of dermatological cream.

"This won't cure it. But it'll help."

The homeless man offered a smile of yellowing and decaying teeth. He nodded a grateful thanks, and Ollie had to leave that there. Rushing faster up the hill, he weaved through the pedestrians all seeming to walk the opposite way to him and by following the man's directions, Ollie eventually found the restaurant. He peered in through the window with a ridiculous notion of hope, but sighed on not seeing anyone familiar. Scratching his neck, he continued walking past, furrowing his brow, then stopped at the next junction, did a one-eighty, and jogged on back to the restaurant door.

"Welcome," the same waiter from the previous day greeted as Ollie pushed open the door. Plucking out a paper menu from the desk at the front, the waiter then handed it over to Ollie with a smile. "Table for one?"

Ollie nodded, and the waiter gestured for him to follow to a table at the back by the window. He wished he hadn't bothered with the granola earlier. He slapped the menu down and tapped his fingers on the table, glancing out of the window to watch the pedestrians pass on by. He chewed on his bottom lip as the waiter returned, notepad in hand.

"What can I get you?"

Ollie drew in a breath. "I was in here the other day. With a friend. Jacob Monroe. He has a regular table here."

"Oh, yes, Jacob. Loves the American pancakes."

Ollie smiled. "Yeah. You don't happen to know where he lives, do you? Or have a number for him?"

The waiter arched an eyebrow.

"I know that sounds ridiculous. I'm not a stalker. I just really need to get to him."

"I'm sorry, I can't really give out that information."

Ollie hung his head and nodded.

"So, do you want the pancakes anyway?"

Ollie shook his head. "Sorry." Not only did he not have the time to indulge in the breakfast, he didn't want his card declined here yet again.

The waiter collected the menu and walked away to the kitchen. Ollie fumbled back out into the narrow alleyway. Jacob's flat was near here—he knew that. He couldn't remember having walked far on that day. Only a few minutes. He vaguely remembered what the building had looked like. The trouble was, all the buildings appeared the same around these parts.

Realizing he had to do something, Ollie began to walk forward. Slowly. Looking down every street, glancing up at any landmarks he might recall. Just at the point he was about to give up, he saw it. The block of flats. He'd have recognized that front entrance anywhere. The door of no return. He rushed across the road, took a deep breath and slapped his palm on the glass to push it open.

"Fuck!" Ollie cursed loudly as the door didn't budge. He added a childish stamp of his foot, then scanned all the buzzers allocated next to numbers. No names. "Shit." Why hadn't he paid more attention when he'd been there?

He decided to just buzz any old number, starting from the top. The first couple, no reply. Then finally a female voice blasted out from the speaker.

"Yes?"

"Hi, is Jacob in this building?"

"I'm sorry, who are you?"

"I'm looking for Jacob—do you know—"

The click indicated she'd hung up. Ollie tried the next number. This time a man.

"Hi, sorry to bother you, but would you happen to know which flat—"

Another click.

Fucking people these days! Ollie blamed the cold-calling culture. Before that, anyone would have let him in. He did in his own flat. Okay, in hindsight, he knew that was foolish. *One last try.* He buzzed the final number. The elderly lady's voice was shaky but kind. Ollie could do kind.

"Hello, ma'am, my name's Ollie. I'm a nurse. I've been called here to see a man called Jacob. Trouble is I've forgotten the flat number."

"Oh, dear. Is that young man hurt?"

"I don't know, ma'am." It wasn't a complete lie. Jacob could be hurt. Emotionally, perhaps. "If you could just buzz me in, I'll be able to find his door." That he wasn't sure of, either.

"Um, oh, I see, well—"

"Mother, I've told you about letting people in! Have you not learned from the last time?" A man's voice barked down the receiver and Ollie nearly punched the wall. "Go away. Stop harassing my mother or I'll report you."

Click. Fuck!

Ollie growled. He spun around and glanced out to the road. He fished his phone back out. There was nothing on the display other than a few notifications on his social media feed. He slumped back against the building's wall and slid to sit down on the floor, knees hunched to his chest. Flicking the phone around between his fingers, he racked his brain. His screen lit up with a notification of a Like for his profile picture. Ollie rolled his eyes and thought he should probably change that photo. Suddenly, he sparked to life.

He swiped his phone, clicking on the Facebook app. He typed Jacob Monroe into the Search button. Several options came up. None of the pictures were of his Jacob. A couple of silhouettes. He clicked on one. Profile hidden. *Of course it would be.* Jacob was a hacker. He knew how to hide his online presence. Even knowing it was futile, Ollie Googled him. Was this bordering on stalking? Quite possibly. But Jacob had done the same to him.

The building's entrance door suddenly swung open, the loud clang startling him. Ollie whipped around to peer up to the vacating resident, his heart hammering. The young lady, business suit and flowing blonde locks, gave him a confused and apprehensive smile. Ollie offered up his sweet and genteel one before returning to his phone. He then attempted to stand, splaying his hand on the bricks to aid his inelegant heft up.

"Hey!" Ollie called to the lady as she tottered on her kitten heels up the path.

The lady turned.

"You live next door to Jacob."

The lady nodded, confusion spreading across her dainty features. Ollie pinned all his hopes on this stranger in front of him.

"Is he in? Have you seen him? Can you let me up there?"

"I-I–"

Ollie bundled up toward her. He grabbed her hand and squeezed. He widened his eyes behind his glasses' lenses and pleaded with her silently.

"Please. I have to reach him. It's about his daughter."

"Daisy?"

"Yes. Please, do you know where he is? Do you have his number?"

"I don't think I should give out his number." She shook her head. "Nor really let you into the flat."

"I was here the other day. With him. I saw you. Do you remember?"

She bit her lip and nodded, then glanced away. "Look, I can't let you in. We've had all sorts of trouble with unvetted visitors. It's not fair on the others."

Ollie let go of her hand and stepped back in defeat. "Can you at least tell me which flat number he is?"

"Fourteen."

Ollie beamed. "Thank you, thank you." He twisted back to the main entrance.

"He's not there, though. He left. Couple of hours ago."

Ollie's whole body deflated. So close.

"I think he was going to work. Said he had some things to sort out."

Ollie nodded. He offered up a grateful smile and simply resigned himself to the fact he had to wait for Jacob to come to him. If he ever did.

"He works at the Accelerator. Old Street." The lady nodded to Ollie's phone. "Google Maps'll find it."

* * * *

It didn't take long to find the glass-fronted office block using his maps app. Plus the building was slap-bang in the middle of the newly named Silicon Roundabout in Old Street. Ollie cursed himself for not remembering that tidbit of information Jacob had let out in their limited conversation. All the new media and software companies had moved into the area, sharing information and kicking off start-up companies all dealing in things Ollie knew fuck all about. He just knew it was some online, media, IT setup. Apps, software, that sort of thing.

The Accelerator was a 'business incubator', according to the plaque on the front that Ollie found himself rereading over and over again rather than pushing open the blasted door. It meant the place housed several start-up companies in the early stages of their business ventures, like Jacob had mentioned about his company. Trouble was, he hadn't mentioned the sodding business name. And while Ollie had been thankful that Jacob's next-door neighbor had gotten him this far, he felt back at square one.

He peered in through the glass front at a middle-aged lady receptionist, headset on, seated at the desk. She wore a suit. This didn't look the suit kind of place. It was all hipster and cutoffs. Ollie glanced down at himself. Puffer jacket, cheap jeans that he'd kept in his work locker and beneath the coat, he was still in his work scrubs top, having not found a jumper to change into. He caught his reflection in the window and tried to sort out his hair. It didn't help any. His face was in even more of a state. He was now clearly running on empty.

The lady at reception whipped off her headset and caught Ollie's eye through the glass pane. He immediately smiled. She cautiously offered one back. Ollie then realized he had to go in or he was in danger of looking like a stalker. Again. He wouldn't be surprised if his photo started showing up online asking if anyone had seen this shifty-looking dude. So, putting on his best practiced smile, Ollie curled his hand around the metal door handle and yanked it open.

"Good morning," the lady welcomed. "Which company are you here to see?"

Ollie paused at that. He glanced down the sign behind her detailing the ten or so businesses that resided in the building. They all had stupid names like Z4 or Hollabox. Ollie couldn't even hazard a guess what the companies did, let alone which one Jacob might work for. There were none called IT Hacker for a start.

"Um." Ollie decided to use what he did have in his arsenal. He smiled. "Does Jacob Monroe work for one of those?" He pointed behind the desk to the display sign hanging on the wall next to the large plasma screen displaying some news channel.

The lady cocked her head. "I'm not really meant to give out personal information."

"Okay." Ollie tried a different tack. "I'm here to see Jacob Monroe."

The lady arched an eyebrow. "And which company is that, sir?"

Ollie narrowed his eyes and shoved on his less-condescending-than-her smile. "Z4?"

She shook her head.

"Hollabox?"

She shook it again.

"Bumbleberry?" His voice elevated unconvincingly.

The lady inhaled a deep, annoyed breath. Ollie sighed.

"Am I going to have to read through them all?"

"I sincerely hope not." The lady harrumphed and folded her arms.

Ollie was about to give up when the front doors banged open and in walked a younger girl with funky pink hair, denim dungarees visible beneath her parka. The tinny music from her headphones wafted into reception and she waved at the woman behind the desk. She banged the Call button on the lift, then stared at Ollie. Flicking out the buds from her ears, she approached. Ollie, a little off guard, smiled back.

"Ollie?"

"Yes," Ollie replied cautiously.

"Oh, my God!" The girl bundled him into a hug.

Ollie tapped her back. He had absolutely no idea who this girl was, but she seemed pleased to see him, and so he didn't want to break the poor girl's reunion by actually asking. She pulled away, gripping the tops of his arms, and cocked her head.

"You don't remember me, do you?"

Ollie shook his head. "Sorry."

The girl chuckled. "It's okay. I didn't have pink hair back then. Blonde usually." She ruffled her shoulder-length locks. "But I did this for charity. Plus, no nose rings allowed on the ward, obviously."

Ollie narrowed his eyes, racking his brain.

The girl laughed. "Two years ago, I was in St. Cross for my heart surgery. You were the student nurse. You made me laugh so hard one day my catheter fell out."

Ollie's mouth hung open. He burst out laughing. "Yes. Yes! Blondie. You loved Blondie. Which is weird for a sixteen year old."

"Still do. And the name's Summer."

"Summer. Yes, I remember now. Sorry."

"No worries. I'll bet you care for so many children, names aren't important pieces of information for you to retain."

Ollie snorted. "Yeah, true."

"You still work there?"

"Yeah. I do." He didn't add in the 'thank God' at that point, although he mentally said it. "What are you doing here?"

"I'm at uni now. Thanks to you."

"Me?"

"Yeah. You talked me into it. When I thought my life was over. When I said I wouldn't be able to do all the things the girls in my class were going to do. When I cried on your shoulder about my scar. You told me I'd be a force to be reckoned with one day. You told me I'd change the world. You told me I would be a heroine."

Ollie smiled, nodded, vaguely recalling the conversation.

"So, I do social enterprise at London Met. They give me an incubator here along with other student start-up companies. I'm running my own charity, helping kids get back their self-esteem after surgery."

"That's amazing." Ollie beamed with pride. "Truly. Well done."

"Thanks. Early days. Looking for some sponsors to get us off the ground. But I'm excited." Summer peered over Ollie's shoulder to the stern woman on reception. "What are you doing here, more to the point? Apart from disturbing Wanda's coffee break."

"Oh, I'm trying to find a friend. He works in this building, but I'm not sure which company and, well, she's not very forthcoming with that information."

"Wanda's from a temp agency. Used to working in big businesses. Runs the front desk like it's Saatchi and Saatchi."

Ollie laughed and shot a look over his shoulder. Luckily, the receptionist had just answered an incoming call and wasn't listening in to their conversation.

"Who's your friend?" Summer asked.

"Jacob? Monroe."

"Oh, the man whose little girl just had heart surgery?" Summer gasped and squeezed his arm. "Were you her nurse too?"

Ollie could only nod. Summer smiled, then shot another glance over to Wanda, still talking on her headset.

"Wanda, I'll take Ollie up to Whiz Tech."

Wanda opened her mouth, but Summer pulled on Ollie's jacket and practically threw him through the open doors of the lift. Wanda waved a frantic hand, and all Ollie could do was offer up yet another smile along with a shrug as the doors whooshed closed.

"Thanks," Ollie said as the lift began its ascension.

"Least I can do after what you did for me."

Ollie nodded, swallowing down the ridiculous fear he suddenly had bubbling inside his gut. He was here to deliver news about Daisy. That was all. Anything else was just…a bonus? Ollie hung his head, picking at his fingernails. He desperately tried not to think about the possibility of rejection.

The doors slid open and Summer waved.

"Bye, Ollie. It was so lovely to see you again and to thank you properly."

"Good luck with everything, Summer."

Ollie stepped out of the lift into a spacious open-plan office. All gleaming white. All new. All laptops on workstations rather than personalized desks. No phones other than mobiles. A whiteboard with various scribbles on it. There were a dozen or so people hunched at desks. Two stood by the watercooler in true office cliché. All in casual attire, to the point Ollie couldn't even tell which one the boss would be. Ollie hadn't ever worked in an office. He couldn't think of anything worse than to be stuck at a desk. But the office staff at the hospital, like Kwesi, all dressed pretty smartly. And it was obvious who management were. They were decked out in suits. Smart suits. Silicon Roundabout really was a modern-day workforce, unlike the NHS.

Ollie finally spotted him. Spotted the mound of dark curly hair hanging in tails around his face as he squashed his cheeks in his hands, bent over a laptop screen. The concentration on Jacob's otherwise handsome, chiseled features brought out furrowed lines along his forehead. His stubble protruded, and the dark rims around his eyes were evidence that he hadn't slept much either.

Ollie felt as though he was walking through snow as he trudged closer. One of the watercooler girls, cutoff denims and smiley-face emoji T-shirt, curled a hand around his arm to stop him getting any closer.

"Can I help you?"

"Uh, yeah." Ollie nodded over to Jacob's desk. "I'm here to see Jacob."

"Are you his eleven o'clock?"

Ollie glanced down at the girl. He didn't even want to think about what his first thought was to that statement. Did Jacob take time slots for all his 'clients' in the city? Ollie opened his mouth to speak but jumped at the sound of a desk rattling.

"Ollie?" Jacob stood, bashing the desk with his knees, making his cup and limited equipment clang together and sparking interest from the rest of the office drones.

"Hi," Ollie breathed. "Sorry, I just have something for you."

The girl eyed Jacob suspiciously before turning that suspicion on Ollie.

"How did you know where to find me?"

"You don't have to be a hacker." Ollie grinned. "A nice smile can get you all sorts of information too."

Jacob gaped at him, and the blood rushed around Ollie's body. Jacob wasn't saying anything, nor was he reacting. He was just staring vacantly, until his lips curved upward.

"I can imagine that smile gets you most things."

"Not everything."

The girl seemed to take a hint and pushed off to wherever her impersonal desk resided in the office. Ollie tugged the letter from his pocket. It had gathered a fair few creases from being shoved in there all morning.

"Daisy was discharged yesterday," Jacob said, head bowed. "When I wasn't there."

"I know – "

"I tried to contact her. Tried to get to her. Been trying all night. But I'm too late." Jacob glanced away, his lips trembling. "So I came to work to see if I can get some legal representation from the company, as there's no way I can afford it with all the maintenance I have to pay," Jacob babbled on, not letting Ollie get a word in. Clearly his mind was on overdrive, thinking a dozen things at once. "Although, I think it's pointless." Jacob closed his eyes. "No one ever backs the father. Especially one like me. I deserve this."

"No, you don't." Ollie tilted his head, locking onto Jacob's gaze. "That's why I'm here." He tried to flatten the letter out before handing it over. "It's your copy. Becky will have received hers."

Jacob came around his desk, slipped the letter free from Ollie's hand and scanned the words. He peered up, brow furrowing. "Does this mean?"

"It's a letter recommending she stays in the country. I can't guarantee it will be followed, but if Daisy is taken and has to receive medical treatment, which she will as she'll need her medication, the authorities will be notified of this." Ollie shrugged. "Becky knows she can't take Daisy to Ireland without a fight. There's still time for you to get custody back."

Jacob's eyes darted across the words on the page. His chest rose. As he looked up, the pain in his features caught Ollie raw. It took him a moment before he realized what Jacob must be thinking. He'd opened his mouth to speak when Jacob cut him off.

"You did this?"

"Dr. Rawlings did that. It's the best he can offer you."

"Right." Jacob folded the letter, avoiding looking Ollie in the eye. "Megan? Can you cancel my eleven o'clock and order a cab? I need to get across town."

"Sure thing," the girl from earlier replied from across the office.

"Jacob—" Ollie started.

Jacob shook his head and scurried back around his desk. "It appears I've gotten a lot of things wrong recently." He spoke almost to the floor. "I need to rectify them. Immediately."

Ollie hesitated, waiting foolishly for something more. Jacob took his seat and frantically began typing, no more eye contact his way. Ollie wanted to scream out. Instead, the buzzing office kicked into a life that he wasn't part of. So he turned and headed back to the lift.

To say he didn't feel disappointment was an understatement. But what could he really have expected? He'd done what he'd gone there to do. He'd brought a family together. He purposely ignored Wanda in reception and headed straight to the exit. The raging snowfall hit him in the face and felt like splats of icy reality. He slid his glasses off to let the flakes trickle into his eyes, masking the moisture already forming.

Slipping his glasses back on, he took one step forward but was suddenly grabbed from behind and whipped around.

"Shit, Ollie, I know this is none of my business. You're clearly back with the doctor. Fuck, perhaps you never left him." Jacob closed his eyes. "But did you have to—"

"No." Ollie shook his head. "No, I didn't. And I'm not with him. Not anymore."

Jacob dug desperate fingertips through the stuffing in Ollie's puffer jacket and squeezed his arms. He met

Ollie's gaze beneath his thick lashes, then nodded, let go and stepped back.

"Thank you."

"Jacob, I—"

Ollie was cut off by the office doors swinging open and Wanda marching out onto the pavement.

"Mr. Monroe, your taxi is waiting around the corner. He says to hurry."

Jacob shoved back his hair. "Thanks, Wanda."

Wanda gave Ollie a suspicious glance before clanging the doors shut again.

"I need to go," Jacob scrubbed a hand down his face.

"Of course." Ollie adjusted his glasses, preventing anything seeping out from behind those lenses that would no doubt give away his disappointment and gut-wrenching feelings. *Fucking New Year's resolution!*

A loud, impatient car horn startled Ollie, and Jacob waved over at the black private-hire sedan taxi parked up on the edge of the side road next to the building.

"They charge a fortune for waiting," Jacob muttered.

"Sure. Go." Ollie waved him off. "I need these four days off to sleep, anyway."

"You not working tonight?"

"No. Four days off, then I switch to days."

Jacob nodded and stroked Ollie's cheek with his thumb. That brush of fingertips sent delightful shivers along Ollie's skin. But nothing further was uttered because Jacob jogged over to the taxi and bundled in. As the car drove into the main Shoreditch High Street traffic, Ollie couldn't watch.

Chapter Sixteen

Administering the Medicine

Ollie jumped out of his shower, grabbed the towel from the rail and scrubbed it over his hair. He glanced in the mirror and took a long, hard look at his reflection. The hot waterfall and steam had managed to sort out most of his complexion, but he was still too pale for his liking. He really had to think about using that voucher for the tanning place soon. Four days off meant he should be able to squeeze it in, now there wasn't anyone demanding his leisure time anymore.

He trudged through to his bedroom and yanked open the wardrobe. The day had passed without a peep from Jacob. Or anyone. Having been wishing for the luxury of being alone, now that he had it, he didn't seem to like it. He shook his head, beads of water dripping from his hair onto his carpet and bedspread, and searched for something to wear. He decided on a pair of slim-fitting baby-blue jeans and a simple T-shirt. It wasn't like he was going anywhere. He could have headed to the pub, or maybe even a club and danced his woes away, but the niggling hopeful feeling kept him housebound.

He sauntered through to the kitchen. He'd been to the supermarket earlier and stocked up on all the food items that Elliot would have reprimanded him for. Luckily, Ollie's credit card still had space on it to pay for all the stuff. He'd chilled some cheap white wine and planned to consume most of that bottle by himself to drown his sorrows on his comfortable sofa. He flicked on the television to a low and mellow music station and paced. He couldn't sit. He was too antsy and feared if he actually parked his arse on the sofa, his body might take over and tell him to sleep. He was grateful when his phone rang to give him some distraction from the foolish and hopeless pacing.

"Hey, T," Ollie said into his mobile.

"I cannot take the suspense anymore. Are you trying to make me fail my resolution too? I have very nearly opened my emergency pack of ciggies."

Ollie slid open the balcony door and the wind chill bit at his bare arms and wet hair. It was welcome, though. It slapped him awake. "The very fact that you have emergency menthols tells me you weren't taking the quitting seriously." He checked the winter plants that hung on the railings in various colored pots. "Suspense over what, anyway?"

"Don't play that dumb card with me. Are we or are we not still nursey pals? I mean, I've been thinking and I'm just not sure I can handle a night shift without you there. Or a day shift. And, before you bang on, I am aware that this shouldn't be about me and it's clearly a more worrying time for you. But seriously, bae, I'm having palpitations at the thought of only having Patty to talk to. No one else understands my love of pink hot chocolate. I'd have to quit that too, and I can tell you now, Ollie Warne, giving up smoking is not as easy as the sodding commercials for nicotine gum or the blasted government health guidelines claim."

"I can tell."

"So perhaps, maybe, if you are leaving, I will leave with you. I'll quit. In protest."

"You're going to quit cigs, pink hot chocolate and your job?"

"Yes. For you, I'll quit anything."

Ollie smirked, resting his elbows on the balcony railing and glancing up at the night sky dotted with twinkling stars. Not a cloud in sight. *No wonder it's so fricking freezing.*

"Will you quit dating sites?"

"Why the fuck would I do that?"

"Because it's just as unhealthy as the rest of the list."

Taya sighed heavily down the phone. "I will definitely think about quitting Plenty of Fish. But if I'm quitting my job, then I can't afford the Match fees."

Ollie laughed. "Good."

He stood straight as a bundle of noisy people vacated the Tube station across the road. Ollie's stomach fluttered as he caught sight of a familiar tumble of dark locks on a wrapped-up-for-winter male—

"I have to go."

"Don't you dare—"

Ollie did dare, and he hung up. But he wasn't that much of a bastard. Plus, he knew he'd never get any peace if he didn't give the girl something. So, he quickly composed a text.

Job safe. Elliot and I over. It looks like I have a visitor.

Ollie rushed out of the balcony and closed the door. He took one last look at himself in the mirror, blew into his hand to smell his breath, and adjusted his jeans that had slipped down his hips to reveal his arse crack. His phone vibrated in his hand.

That's all I get? I thought of something else to quit. You.

Ollie chuckled. His mobile immediately pinged again.

Love you xx

The buzzer screeched around the flat, and Ollie was about to switch off his phone when yet another ping came through.

FFS Ollie, you utter bastard, tell me who it is!

Ollie sighed, then whooshed his thumbs across the keypad.

Jacob. Now bugger off.

So this whole 'not feeling a thing' didn't work out?

Are you smoking?

Yes.

Let's just say our next new year's resolution is to not have a new year's resolution.

The buzzer sounded around the flat again, this time not stopping. Ollie shut the phone off, chucked it through the open door of his bedroom where it bounced onto the mattress, then slid over to the entry phone.

"Can I help you?"

"Hi, it's Jacob. Can I come up?" Jacob's voice made Ollie's spine tingle.

"No."

Silence. Ollie laughed and pressed the buzzer to unlock the downstairs door.

"Get up here."

The creak and slam from downstairs made the building rattle. Ollie unlocked the chain from his flat door and held it open with one outstretched arm. The slaps of feet up the fire stairwell were timed in perfect unison with Ollie's heartbeat. As Jacob emerged onto the third-floor landing, wrapped up in a long black coat and scarf, cheeks flushed, he ran his fingers through his hair to ruffle it away from his face.

At the distress in Jacob's eyes, Ollie's stomach plummeted. The previous skittish fluttering at Jacob having turned up at his flat meshed uncomfortably with the overriding fear that this wasn't to be a pleasant reunion.

Jacob paused in front of him. Ollie swallowed.

"You okay?" Ollie finally asked, his heart hammering.

Jacob exhaled a weary breath, and Ollie's whole body felt as if it was sinking into the hardwood flooring and seeping down into the flat below. But he was wrenched back up as Jacob stepped forward and slammed his lips onto Ollie's. He pushed Ollie through into the flat, kicking the door closed behind them. Jacob wrapped his arms around Ollie, staggering him backward, digging his fingers into Ollie's arse.

Jacob pinned him against the wall and kissed him, grinding his body into Ollie's. The kiss slowed, as if Jacob had realized his haste and decided to calm it down a notch. Just one last entwine of tongues before Jacob pulled away, shoving his hair back.

"How do you do it?" Jacob breathed.

"Do what?"

"Make me want you so badly on first sight?"

"Oh, that old thing." Ollie bit his lip. "It's a talent."

"Yeah." Jacob shuffled away, uncurling his scarf from around his neck. "We should talk."

Ollie's playful smile dissolved. His whole body felt cold. Perhaps he should have wrapped up warmer, like Jacob was. Ollie nodded, doing his best to mask the fear that bubbled throughout him, and waved a hand for Jacob to follow him to the living room. Ollie went straight to the kitchenette and yanked open the fridge. Normally he would have used that to cool his hot sweats, but Jacob's words had done that all on their own.

"You want a drink?" Ollie called from behind the fridge door.

Jacob slipped out of his coat, laying it down on the armrest of the sofa. It revealed a different shirt from the one he had worn earlier at work. This one was plain white and gripped tightly along his back. As Jacob folded his arms, the short sleeves stretching over his biceps, Ollie couldn't help but stare. The hair revealed through the top couple of open buttons was enticing enough for Ollie to want to rage his tongue through it. As Ollie trailed his gaze to Jacob's face, Jacob arched an eyebrow. Ollie smiled and nodded toward the fridge.

"Wine, beer, orange juice." Ollie scanned the rest of the refrigerated contents. "Milk. Sparkling water."

"Sparkling water?" Jacob chuckled.

"It's when I like to pretend I'm having a drink. Put it in a wineglass and it's almost the same as cheap prosecco. Just without the hangover."

"I'd love a wine."

Ollie nodded and turned to pull out the chilled sauvignon. The fact the man wanted wine could be down to one of two possible reasons. Ollie didn't dwell on the one that said Jacob was delivering bad news. Rummaging for the corkscrew in the kitchen drawer, he didn't notice Jacob come up behind him until strong arms wrapped around his waist and Jacob kissed his neck.

"Don't look so worried," Jacob whispered into his ear.

"What?" Ollie yanked the cork out of the bottle to a deep pop.

"I want to take you to bed. Right now." Jacob tugged at Ollie's earlobe, his deep rumbling voice going straight to Ollie's groin. Perhaps tight jeans hadn't been the right thing to wear either. "But all in good time."

Ollie wriggled against Jacob's body. "Let up, then."

Jacob stepped away, and Ollie poured the wine into two purple-frosted glasses. Jacob took his and immediately swallowed a large glug.

"Did you get to Becky?"

"Yes."

"And?"

Jacob swished the glass, peering into the liquid. "It's what I need to talk to you about."

Ollie nodded and pointed at the sofa. They took positions almost identical to the ones they'd taken the previous day. Jacob hung his glass between his legs then met Ollie's concerned eyes.

"She's staying here."

"That's great."

"For the time being."

"Okay." Ollie thought that would have been a good thing but Jacob's hunched exterior and brooding expression had him confused.

"I got a lawyer. I'm going to fight for shared custody. Again."

"Okay." Ollie was still apprehensive about where this was going.

Jacob plonked the glass on the table and faced Ollie.

"It means I need to be a father. A real one, this time. I need to be there for her. I need to show I can be what she needs. I need to make my place a home. I'll need to figure out how I can get her to school."

Jacob was babbling, so Ollie leaned forward and slid a hand onto his knee.

"You can do all that. I'm sure."

Jacob nodded, then leaned back against the sofa. "I told work I can no longer do the far-flung business trips on a whim. They seem okay with that. We can do most of it by conference calling anyway, but they usually like an in-person meeting. We'll work around it."

Ollie nodded in turn. There was something more to come, and he braced for the impact.

Jacob sighed and rubbed a hand along his temple. "I have to prove I'm stable."

"That's understandable."

"I told them I was in a relationship. I know that might have been a stupid thing to do. I just needed to prove I'm stable."

"Right…"

"But, also, maybe, because…" Jacob hung his head and mumbled to the floor, "I really want that."

Ollie didn't say anything. His mind was going ninety to the dozen about that revelation. Mostly he reflected on how Elliot had often pretended the same thing—that he was in a heterosexual relationship. That probable hidden family on the third floor of the doctor's house flashed before Ollie's mind's eye. Being so damn secretive had deflected any attention Elliot received for being in his forties and still single. Some believed he was married to his work. Others, including Ollie, believed he did have a secret family. Ollie knew the truth now. And it killed him to think that this was where things were going with Jacob. Ollie couldn't help but chuckle at the irony of his last conversation with Elliot. That he had wanted to be open. Out. Proud. Well, that hadn't lasted. Much like his New Year's resolution.

"Ollie?"

Ollie had been staring into space.

"I want that with you."

Ollie blinked. Rapidly.

"And I know I should have asked first." Jacob rested a hand on Ollie's knee, his fingers trembling. "And I know this is fast and we barely know each other. And I know"—Jacob closed his eyes—"this sounds a lot like I'm using this situation." He opened them again to gaze upon Ollie. "But I think I can do this. I want to be with you. So, if that isn't what you want, which is fine, then I'm afraid I can't do casual hookups. Not anymore."

Ollie breathed out the air he'd been holding in to the point the papers on the coffee table floated in the breeze. He leaned forward and dropped his glass onto the table. He took Jacob's face in his hands and kissed him.

"Okay." Ollie cleared his throat. "Well, you see, there's something I should probably tell you."

Jacob waited.

"I stupidly made this New Year's resolution."

Jacob brushed Ollie's lips with his own. "What was it?"

"To not feel a thing. Casual hookups, no feelings."

"Ah." Jacob slumped back.

As much as Ollie wanted to pull him up, he knew he needed to explain. He was done with secrets. Hiding the truth. If he was to have a healthy, adult, relationship, one that was a million miles away from what he had had with Elliot, then it needed to start with a clean slate.

"My relationship with Elliot sucked me dry. I was young, naive, vulnerable and desperate for someone to love me. I love my father. I do. But I lost him. Long before he lost himself. Tilly required so much attention that I couldn't get what I needed from him. I guess Elliot provided that for me. He took control of my life. He looked after me. He gave me what I needed."

Jacob sucked in a breath. Ollie felt like he wanted to say something. Cut in, perhaps. Ollie would know he didn't want to hear everything Ollie had to say. So, he tried to get it over with as quickly as possible. *Rip the Band-Aid off.*

"I fell for everything he said and did. He used me, yes. But I used him too. I used him to prevent myself from actually having a normal relationship. To have a reason not to fall in love. Not to feel. Because, shit, it hurts when you do, right?"

Ollie curled a finger under Jacob's chin and raised it to meet his gaze.

"But I came to my senses. You helped me do that." Ollie smiled. "Now I realize what I was missing. That feeling something doesn't make you weak. It makes you whole. It makes you alive. And, God, Jacob, I want to be alive with you."

Jacob swallowed. He closed his eyes for a brief moment before taking Ollie's hand and squeezing it. "I've never been in a relationship with a man before," he admitted.

"I know." Ollie wasn't sure what the statement was meant to mean.

"Everything I did with Becky was wrong. I know that. I'm still paying the price for what I did to her."

Ollie nodded, listening, his heart beating.

"I won't be perfect, Ollie. It'll take some getting used to. But, right now, here, for the record, I will never, ever, make those mistakes again. Not if I am with you."

Ollie licked his dry lips, then curved them into a smile.

"Well, then." He waved a hand. "I guess I need to change my resolution."

"Yeah?" Jacob arched an eyebrow.

"I vow to start this new year with a boyfriend."

Jacob chuckled, his hair falling around his face.

"But I do have a list of requirements to meet my high standards."

"And they are?"

Ollie leaned back and held up his forefinger. "One, tech whiz, so when I forget my passwords I can still get into my bank account." Ollie flicked up his middle finger to join the counting. "Tons of hair in all the right places." Ollie ruffled his hand through Jacob's curls, brushing them away from his face. "I'm also willing to accept the wrong places." Jacob laughed. Ollie held up his third finger. "Seafood pizza lover." That was a deal clincher right there. Fourth finger. "Doting dad."

Jacob opened his mouth to speak.

"Wait!" Ollie held up his hand. "Five—must be smoking hot." Ollie picked his glass back up and took a sip. "Know anyone?"

"So, you have four days off?" Jacob questioned.

"Uh-huh."

"Then you won't be working nights?"

"Nope. Not for a couple of weeks."

"Can I see you?"

"For which nights?"

Jacob inhaled. "All the nights."

Ollie's heart thumped and his gaze followed Jacob as he stood. Ollie then choked on his drink as Jacob began unbuttoning his shirt. The wine dribbled out of the corners of Ollie's mouth as Jacob ripped off his top and threw it to the floor. He leaned forward, licked Ollie's chin, and delved into his mouth to devour the trailing liquid. "And how does this night-to-day shift work, anyway?" Jacob panted. "Where's your body clock at now?"

"Well." Ollie ran a hand through Jacob's chest hair. "After the last night shift, I don't sleep through the day. Twenty-four hours awake means come that evening, I'm so shattered, I fall into a coma to start the next day back on real time."

"Last night was your last night shift?" Jacob kissed his neck.

"Yeah."

"Wow." Jacob leaned away and hung his head. "You must be exhausted."

Ollie sat forward, tugging Jacob back to him and whispered in his ear, "I slept all day."

Jacob peered through his hair to meet Ollie's gaze. He smiled. Ollie winked, but was stumped from doing anything further when Jacob rammed his mouth onto his and kissed him. Not that Ollie minded. It was his New Year's resolution, after all.

To feel every inch of Jacob.

Want to see more from this author? Here's a taster for you to enjoy!

St. Cross: Won't Be Fooled Again

C F White

Excerpt

The yellow toy candy egg that was perched on the shabby chest of drawers wobbled with every foot stomp from outside. It stared at him. *Mocked* him. Forced him back to a life he'd tried escaping.

Pacing the dishevelled bedroom in his fifth-floor flat, Callum scraped his hair back and tied it into a messy topknot. With nothing more than a pull-out bed and a wardrobe, the space was so small that his uneasy strides took him full circle. *This bloke cannot get here quick enough.*

He had to swat away the beads of sweat sprinkling his bottom lip with the ball of his thumb—his fingers were useless with trembling. He wiped his hands down his ripped jeans then rubbed his palms together, needing his hands back at full function. *Get a fucking grip. It'll all be over in a minute.* Adrenaline had him jumping on the spot and the crash of his heart pained his chest with every energetic leap.

Fuck. All. This. Shit.

Deep thuds from above and below pounded louder, like a herd of fucking elephants were marching down the communal stairway opposite his single occupancy. *Why can't these people use the damn fucking lifts?*

Catching his reflection in the smeared mirror hanging on the wardrobe by one rusty nail, Callum paused. Not for thought – more for context. He glanced away just as quickly. The clothes strewn about the room covered every inch of the grey tiled carpet and his fraying rucksack propped up by the door was ready and waiting for his swift exit. His stomach growled, which temporarily masked the heavy stomps from outside. At least after this, he'd have a bit of dough and could buy a decent meal. He'd had enough of the tinned crap from the food bank.

The candy egg caught his eye again. *Just one?* No one would know. Might take the edge off.

Fuck. He needed gloves. He ransacked the flat – every room, every drawer, every cupboard, under every discarded item of clothing – stopping in the living area for composure. He checked in his stone-washed-jeans pockets, a last resort. *Come on!* Snatching his bag, he then ripped open the zip with trembling fingers. He hung it upside down over the once-red fabric sofa that was now stained with varying amounts of he didn't want to know what. Nothing of interest fell out. Just the two throwaway phones. He checked the display on one, then switched it off, smacked it against his leg to release the SIM card and stamped on it with his steel-toe-capped boot.

The front door rattled on its hinges and Callum's heart leapt into his throat along with a sizeable amount of bile. He peered through to his bedroom just in time to witness the plastic egg falling from the chest of drawers and being captured within the soft cotton of a tattered jumper. *Bollocks*. He couldn't touch it. He couldn't. Not without the damn gloves.

Bang, bang, bang. Knuckles rapped the front door, drilling through Callum's temple and whatever resolve he might still have had left. *Thank fuck.*

Pulling himself together, he trampled over the clutter to flick the latch up, making the clang ricochet off the oppressive walls. He nudged open the door just enough to fit his face through the gap.

An Indian man stared back at him, eyes wide. "Gotta get out, son. Fire."

"*What?*" Callum clung onto the door, unwilling to open it farther.

"Leave everything. It's spreading." The man, Callum suddenly recalled, lived three doors down from him in one of the larger flats. This was the longest conversation they'd ever had—Callum had become a bit of a recluse.

As his grip released, the door drifted open wider to reveal a horde of families rushing down the fire escape steps opposite. All panic-stricken. No forming an orderly queue. His neighbours halted up ahead by the stairwell—four young girls all clinging to their mum's skirt, glaring in frustration as the woman yelled something to him in her mother tongue.

The man responded to her in a quick-fire language that Callum couldn't decipher, then, with fear apparent in his dark eyes, gripped Callum's arm. "Please. Come."

"Wait." Callum held up a finger, when the sudden stench of thick smoke drifted to his nostrils. He coughed.

"Now!" The man yanked him again, but soon gave up when fog clouded around his family. He left, rushed to their aid and ushered them all down the stairs.

Callum's eyes streamed. He couldn't leave. He couldn't. Not yet. *Not now, for fuck's sake!* He looked through the flat to his bedroom, to his bag, his stuff, his life. The plastic toy egg—

Then he slammed the door shut behind him and lunged for the staircase.

Slapping a palm on the railing, he paused. Others bundled past him, bashing him in their hasty retreat. Callum's legs wouldn't move. He shut his stinging eyes for a moment, then, when he opened them, peered along the corridor to the flat at the end. The door was shut.

Shit.

Growling, Callum launched himself off the steps and ran the length of the corridor, landing with a balled fist at number fifty-nine. He banged, hard, coughing through the surrounding smoke and the rising heat enveloping him. *She could have left already?*

He'd never forgive himself if he didn't find out for sure.

Stepping back, he lifted his leg and lined up the outsole of his heavy-duty standard work boots at the door. He sucked in a deep breath that was clouded with bristling fumes, then slammed his sole, full force, onto the PVC. The pressure-pain ricocheted up his leg to his hip and the door flung open, ripping half the wood from the frame along with it.

Coughing, Callum bolted inside the flat. "Eve!" He held his sleeve up to his mouth as he stormed through the corridor.

The living area was vacant, no one inside. The kitchen opposite also empty. Farther still, he pushed open the door to the first bedroom. Neatly kept, not slept in. Not for years. Callum's heart sank through to his feet.

"Callum! What are you—" Eve's tight braids that had used to be wound into an on-the-top bun were left dangling over her shoulders as she emerged from the main bedroom. Her hair used to be solid black, but now there were speckles of ash white running through, serving Callum a dreaded reminder of how long it had been since he'd last seen her this close. But he couldn't think about that now. Or they'd both be dead and buried, like the past was supposed to be.

"Fire. We need to get out." Callum's mouth was dry, but he ignored the parch in his throat to grab her arm.

"What? Callum, no!" She resisted, yanking away from him. Her long night dress was only mildly covered by a towelled dressing gown that hung down to a cast on her left foot. He'd heard about her fall, but he hadn't had the guts to ask how she'd been doing. He hated himself for that. "Fires are contained to the flats. We stay put and secure the doors."

"*Everyone* is leaving." Callum's panicked voice elevated in urgency and he widened his eyes in plea.

The screech of a long and loud blast from the internal fire alarms burst through to the room and Eve staggered back.

"Your door's broken now, anyway!" Callum dug fingertips into the soft fibres of Eve's dressing gown as smoke trailed in through the open front door and down the corridor. "Auntie, please." The endearment fell from his tongue without conscious thought, even if he hadn't uttered the word in so long. He had no right to call her that. He didn't deserve it. Not anymore.

Eve bit her bottom lip, drawing troubled eyebrows in. She stared at Callum, her chest rising. And for a moment Callum thought this would be how it all ended. And wouldn't that make for a piece of fucking irony? Eventually, though, she nodded and allowed Callum to usher her out of the flat. She had to hobble, the cast on her foot making it difficult to walk, let alone rush. Callum stayed at her side, coughing through the rising fumes and taking all Eve's weight for her.

As they reached the stairwell, the smoke had thickened, distorting much of Callum's view and preventing any clean air from reaching his lungs. Grabbing Eve's wrist, he held her towelling sleeve to her mouth. "Breathe through that."

They tumbled down the first flight, awkwardly falling into each other or the wall, to stop at the separating landing. A little boy, no more than five or six, stood against the wall and wailed, calling for his mummy.

"That's Thomas!" Eve choked out the boy's name in urgency.

Callum didn't think. He rarely did. With a clenched jaw, he let Eve go and grabbed the boy to haul him up to rest on his hip. The boy wrapped thin, quivering arms around Callum's neck and clasped his hands together.

If this fire didn't kill Callum, strangulation would.

"Where is his mother?" Eve asked.

"Everyone left, Auntie." Callum tapped the boy's arm, attempting to loosen the kid's tight grip. It didn't work. Delving deep to find a courage he didn't know he had, he linked his arm through Eve's and hobbled them all the rest of the way down the stairs.

As they emerged into daylight, he set the boy to the ground but clung to his tiny, trembling hand. He wasn't sure it was any comfort to the snot-nosed kid, but, for some reason, it was to Callum.

"You're all right, yeah?" Callum wasn't sure if that was a question, or just hope vocalised.

The little kid didn't answer. Which was okay with Callum. He wouldn't have known what to do if he'd been given the negative anyway.

"Thomas!" A woman's petrified scream sounded up ahead. Her approaching voice was distorted by the other sounds that rippled Callum's skin. He could see her mouth moving, but no words were decipherable. Slipping down onto her knees, the panic-stricken woman snatched the boy to her chest. "Eve!" She stood. "Thank you! I lost him on the stairs. Are you okay?"

Eve shook her head, tears trailing down her cheeks as she slipped away from Callum and into the woman's outstretched hand.

"Let's get you to an ambulance."

Dazed, confused, Callum lost them all. Alone, he stumbled up the path and passed the fenced-off playground, where the one lone swing swaying in the breeze appeared as inviting as it ever had. Bashed, Callum was forced back to the present, his head a haze of cotton wool. Dozens of firemen decked out in full head gear rushed toward the entrance of the building.

Only once he'd reached the pedestrian walkway littered with onlookers did Callum stop and turn.

Flames sizzled from the fourth floor of the block and drifted upward, blurring the outline of the concrete. Gasps, cries and sobs stabbed Callum's eardrums, whilst flashing emergency lights, thick black smoke and bright orange sparks saturated his vision.

Involuntary retching pained his chest. He couldn't get a handle on himself. Bending double, he threw up into the gutter, his limited stomach contents now discarded down the drain for the rats to consume.

"You okay, mate?" A light tap to his back stopped the pitiful display.

Callum stood, tufts of hair falling from the band to irritate his eyes, but he could still see the concern flickering behind the fireman's shielded mask. "Yeah."

He nodded and looked back up at his childhood home. "Lucky escape."

Never a truer statement.

Sign up for our newsletter and find out about all our romance book releases, eBook sales and promotions, sneak peeks and FREE romance books!

About the Author

Brought up in a relatively small town in Hertfordshire, C F White managed to do what most other residents try to do and fail – leave.

Studying at a West London university, she realised there was a whole city out there waiting to be discovered, so, much like Dick Whittington before her, she never made it back home and still endlessly searches for the streets paved with gold, slowly coming to the realisation they're mostly paved with chewing gum. And the odd bit of graffiti. And those little circles of yellow spray paint where the council point out the pot holes to someone who is supposedly meant to fix them instead of staring at them vacantly whilst holding a polystyrene cup of watered-down coffee.

She eventually moved West to East along that vast District Line and settled for pie and mash, cockles and winkles and a bit of Knees Up Mother Brown to live in the East End of London; securing a job and creating a life, a home and a family.

Having worked in Higher Education for most of her career, a life-altering experience brought pen back to paper after she'd written stories as a child but never had the confidence to show them to the world. Having embarked on this writing malarkey, C F White cannot stop. So strap in, it's gonna be a bumpy ride...

C F White loves to hear from readers. You can find her contact information, website details and author profile page at https://www.pride-publishing.com

www.ingramcontent.com/pod-product-compliance
Lightning Source LLC
Chambersburg PA
CBHW032029240626
47154CB00003B/842

* 9 7 8 1 8 3 9 4 3 8 1 5 8 *